High Frequency

FREYA BARKER

HIGH FREQUENCY

Copyright © 2024 Freya Barker

This book is a work of fiction and any resemblance to any place, person or persons, living or dead, any event, occurrence, or incident is purely coincidental. The characters, places, and story lines are created and thought up from the author's imagination or are used fictitiously.

Cover Design: Freya Barker
Editing: Karen Hrdlicka
Proofing: Joanne Thompson
Cover Image: Golden Czermak — FuriousFotog
Cover Model: Joey Berry

FREYA BARKER

just ordinary people with extraordinary stories

When the rug is pulled from under Detective Sloane Eckhart, she leaves the Billings PD and returns to Libby, Montana. Eight years ago she left with her pride and the promise of a future, but her heart was broken. On her return, there is no pride left, no prospects to speak of, but at least her heart is safely secured in the back seat.

Still, a bit of groveling, a kind offer of help, and a brand-new job with the sheriff's office quickly gets her back on her feet.

High Meadow will always be home to Dan Blakely. Working with horses, being part of the HMT search and rescue team, and now building his own home right next door checks all his boxes. Only one thing is missing, but that dream walked out the door a long time ago.

Still, his life is good, steady...and perhaps a little boring.

That quickly changes when the rescue of a young, teenage girl, places the new sheriff's detective squarely in his path. He's not bored now, doing his best to keep her safe, even as their past holds them back while they fight for a future.

One

Dan

I take a last look at the sun going down over the mountains on the other side of the Fisher River; a view I'll never tire of.

Time to wrap up this quiet celebration for one.

Picking up my hat from the pile of logs I set it down on, I slap the dust off, and fit it back on my head. Then I tuck the two empty beer cans in my saddlebag, take Blitz's reins in my left hand, and swing myself in the saddle.

Blitz isn't mine—he belongs to my boss—but I'm the only one he'll tolerate on his back. Every so often I take him out for some exercise, giving my regular mount, Will, a well-deserved break.

Despite getting up there in age, the prized Arabian stud still dances restlessly, shaking his head when I settle my weight in the saddle. It's mostly for show these days—a lot of his younger fire has dissipated—but I indulge him with a tug on his reins and a firm, "Whoa."

Then I press my legs in his sides and steer Blitz back

toward the ranch, leaving my newly cleared piece of land behind. Monday we'll break ground.

Six years ago, Jonas Harvey—my boss and owner of the High Meadow Ranch and High Mountain Trackers—parceled off a wedge of his land bordering the Fisher River. His former Special Ops teammate and friend, Sully, bought six of the twelve-acre parcel—the widest section closest to the highway—and built a new house there.

That left the narrower stretch along the river farther away from the road. I was blown away when Jonas offered that to me at a steal.

Never in a million years could I have dreamed of owning an actual piece of these beautiful Montana mountains. Me, a high school dropout, forced to get a job when my mother was fighting a losing battle with colorectal cancer. The only one I was able to find was as stable help at High Meadow Ranch. Jonas gave me a chance, and even though I almost blew it several times, I'm still here now, after all these years.

I'm still part of the crew responsible for managing the daily running of the ranch and breeding facility, but for the past decade or so have also been a proud member of the High Mountain Trackers, Jonas Harvey's mounted search and rescue team. A far cry from the teacher I once aspired to be, but I wouldn't trade this life for the world.

And now, six years after I bought my own little slice of paradise, I've saved up enough to start building my dream home.

I plan to do a lot of the work myself, and some of the guys have offered to help as well, but for the foundation and framework I've hired contractors. A family-owned specialty log construction company in Heron, Montana—a little over an hour from here—is prepping the logs that will make up the walls of my house, and a truckload of lumber we cut from my land went to a mill outside of Libby to be cut into planks for flooring.

Ideally, we should've broken ground back in the spring, but getting the schedule for the different trades to line up had been a bit of a challenge. As a result, we got a late start, and the house likely won't be move-in ready before winter hits as I'd hoped, but we should be able to get the roof on before the first snow flies.

So for now, I'll stay living in one of the employee cabins at the ranch. I'm not really in a hurry, although I know someone who may disagree, even though it shouldn't impact her either way.

Which reminds me, if I'm supposed to meet Shelby at eight at The Salt Lick, a local hangout in town. I'd better hustle or I'll be late.

Forty-five minutes later, showered and cleaned up, I stop the truck at the end of the driveway to check traffic on the highway before heading toward Libby. To my left, I catch sight of an older, burgundy Jeep turning onto the dirt road that leads to Sully's place and my property beyond that. I don't recognize the vehicle, but the brief flash of blond hair behind the wheel seems familiar.

The image of a pair of stormy blue eyes, a slightly upturned nose, and the stubborn set of a shapely mouth immediately comes to mind. Followed closely by a confusing collection of emotions I have no interest or time to examine.

Whoever is driving that Jeep, it's none of my business.

I shake my head to clear it before pulling onto the road to Libby.

I have an appointment to keep.

"Oh. But I thought..."

She lets the sentence trail off, a blush crawling up her face as realization sets in.

"I probably should've been clearer," I volunteer, even though I'm not sure how I could've made, *"I'm not in the market for anything long term,"* any more straightforward.

To my horror, tears pool in her eyes and threaten to spill over. Oh no. I don't like crying, at all. It makes me very uneasy.

"Look, I'm sorry if I misrepresented myself in any way," I try.

"I guess I thought you were including me in your future when you asked my opinion on the house," she explains with a sniffle.

I remember she was at my place a month or so ago and asked about the drawings for the house I had spread out on my kitchen table. At the time, I was deciding whether to go with a simple front porch or to wrap it around one side to where the door to the mud/laundry room is going to be. I mentioned my dilemma and she pointed out it might be handy to have a dry outdoor spot to drop muddy boots before tracking dirt into the house.

It was a valid point and I opted for the wrap porch as a result, but it seems like an awfully big leap to go from there to planning a joint future.

I do my best to curb my annoyance. It's not like I want to hurt her feelings any more than I need to, Shelby is a nice girl.

Her parents own the feedstore in town and I remember seeing her around from time to time years ago. Apparently, she got married to a truck driver from Eureka and ended up moving there. Then suddenly this spring, she was manning the cash at her parents' place again, and we got to talking and hit it off. She made it clear she'd just gone through a messy divorce and was looking for something very casual, which suited me just fine.

Then she called this morning to let me know we were expected for dinner at her parents' place this weekend, and it became clear somewhere along the past few months her expectations changed.

Sadly, mine have not, which is why I asked her to meet me tonight to set the record straight.

"I'm sorry," I repeat, because what else is there to say?

She nods and takes a small sip of the wine I ordered for her, seeming to pull herself together. Then she plasters on a smile and blows me away when she asks, "So, your place or mine?"

Twenty minutes later, I close the door of her little blue car and step back, as a crying Shelby peels out of the parking lot.

Needless to say, she did not take my rejection well, and I'm actually pretty pissed myself. I'm not a player, I don't lead women on, or make empty promises, and yet I've just been made to feel like a goddamn villain in the public drama she created back there.

From here on in I'm sticking close to the ranch. I do better with horses than I do women.

Sloane

"Ohmigawd! So cute!"

I manage a grin at Carmi's excited outburst, as she pulls

open the rear passenger door and pokes her head inside. I barely have the chance to put my Jeep in park.

Getting out of the vehicle, I catch sight of my uncle walking up, his eyes zoomed in on me. I recognize both the concern and the anger I was expecting.

He has cause.

My phone call last week must've come as a shock. Years and distance had made those a rare occurrence, Mom is the one who would serve as an information relay, of sorts, since I took a job with the Billings Police Department and left.

Last time I saw my uncle and his family was October last year at the goodbye party for my mother and stepfather at their place in Brigham City, Utah. Mom and Steve were embarking on their years-long dream of moving to a life on the beach.

They found it in Panama, where the temperature is the same year-round, and life moves at a slower pace. With the proceeds of the sale of their house in Utah they'd been able to purchase a sprawling beachfront property, which they've turned into a profitable bed-and-breakfast.

I haven't been to visit yet, but I've seen pictures.

Anyway, there are a myriad of reasons why Mom and I haven't been in touch a whole lot these past few months. There's a couple of hours of time difference, and with my crazy busy schedule it's been hard to find a good moment to connect, so we've mostly been emailing back and forth. At least, that's the excuse I've been hanging on to.

Of course, that is not going to last. Not now.

"You look like shit," are the first words I hear out of my uncle's mouth before I'm wrapped up in his arms.

With my face pressed against his wide shoulder, it's hard to hang on to the stiff upper lip I've been sporting for a while now.

"Sully, let go of her already," Pippa firmly orders her husband.

I'd been so focused on my uncle; I hadn't seen her walk up behind him. Next, I'm hugged to a much softer body but her grip is equally strong.

"Mom, look how cute!" my little cousin gushes.

"You're gonna wake her up if you keep squawking like that," Sully grumbles.

By the time I step out of Pippa's hold, Sully already has the baby seat out of the Jeep.

"She's precious," she observes, shooting a warm and encouraging smile in my direction.

I'm grateful for it.

"Leave your things. I'll grab them later," Sully orders over his shoulder as he starts walking to the house, carrying the car seat.

Pippa shoves her arm through mine, as we follow along behind him, and gives me a squeeze.

"I'm so glad you're here."

Not sure the same can be said for my uncle. I've been so worried coming here might turn out to be another in a series of mistakes I seem to be making.

That's the problem when you start off with one lie, even if only by omission. It leads to others, until you've created a situation where anything you do or say simply compounds on your problems.

So yes, I'm grateful for Pippa's show of support. I had a feeling she may understand better than most why I made the —arguably unwise—choices I made, which is why I'd dialed her phone number instead of my uncle's last week when the shit hit the fan. Like a coward, I'd left it to her to inform him.

It's no wonder he's pissed. I'm surprised he even hugged

me, given I just showed up with a daughter he didn't hear about from me.

~

"What the hell were you thinking?"

I almost laugh at his exasperated question. One I've asked myself countless times over the past ten or so months since seeing that second red line appear on the pregnancy test.

The truth is, I wasn't thinking. Or maybe I was thinking too much. Hell, why not blame it on hormones. The result is the same; the giant mess I find myself in now.

"Sully..." Pippa, who just walked in, puts a gentling hand on my uncle's rigid shoulder. To me she directs, "Hope you don't mind, Carmi is sitting on the floor next to the Pack 'n Play, watching Aspen sleep."

"That's fine. Once she's out on a full stomach, there's little that'll wake her up."

The full stomach was courtesy of the bottle Pippa volunteered to give her while I helped a brooding Sully empty out the Jeep before the dark of night set in.

I was able to nurse Aspen the first eight weeks after her birth, but I weaned her before I had to go back to work. Working as a detective with the very busy Billings PD doesn't exactly lend itself to pumping breast milk. My heart still aches at that decision, but I didn't really have a choice at the time.

Now, barely two months later, none of it matters anymore.

"I'm still waiting," Sully grumbles.

This is the part I hate most; disappointing him. God knows I did plenty of that in my younger days. But I'd earned his respect in later years, which makes coming clean now a bitter pill to swallow.

"I thought I had a handle on things," I offer meekly.

From the flare of his nostrils, I deduce that was not a satisfactory response.

"Aspen's pregnancy was not planned," I try again, starting at the beginning this time. "At first I kept it to myself because I needed time to figure out what I was going to do."

"Of course," Pippa agrees, earning her a sharp look from her husband.

"Fine, but clearly you figured it out at some point because she's here. Except you failed to inform your family."

I don't know whether it's his sharp tone, or his accusation that ends up pushing my buttons, but in an instant I'm twenty years old again, and all my defenses are up.

"And what?" I snap. "Have Mom give up on her and Steve's dreams? Because you know she wouldn't have left had she known, and this was my problem to solve, no one else's."

"What about the father?" Sully demands, not backing down.

It was inevitable the question would come up sooner or later. It doesn't shock me, but his next comment does.

"If you even know who it is."

"Sully!" Pippa scolds. "That's out of line."

She's right, and I can see from the way he winces he knows it, but that doesn't make the sting any less. The sad part is, I almost wish I didn't know who her father was, since he turned out to be the biggest mistake of my life.

Sick to my stomach, I get to my feet.

"I need to go to bed."

Before anyone can stop me, I rush upstairs where I find

Carmi sitting on the edge of my bed. I'd forgotten about her.

Blinking a few times and forcing a smile on my face, I give my cousin a quick hug.

"Thanks for looking after her."

"Are you waking her up?" she asks expectantly.

"Not until the morning. I was actually going to bed myself, but maybe you can give me a hand changing her diaper tomorrow morning when we get up?"

"Sure!"

I involuntarily chuckle at her enthusiasm. I'm sure it'll wane when she's first introduced to one of Aspen's impressive diaper explosions.

As Carmi almost skips out of the room, I close the door behind her and—forfeiting my toothbrush and pajamas—crawl into bed fully dressed. I roll on my side so I can look at my daughter's perfect little face in her travel bed, pulling the covers up to my ears.

It's just you and me now.

Two

"You're awake."

Aspen's eyes find me without a problem, and I'm greeted with a wide, gummy smile.

Obviously, her sunny disposition first thing in the morning is not something she inherited from me, but I'm grateful for it. That smile does more for my mood than a good jolt of java, although it's the smell of fresh coffee that first woke me up.

Her hands come up and grab at my hair when I bend down to blow a raspberry in her neck. I smile against her skin when I hear her excited, "Gah."

She's really starting to vocalize, testing sounds and volume, occasionally startling herself. Already it feels like every time I look away she's developed some new skill or hit a next milestone.

Carefully untangling my daughter's little fingers from my hair, I look down in her pale blue eyes.

"Can you keep yourself entertained for two more minutes while Mommy gets dressed?"

I turn on the mobile Pippa dug out of a box in the garage. It turns out she kept quite a few things from when Carmi was a baby, which is helpful since most of Aspen and my things are packed in a storage facility back in Billings, waiting for me to find a place of my own.

Today is hopefully the first step in that direction.

I drop my towel and dig through the clothes I moved into the closet when we got here last week. I need something professional-looking to wear for my interview today. I finally got a call back from the sheriff's office yesterday. The same sheriff's office I spent nearly four years working for almost a decade ago, before I moved to Billings.

Back then Wayne Ewing was sheriff, but he retired shortly after I left. For a few years after that some other guy held office until Ewing's son, Junior, was voted in. I remember Junior, who was a deputy back when I was. He's who I have an appointment with this morning about a possible job.

Sully offered to talk to Jonas about me working in some office capacity for the High Mountain Trackers team, but I have a little too much pride left to allow my uncle to beg for a job for me. Let alone an office job. I'm keeping my fingers crossed I can get my old position back at the sheriff's office. It'll be a substantial step back for me, both career-wise and financially, but my life circumstances have changed. Besides, the cost of living is less in Libby than in the big city.

I check my reflection in the mirror on the back of the door. I think I look professional enough in navy slacks and my white dress shirt. My short hair doesn't require more than a quick comb and I haven't bothered with makeup in years.

"All right, baby girl, are you ready to get dressed?"

"Sloane?"

I turn my head to find Pippa standing in the doorway, a concerned look on her face.

"Hey. We were just on our way down."

"There's been a change of plans. Carmi just tried to slice off her finger cutting an apple. She's going to need stitches."

"Oh no. Is she okay?"

Stupid question, of course she's not okay.

Shit, my interview. Pippa was going to watch Aspen.

"She's a tough cookie, but I really should get her to the ER."

"Of course. Go."

I wave her off. I'll have to take Aspen with me to the interview. Not the first impression I was hoping to make, but I have no choice. This is life as a parent, I just hope Junior is open-minded enough to not turn that into a strike against me.

"Take her to Sully. I just talked to him; he's working at the ranch office today. Between him and Ama, they can watch Aspen while you go to your interview."

Ama works at the High Meadow ranch. She wears many hats: she runs the kitchen, looks after housekeeping, does the ranch administration, and also happens to be married to one of my uncle's teammates. I have no doubt she's well-qualified to take care of my daughter.

Still, the idea of going to the ranch, when I've so carefully avoided showing my face there, is making me a little nervous.

One way or another, it looks like today might turn into a day of confessions.

Sully had agreed to put off talking to Mom for a week to give me a chance to get my shit together, and today would mark my cutoff. I'm hoping to at least have a job lined up before I'm forced to talk to her. It's not going to be a fun conversation, regardless, but being able to show her I'm taking care of things will hopefully ease the way.

Mom never liked Jeff; thought he was a waste of space. Which, in hindsight, she was right about, although I hate to admit it. I think the fact he was nothing at all like any of the men who had been prominent in my life up to that point is what made him attractive to me.

He was different, all right. When I met him, he was working as a bartender at a pub down the block from the precinct. Good-looking, charismatic, funny, and he definitely had a way with words, singing poetry while slinging drinks. According to him, bartending was just to pay the bills while he pursued his dream of making it as a music artist.

What can I say? I ignored all the signs. Not even the fact he was forty-two and still rooming with two buddies was enough of a red flag. Granted, I had no illusions of any kind of long-term relationship, not until I found myself pregnant. Then everything changed.

At first it looked like he would step up to the plate, vowing to be there for me and our child. He moved in with me, quit his bartending job since he made less than I did as a detective for the Billings PD, and would work on his music from home while taking care of the baby.

He lasted a little over a month alone with Aspen at home. Then one day when I was at a doctor's appointment with Aspen, he cleared out. By the time I got back, any and all evidence of Jeff was gone from the apartment. He did leave me a note, stating he was destined for greater things and parenthood was holding him back.

I don't like admitting failure, and for all the mistakes I

made in my life, putting my faith in that loser was the biggest mistake of all. There's no doubt my mother will find a way to pry the whole sordid story from me. Pippa has been running interference for me with Sully, reminding him I'll tell him what happened when I'm good and ready to, but I don't think even Pippa can save me from my mother's determination.

"There she is."

I can't even get through the door before Sully plucks my daughter from my arms. He must've been lying in wait for me.

Not a word for me, as he turns his back and carries Aspen down the hallway to the large ranch kitchen. I follow, carrying the diaper bag I quickly packed, but to my relief only Ama is in the kitchen.

"Oh, isn't she precious," Ama mutters, wiggling her fingers as she reaches for her. "Gimme that little nugget."

Sully presses a kiss to Aspen's downy head and reluctantly hands her over.

"It's that I know you have an appointment," Ama directs at me with a stern look. "But when you get back to pick her up, I'll be waiting for an explanation."

Shit. If there is anyone more single-minded than Mom, it's probably Ama.

I'm afraid after today my poor life choices are going to be public knowledge.

Dan

. . .

"Don't move."

The young girl is shaking so hard, I'm surprised she hasn't already fallen off the side of the cliff she's desperately hanging on to twenty feet below me.

"I'll be right down there to get you," I promise.

I back away from the edge and grab the extra harness Wolff holds out for me, clipping it on to my belt. I plan to rappel down and hope to hell the girl hangs on long enough so I can get her hooked up.

When we got the notification from the sheriff's office early this morning, I didn't think we'd actually find someone out here. They'd gotten a call from a couple of hikers who'd walked down off Kenelty Mountain at the crack of dawn. The two had planned to spend the night on the mountain, but were woken up by screams in the middle of the night. When they went to investigate, they found a backpack, and spent some time looking for the person it might've belonged to, but without much success. So, they ended up packing their gear, grabbing the backpack, and hiking back to the trailhead from where they were able to call for help.

The trailhead is actually almost directly across the Fisher River from my little piece of property, so rather than loading the horses onto the trailer and driving around the long way, Wolff, James, JD, and I saddled up and crossed the river on horseback.

James Watike is part of the original High Mountain Trackers and married to Ama, who rules the roost back at the ranch. Of all of us, James is by far the best actual tracker. He could pick up the trail of a field mouse.

James, Sully, Bo, and Fletch were all part of a special ops

tracking team under Jonas Harvey's command, and when each of them aged out of special forces, they all followed Jonas to the High Meadow Ranch.

JD is James and Ama's son, and he, Lucas Wolff, and myself are the more recent additions to the HMT team, which is now eight men strong. I know Jonas would eventually like to add one or two more, but the one person he has his sights on—his own stepson, Jackson—is playing hard to get.

"JD, did you get the rope anchored?"

I turn my head to catch him give the thumbs-up, while Wolff double-checks my gear. Then I test the rope, leaning my weight against it. It feels sturdy enough. Time is of the essence and my main concern is getting to the girl, I have to trust my teammates to get me back up.

"Ready?"

At Wolff's nod, I step back so my heels are hanging over the edge. Then I lean my body back, letting the rope take my weight.

As I rappel down, I kick loose a few stones that bounce down the rock face, narrowly missing the girl. I freeze, worried she might startle and let her tenuous hold slip, but she doesn't even seem to notice. The poor girl appears almost catatonic. I don't notice until I'm at face level with her how young she really is. She's no more than a teenager.

I can hear the clacking of her teeth chattering, and her whole body is trembling. I expected to find her eyes closed, so I'm surprised to find them wide open but empty. She appears to look right through me.

The girl's fingers are jammed into a crevice running just above her head, and only the toes of her white sneakers rest on the narrow ledge. Very carefully I position myself behind her, bracketing her body with mine. This way, if she lets go for any reason, I can use my body to prevent her from falling.

"Hey. I'm Dan. I'm going to put a harness on you, okay? All you have to do is stay still, and I'll have you out of here in no time."

There is no response, and no reaction when I secure her in the extra harness. There is no way I can send her up on her own so I fasten her to my front. My legs are long enough, I'll be able to walk us both back up the wall.

"Wolff?" I yell up.

"Yup."

"We're ready to come up. Together," I add.

It takes a bit to pry her cramped fingers from the rock crevice, and once I do, her entire body goes limp in my arms. When we're pulled over the edge a few minutes later, the only thing keeping her upright is my arm banded around her waist.

"This is Lucas," I mumble to the girl. "He's going to help you out of your harness, okay?"

"Spoke to Ewing," JD says in a soft tone as he walks up. "He'll be waiting at the trailhead with the EMTs."

Good, because this poor kid needs medical attention. I don't know what happened to her, or how she got out here, but I suspect it was nothing good.

While Wolff takes charge of the girl, James, JD, and I pack up the gear. Then we mount up—Wolff has the girl in front of him—and, barely half an hour later, James leads us into the small parking lot at the trailhead. An ambulance and two sheriff's vehicles are waiting for us.

It's not until Wolff has carefully lowered the girl into the hands of the waiting medics, and they finish securing her to the stretcher, I notice the blond woman on the far side of the ambulance, standing beside Sheriff Junior Ewing.

I'd tried hard to ignore the glimpse I caught of the blond hair behind the wheel of that Jeep last week. Sully didn't mention anything, and I convinced myself I must've been wrong. It couldn't have been her turning into the driveway.

Except, there she is.

"Is that...?" JD starts.

"Well, I'll be damned," James mutters beside me.

I don't have words.

There was a time I thought we were friends, but friends don't take off without a word, which is exactly what she did. I tried a few times to get a hold of her, maybe get an explanation from her, but she never got back to me. I may not be college-educated or book-wise, but I'm no fool, I can tell when I'm not wanted.

Since then, the few times her name came up I removed myself from the conversation. I should be long past what felt like a betrayal at the time, but seeing her standing there, just steps away, still burns in my gut.

I know the exact moment she recognizes me, when those blue eyes of hers widen slightly and she instantly pushes her shoulders back and juts out her chin.

Nothing's changed, she's still stubborn as fuck.

"Did you know she was back?" James asks.

"Fuck no," I grumble.

I hope she's only visiting, but when I see her climbing into the back of the ambulance with the sheriff, I have a nasty suspicion it won't be the last I see of Sloane Eckhart.

Just what I needed.

Three

SLOANE

Talk about hitting the ground running.

I haven't even been officially hired yet, but Sheriff Junior Ewing told me to tag along into the mountains. I'd barely been in his office long enough for him to explain it's a brand-new position he is looking to fill. One born out of necessity, from what I understand.

Libby's small police department had all but disintegrated over the past years after a scandal took out some key players, leaving the Lincoln County Sheriff's Office to pick up the slack. The LPD is slowly being built up from the ground again, but not fast enough to meet the growing demands on law enforcement as crime is rising. Even in small-town Montana.

According to Ewing, it's not easy finding experienced law enforcement officers willing to relocate to Libby, let alone take a pay cut, given the limited budget the Sheriff's Office has to work with.

The position is for a detective who would report to the sheriff but is expected to also work together closely with the tiny Libby police force, which currently is only three. A full-time job with flexible hours, depending on caseload.

I could barely contain my excitement when he outlined it, it's like the position was made for me. I was going to ask for a day or two to figure out childcare for Aspen. Pippa offered, as did Ama, but both of them work too. I'm going to need a better plan than simply counting on family.

Of course, that's when Ewing received that phone call and I suddenly found myself ushered out of his office and into his cruiser. He mentioned a couple of hikers hearing screams overnight and finding a backpack. A search team had just located a young girl clinging onto the edge of a cliff. He suggested I might come in handy in talking to the girl.

"We found her name in the backpack, it's Chelsea Little-ton. Only fourteen years old," he explains as we turn south on Hwy 2. "She's from Columbia Falls, was reported missing this past weekend. Apparently, she took off on Friday after an argument with her parents, who thought she'd be back after she cooled off. They spent all night looking for her and when she still hadn't shown up Saturday, they called it in."

It's Tuesday now. She's been missing for four days. How does a fourteen-year-old girl get from Columbia Falls—which is northeast of Kalispell—to the mountains just south of Libby? That's about a hundred miles, a long-ass way to come without transportation.

"She's a long way from home," I think out loud. "No way she got here under her own steam. Are you sure it's the girl?"

"Not confirmed yet—apparently, she's not talking—but it would be a bit of a coincidence to find a young girl matching the description of a missing person in the middle of nowhere, less than half a mile from where the backpack with her name was located," he points out.

True enough, but I know from experience, drawing conclusions without supporting evidence can be a dangerous habit to get into for an investigator. Assumptions don't get very far in court.

"Is she hurt? Any signs of visible trauma?" I ask.

"We'll find out when we get there. EMTs are en route."

We drive in silence, lost in our own thoughts, until Ewing steers the cruiser onto a dirt road leading up the mountain on the other side of the Fisher River.

"You know," I start, unable to stop thinking about the four days the girl has been missing, and all that could've happened to her during that time. "If it *is* Chelsea, she didn't get here by herself."

I glance over to find Ewing looking back at me.

"Yeah, I know," he confirms. "That's why I figured it might be easier for her to talk to a woman."

Clearly, he's thinking along the same lines. There's no way you can work in law enforcement, seeing what we see on a daily basis, and not have your mind go there. There are some sick individuals out there. The ambulance is not far behind us as we pull into the small parking lot at the base of the trail.

"They shouldn't be too long," Ewing announces as he gets out from behind the wheel.

I follow suit and get out of the cruiser as well, taking a deep breath in.

I've missed this; the scent of pine, soil, and cool, fresh mountain air. Living in Billings turned me into a bit of a city girl, and I haven't really ventured out much since returning—I've mostly stuck around my uncle's house this past week—but in this moment I realize how much more at home I feel here in the mountains.

I didn't grow up here—initially my only tie to this area was my uncle living here—but there is a reason why I ended up here twice when my life hit a roadblock. As much as I've tried to deny it, this place is where I feel grounded and connected.

I'm just joining Ewing at the back of the ambulance where he's talking with one of the EMTs, when I hear the distinct sounds of horses approaching. The light rattle of a bit, the creaking of a leather saddle, the soft thud of horses' footfalls, and a distinct snort of alert as our presence is sensed.

Lucas Wolff is first to appear out of the trees. When I first started working as a sheriff's deputy, he was still a federal agent with the FBI, but has since left the Bureau and joined the High Mountain Trackers' team.

I'm not looking at him though, my eyes are focused on the pale, young girl slumped in front of him in the saddle. Her eyes are open but staring off in the distance. I get the sense she's not even aware of her surroundings.

The EMTs have already removed the stretcher from the back of the rig and approach the lead horse. I watch as Wolff eases the girl down into the EMTs' care. She barely even responds as she is strapped down on the stretcher and loaded into the ambulance.

"I want you to hop in there with her. See what you can find out," Ewing instructs me in a low voice.

There's a prickle at the back of my neck that has me whip my head around. My eyes slam into a pair of hazel ones, and in one instant it's like the past eight years didn't happen. He was angry then too. Seeing him is like a sledge-hammer to the chest, stealing my breath.

He's matured. His face is no longer clean-shaven but sports dark, scruffy facial hair. He has also filled out, his shoulders wider, and overall bulkier than I recall. Dan was always tall, but now he looks imposing, especially on the back of that big sorrel he's riding.

The man has definitely not lost in appeal with age, and I feel my body responding.

Regret floods me, along with a wave of emotions I do not wish to put on display, so I straighten up, lift my chin proudly, and turn back to what I was brought out here to do.

For the sake of self-preservation, I resolutely push any thoughts of Dan from my mind.

In the back of the ambulance, Rick, the EMT, instructs me to sit on the bench by the girl's feet while he starts an IV on her. She doesn't seem to flinch with the poke of the needle, so I doubt she'll be responsive to me, but we'll see. One way or another, I'll find out what happened to her.

I glance out the small back window when the ambulance takes off a minute or two later and catch sight of those same eyes, still scrutinizing me closely.

Dan

Thankfully the guys don't razz me on the way back to the ranch, but every so often I catch a curious glance. I ignore those, needing a chance to recover from that blast from the past.

In the grand scope of things, eight years isn't that long, but at times it almost feels like a former life and I was a different person. When I think back to the last time I actually saw Sloane, I almost don't recognize myself.

I remember we were at the ranch, where Ama and Jonas's wife, Alex, had prepared a light lunch for everyone after the funeral. Thomas, Jonas's father, had brought out a bottle of twenty-year-old whiskey. I remember Ama having a fit, because the old man wasn't supposed to be drinking alcohol or smoking his smuggled Cubans due to a heart condition, but that didn't stop him.

I recall he ushered me out on the porch and into one of the rocking chairs, where he then proceeded to pour me about four fingers of the stuff in a tumbler. He handed me the glass, told me not to try and bury my pain, and left the bottle on the small table beside me. Then he went back inside, leaving me to grieve the loss of my mother who we'd just buried.

All I remember is putting a good dent in that bottle and then crying like a baby. At some point Sloane was there, pulling me out of the rocking chair before walking me back to my cabin and putting me to bed. I never saw her again.

"You doing okay?" Wolff asks when we walk our horses into the barn side by side. "I wasn't expecting that," he adds.

He briefly looks at me as he wraps his horse's lead to the stall door.

"Me neither," I confirm, instinctively knowing he's referring to Sloane.

"Must be tough," he probes.

I get along with all of my teammates but I'm probably closest with Lucas, even though he is a few years older. He lives in the cabin next to mine—the other guys all live elsewhere—and since neither of us are big on hanging out at one of the bars in town, we tend to stick around the ranch. We've spent quite a number of long, boring nights—especially during the winter—playing cards or watching movies.

We've also had some conversations, so I know a bit about him and he knows me better than most. It's possible in one of those—often alcohol-infused—talks, I may have let on how much Sloane's abrupt departure impacted me.

Which is why I'm inclined to answer instead of shutting him down.

"Harder than I'm comfortable admitting," I confess.

I slide Will's saddle off his back and drop it over the top of his stall door. Then I grab a handful of straw to rub him dry. On the other side of the aisle, Wolff does the same with his horse, Judge.

"You cared for her."

I shrug. "I thought we were friends."

I notice Wolff staring at me as he repeats, "You cared for her."

Shaking my head, I return my attention to grooming my horse.

"Didn't realize how much 'til she bailed on me right after my mother died." I toss down the straw and remove Will's bridle, opening the stall door for him. "Then I got pissed when she ignored me, not responding to messages or texts."

"You're still pissed," Wolff concludes.

"Fuck yeah," I respond, closing the door and grabbing the saddle. "She took off without a word, was gone for eight years, and suddenly she's back. Damn right I'm pissed."

Then I return my gear to the tack room and almost bump into Wolff when I walk back out. He blocks my path.

"Means you still care," he imparts, not giving me a chance to counter before he steps around me.

I dismiss his comment and walk out back to grab one of

the utility ATVs, so I can check on the guys doing repairs to the fencing on the north pasture. But throughout the afternoon, his words keep playing through my mind.

When I return to the ranch at the end of the day, I catch sight of the dark red Jeep I now know belongs to Sloane. What the fuck is she doing here?

I return the ATV and instead of hitting up the big house for an early dinner, as I'd intended, I start walking toward my cabin. I probably have a couple of eggs I can fry for dinner—that's about the extent of my culinary skills—but I'm not in the right frame of mind for a confrontation with her.

Unfortunately, that choice is taken from me when she steps out the front door just as I pass by the steps up to the porch. She freezes when she spots me, and I come to a dead stop when I notice she's carrying a car seat.

It's like time is suspended and all the air is sucked from my lungs.

A punch of sharp pain hits my gut the moment my brain processes what I'm looking at.

A baby? *Sloane?*

"Hey, Dan," she says in a soft voice, moving to the top of the steps.

My eyes are fixed on the white bundle packed in the carrier. I can't see more than a little bit of a forehead and a shock of dark hair peeking out.

"This is my daughter, Aspen," she explains, brushing the blanket out of the way to reveal a small, sleeping baby.

Then I let my eyes crawl up Sloane's body and register the added curve to her hips and fullness of her breasts. I thought she was beautiful eight years ago when she was bordering on thin, but with that body filled out in lush curves she's a fucking knockout.

My body's response to her feels like another goddamn betrayal, and I don't even bother keeping the anger out of my voice.

"Congrats. Hope you're happy."

With that I turn my back and focus on my cabin, forcing myself to walk and not run.

Four

"I'm sorry, what?"

I wince at her tone.

Anger, I could've handled, but the shocked hurt in her voice is so much worse. I'm instantly overwhelmed with guilt and wrecked with second-guessing.

"What is it?" I hear Steve's voice in the background.

"You're a grandmother, Mom. Her name is Aspen," I clarify before adding, "She's four months old."

I hear a gasp, and then a brief rustling, before Steve's voice demands to know, "What the hell is going on? Who is this?"

"It's me, Steve."

"Sloane? What happened? Why is your mother crying?"

Oh yeah, the guilt is thick and bitter in my throat.

"Because I just told her you guys are grandparents."

"You're pregnant?" he asks.

"Actually, I have a baby daughter, she was born the twenty-first of April."

He's silent for a while. All I can hear are my mother's sniffles, and I'm on the verge of tears myself.

This is the problem with bad decisions; the consequences often aren't only yours to bear.

When his voice comes back on, it's carefully measured, but I can hear the barely contained anger.

I deserve it.

"I really hope you have some very good reasons why you decided to keep this information from your own mother."

Lies are what got me here, so honesty is the only way forward.

"I thought there were, but I'm not so sure anymore," I confess.

The first call is long, and painful, and for me humbling and even humiliating. But when Mom calls me back the next day—after giving herself a chance to process the information—we're able to have a more productive conversation. I take the opportunity to tell her about Jeff, not as an excuse, but for the sake of total transparency.

At the end of our talk, she prompts me to tell her about the delivery, which had been fast and furious, and asks for me to send her pictures. At least that's something I can do for her, having chronicled as many moments in Aspen's short life as I'd been able to capture on my phone.

The following day I call back via FaceTime, and watch my mother and Steve fall in love with my daughter. By the end of that call, Mom announces she's coming to Montana for a visit, and I'm determined to have a decent plan in place by then.

My next call is to Junior Ewing to let him know I can officially start first thing tomorrow.

～

"It's a good thing you're so damn adorable, you little stinker."

Aspen is leaking drool and smiling her gummy smile at me while I try to get her dressed again.

We'd been ready to head out the door when I heard a distinct rumbling, much too loud for a body that small. Even before I lifted her out of the car seat, my nose alerted me to what I would find. Good thing I had an extra early start this morning, thanks to a restless night with this little girl.

Teething, already. I wasn't aware babies could start this early, but according to Pippa they can.

Aspen was fussy all night, waking up crying several times, and I finally gave up on trying to sleep. Instead, I surfed the web on my phone, reading up on the milestones and developmental stages of a four-month-old, including what to expect when they're teething. Apparently, diarrhea is not an unusual side effect, hence the impressive blowout requiring a quick hose-down in the tub, and a completely new outfit.

The house is already empty when I carry my daughter back to her car seat, which I'd abandoned by the front door. Sully had been out the door at the crack of dawn, something about picking up a horse in Coeur d'Alene, Idaho. I know Pippa had a busy schedule at her auto shop today but had to drop Carmi off at school first.

Today is my first—official—day at work, which is why Aspen is going to go back to the ranch where Ama and Alex have volunteered to look after her.

I looked into daycare and there is one in town, but they have a waiting list I added Aspen's name to. One of the ladies at the daycare gave me the name of a woman who does home childcare, but she doesn't take babies under six months.

I was starting to panic, wondering if I should pass on the job and coast on my meager savings until I could secure care for my daughter. But when Pippa heard I was considering blowing off the position with the Sheriff's Office, she told me not to make any stupid decisions. Two hours later, I was handed a babysitting schedule for the next two weeks.

Pippa, her sister, Nella, my uncle, Ama, and Alex all have volunteered for shifts. Even Lucy—who is married to Bo and self-admittedly is better with animals than people—appeared to have volunteered for a shift. One thing is sure, Aspen is going to end up with a lot of aunties.

Coming to Libby had been a bit of a knee-jerk decision, and I wasn't sure if it would work out, but it sure looks like I made the right call. They say it takes a village to raise a child, which, in Aspen's case, seems to be a fair statement.

After those first two weeks, my mom plans to be here for the next two, and I have a feeling she won't want to share any time she can have with her granddaughter.

All of that means I should be covered for childcare for the next month, leaving my hands free to get a good grip on my new job.

I'm starting with a return visit to the hospital, where I'm hoping Chelsea—the girl they found up near Kenelty Mountain—has recovered enough from her ordeal to the point she'll be able to answer some of my questions. Something she wasn't able to do when I rode in the back of the ambulance with her a couple of days ago.

Alex is waiting on the porch when I get to the ranch, and I'm able to hand off my daughter and get out of there without bumping into Dan again. After last time, I hope to avoid a repeat of that uncomfortable encounter. Hearing the bitter disdain in his voice once was enough.

~

A car pulls out right next to the main doors to Cabinet Peaks Medical Center, and I slip the Jeep in the vacated parking spot. I grab the small stuffed lion I found at the gift store around the corner, and head into the lobby.

The woman who gets up from the chair next to the girl's bed must be her mother. She looks a little worse for wear, like she hasn't slept in days. Chelsea herself looks better than she did last time I saw her. A little more aware of her surroundings, her eyes no longer hold the blank look but follow me into the room.

"Mrs. Littleton?"

I never met her and am aware I'm not wearing a uniform, so I hold out my hand to introduce myself. She takes it tentatively as she nods.

"I'm Sloane Eckhart. I'm a detective with the Lincoln Sheriff's Department. I rode along in the ambulance with your daughter on Tuesday."

Understanding replaces her suspicious expression.

"Yes, Sheriff Ewing shared as much when he dropped in yesterday. He also mentioned you would be by this morning. Nice to meet you, but please call me Donna."

Then I turn to the bed, where Chelsea looks to have been following the exchange between her mother and me.

"And how are you today?" I ask the girl. "Do you remember me from a few days ago?"

For a moment I don't know if my question registers.

"Horses."

"Yes, the guys who found you were on horseback, and

you got to ride out of the woods on one of them. You remember that?"

This time she nods.

"I brought you something." I hand her the stuffed animal.

"Lion," she identifies it as she tucks it against her chest.

"Yes, I saw him and he made me think of you. Did you know the lion is a symbol for courage?"

Chelsea shakes her head.

"It is. That's why I got it for you, because I thought you were pretty courageous yourself." I flash her an encouraging smile. "Do you think I could borrow your mom for a minute?"

She looks at her mother, who nods and tells her, "We'll be right back."

"How is she?" I ask as soon as we step out in the hallway.

"I'm not sure," Donna says, running a distracted hand through her messy hair. "The doctor says there doesn't seem to be a physical reason for her state. No sign she hit her head or has a concussion or anything, but she can't seem to put together a complete sentence and she seems so confused."

She certainly does. From all accounts Chelsea is a spunky teenager, a bit of a rebel with a sharp tongue. The girl in the hospital bed does not seem like the same person. Of course, we still don't know the full extent of the ordeal she's been through, although the attending physician who saw her when we first came in already told me she suspected sexual assault and would be doing a rape kit.

Bloodwork would've been standard procedure, and I'm curious to know whether anything was flagged on those labs.

Could some drug be causing this lingering fugue state?

Dan

"Sit down a spot, son."

I glance up to see the old man sitting in a corner of the porch, rocking his chair and having his daily drink.

"I should go wash up before dinner."

"Oh, bull hickey. Sit yer sorry ass down and keep an old man company."

Ninety-two years old, a serious heart condition, can barely get one foot in front of the other, but his mind is still sharp as a tack. I don't think any of us—least of all Jonas—would've expected him to still be kicking around, but here he is, issuing orders and making demands.

I love this old man. Enough to forfeit my shower.

The moment I sit down beside him on the porch, he picks up the bell next to him on the small table and starts swinging it. Hard.

In a matter of seconds, Ama comes flying out of the house.

"Keep it down already, old man," she barks. "What do you need?"

The mischievous look on Thomas's face has me bite the inside of my cheek not to laugh out loud. He loves getting under Ama's skin, and most of the time she gives as good as she gets. Today she looks a bit frazzled.

"I'm running low, and young Dan here could do with a beer."

Ama is about to give him what I suspect is an earful, when a high-pitched squeal sounds from inside. She shoots Thomas a dark glare before she ducks back in the door.

Less than a minute later she returns, a bottle of beer in her hand and a baby on her arm. I'm pretty sure it's the same baby I saw Sloane carry out of the house a few days ago. The only difference is this time the kid's bright blue eyes are wide open. If Sloane hadn't already mentioned she had a daughter, the bright pink outfit would've given it away.

"Where's my drink?" Thomas asks as Ama hands me the beer.

"How many hands does it look like I have?" she bites off. "Not to mention I've got better things to do than play bartender for you. Today has been a shitshow of epic proportions. Sully's truck broke down twenty miles outside of Coeur d'Alene so Jonas is driving out there to pick him and the trailer up. Then Alex was supposed to help me look after this little one today, but she was called away for an emergency at the rescue. I have three loads of laundry still to do and have barely had a chance to start the dinner y'all will be bugging me for shortly."

No wonder she looks stressed.

"Well, all you had to do was tell me," Thomas sputters, which doesn't do much to appease Ama.

So I set down my bottle and put my hands on my knees.

"What do you need me to do?" I offer.

Next thing I know, my arms open automatically when she shoves the baby at me.

"Take her."

Ama disappears inside before my brain can come up with an objection.

Any baby experience I have began and ended with Carmi, Sully's daughter, and Fletch's son, Hunter, and that was twelve or thirteen years ago. It's not that I don't like babies, because I do, but the fact this is Sloane's baby is making it a little awkward. Still, I settle her a little better in the crook of my arm.

Then I hear the creak of the rocking chair and Thomas's raspy chuckle and look up. The old fart clearly thinks this is funny.

"You should see the look on your face," he points out as he continues to rock his chair. "I'm guessing young Sloane becoming a parent was a surprise to you as well?"

"Yes," I grumble, just as a little hand slaps against my chin and catches on the short hairs of my beard.

I drop my eyes to Sloane's baby, who has her little face turned toward me. I don't know who the dark hair belongs to, but those blue eyes are unmistakably her mother's.

"Aspen. That's her name," Thomas shares. "Pretty little thing, ain't she?"

She is, especially when her little mouth spreads in a wide, toothless smile.

"You look good holdin' that baby," he continues. "Too bad you let her momma slip away, or that wee one could'a been yours."

Fuck. That stings.

Should've known the old man wouldn't hesitate to poke his finger in the sore spot.

"I'm not the one who left."

The bitter comment slips out before I can check it.

"No, you weren't. You're just the one who let her walk."

Agitated, I get to my feet, shifting the baby to my shoulder as I start to pace the porch.

"It wasn't that simple."

"It never is, son. It never is."

I stop at the railing and look out at a couple of the year-lings fooling around in the front pasture we just moved them to.

I'm still making excuses for my lack of action when it comes to Sloane, but none of that matters anymore. Not when I'm standing here holding the baby she had with another man.

The regret I feel now is too little and much too fucking late.

For a while, the only sound is the creaking of the rocking chair on the wooden boards of the porch. Then Thomas pipes up again.

"It's not too late, Daniel. Never is, when it's important enough."

I open my mouth to point out the pink-clad, pint-sized, proverbial elephant in the room—currently with her little head resting against my shoulder—when I hear the sound of a vehicle coming up the driveway. It's Sloane's Jeep.

She doesn't see me at first—I'm partly obscured by one of the massive beam posts—but her eyes find me as she comes up the stairs. She comes to an abrupt halt when she notices her daughter in my arms. Then a corner of her mouth tilts up in a soft smile.

"She's asleep," she points out.

I have to tuck my chin in to see Aspen's little face. Her eyes are closed, dark lashes fanning on her pale cheeks.

"So she is," I rumble, keeping my voice low in an attempt not to wake her.

"Hi, Thomas," she says, peeking around me. "Is Ama around?"

"In the kitchen," he responds.

"Would you mind hanging on to her for a few more minutes?" she asks me. "I'm gonna pop inside to check in with Ama and grab her things."

"Sure."

I watch her walk inside, and drop a cheek to the top of

the baby's head. She's like a little oven, warm against my chest, and her fine hair tickles my beard. Behind me the old man starts chuckling again, but I choose to ignore him.

As promised, Sloane is back in a few minutes with a diaper bag and a car seat.

"Do you want her in there?"

"Would you mind? The less we juggle her the better the chance she stays sleeping."

I wait for her to pull the straps aside before I lean forward and carefully place Aspen in her seat. Her face scrunches up a bit but she continues sleeping as Sloane straps her in.

"I've got it," I tell her when she goes to pick up the car seat, and carry the seat down the steps to her Jeep.

Sloane opens the driver's side back door and I lift the seat in, clicking it firmly into the base.

"Thanks."

She throws me a faint smile as she carefully shuts the door.

"No problem."

I have a million questions I'd like to ask her, but instead, I shove my hands in my pockets and take a step back as she gets behind the wheel.

She gives me a little wave before she drives off, and I head back up the steps to finish my beer.

The old man is still sitting in the corner, rocking back and forth, clearly not done with the commentary.

"I guess it's a start."

Five

"Eckhart, line two!"

Betty's voice carries clear down the hallway from her office, which is right behind the front desk. It's one of three private offices, the other two house dispatch and, of course, Sheriff Junior Ewing. The rest of us are in an open space at the far end of the hallway, where I have a cubicle with a desk, a chair, a computer, and the ancient telephone which currently has a light blinking.

I pick up the handset and press the lit button.

"Lincoln Sheriff's Office, this is Detective Eckhart."

"Detective, this is Donna. Donna Littleton, Chelsea's mom."

"Yes, of course. What can I do for you, Mrs. Littleton?"

I just checked in on Chelsea yesterday, unfortunately the girl still wasn't talking. Mrs. Littleton had given permission for the girl's doctor to speak with me, but she wasn't able to provide much useful information either, other than to confirm some type of sexual interference had taken place. Blood analysis did not show anything remarkable, but as the doctor pointed out, there are plenty of drugs, which process out of the body quickly, that could've been used to control her.

"It's Chelsea...she was restless last night. Talking in her sleep. A nightmare, I guess."

I immediately sit up straight and pull a pad of paper toward me, ready to make notes.

"It wasn't very coherent though. From what I was able to piece together, she was running from someone or something. She mentioned they were big, and I'm positive she said she was being pushed. Then she started screaming she was falling and something about dead eyes staring up at her." The poor woman stifles a sob. "I feel so damn helpless."

I can only imagine, knowing something horrific has happened to your child outside of your control must be devastating.

"Mrs. Littleton, why don't I drop by, try talking to her again? Perhaps the dream triggered her memories of her ordeal."

"It's Donna, and I already tried that, but the only thing she mentioned again was the dead eyes staring up."

It's not much to go on, but it seems to imply last night's episode may not have been merely a dream, but rather an actual recollection of events. It certainly is more than I had before and would suggest she did not end up going over the edge of the cliff under her own steam.

Maybe I should head back up Kenelty Mountain, have a good look around the area where the girl was found.

"Donna, your call was helpful. It gives me something to work with. Please don't hesitate to get in touch if there is anything else. Is there any word on when Chelsea may be able to come home with you?"

Home for them would mean Columbia Falls, which is a bit out of the way, but we'll make it work. It may be good for the girl's recovery to be in familiar surroundings.

"They tell me it could be as soon as tomorrow."

"That's good. I'll try to pop by tonight or tomorrow morning to touch base with you," I promise.

After ending the call, I go in search of Junior, finding his office empty. Next, I poke my head around the door of Betty's office.

"Is Sheriff Ewing around?"

Betty turns around and scrutinizes me over the rim of the reading glasses perched on the tip of her nose. The five-foot-nothing, silver-haired woman is no less intimidating now than she was all those years ago when I was a fresh new deputy.

She's a permanent fixture here at the sheriff's office. I think she's worked here most of her adult life and knows everything there is to know. Including the whereabouts of our sheriff.

"Gettin' a haircut. What do you need him for?"

I tell her I want to see if I can retrace the girl's steps up on that mountain.

"So? You need to do it, do it."

"Fair enough, but do we have an ATV or something I can use to get up there?"

"In the shop getting serviced, but if you don't want to wait, you can always borrow a ride at High Meadow. Better yet," she adds, turning back to her computer screen. "Get one of those boys to take you, they're the ones who found her."

That gives me pause for a moment. What she says makes

sense, but it would mean stopping by the ranch, when I thought I was safe from encountering Dan today since I left Aspen home with Pippa.

Seeing him yesterday, my daughter in his arms, had been a jolt to the system in more ways than one. It definitely was a dramatic change from our first encounter. Driving home, I couldn't help but replay how natural he looked handling Aspen. I remember Dan being pretty hands-on when my cousin, Carmi, was born.

I think it might have been what made me aware my attraction to him was more than a temporary crush. That appeal still packs a wallop. Handsome, rugged man with a baby, who could resist?

I'd better fortify that shield around my heart. I've made the mistake of following it once before with a painful outcome.

I can't afford to do it again; I have a child now.

Of course, the first person I see when I drive past the corral is Dan, working a large black horse on a lunge line.

Instead of heading toward the house, I pull the Jeep in next to a couple of trailers parked beside the barn.

"Hey," he calls out when he sees me walking up.

I rest my arms on the top of the fence.

"Hey," I return. "Nice animal."

"Yeah, a bit unruly though. It's the horse your uncle picked up from Coeur d'Alene yesterday. This guy was stuck in the trailer on the side of the road for five hours. Apparently, he's not a fan."

"I see."

I note the flared nostrils and darting eyes, as the horse's

ears flit back and forth. I know enough to recognize high anxiety.

"You're back," Dan observes, reeling the horse in slowly. "No Aspen today?"

"No, she's with Pippa."

When the animal is within reach, he gently rubs its nose before taking a firm hold of the halter. Then he starts walking to the gate, which I quickly go to hold open. Then I fall in step beside him as he leads the horse into the barn.

"I'm actually here for work," I explain. "I need to have a look at the trail up on Kenelty Mountain, and I figured it would probably be easiest to do it on horseback. That is, if I could borrow one."

Dan opens the half-door to one of the empty stalls and guides the horse in, before slipping out again and sliding the latch shut. Then he leans his back against it, crosses his ankles, and folds his arms in front of him.

"How long since you've ridden?"

I guess it's a fair question, considering I'm asking to borrow a horse. I'm just not sure the answer will be satisfactory.

"About eight years, I'd say. Give or take," I admit.

Dan

No way I was going to let her go up by herself.

Good thing it's quiet today. No active searches, which is almost unheard of this time of year, meaning plenty of manpower to cover the ranch.

The only ones who aren't around are Jonas, Alex, and

Fletch. I'm not sure what's going on, but I was just coming out of the barn around four—I'd been checking on one of our mares who's about to pop—when I noticed Fletch's truck pulling up to the house. Then I noticed Alex and Jonas coming down the porch steps with suitcases, and getting in before the truck disappeared down the driveway again.

I'm not sure what that was about, but I figure if it's important for me to know, somebody will tell me.

I shift in my saddle to look behind me. It may have been a long time, but Sloane still looks pretty comfortable on a horse. Of course, I saddled Pudding for her, who is one of our most even-tempered mounts. Sloane always was a good rider and doesn't seem to have an issue urging her horse across the river.

"Watch for low branches," I remind her when we get up on the other bank and make our way into the trees.

Wouldn't be the first time someone gets knocked out of the saddle.

When we reach the trailhead, there are no vehicles parked in the small lot, and Sloane pulls up level with me.

"Do you know the exact location where the hikers found the backpack? I'd like to start there."

"Yep. That's where we started our search for her."

It doesn't take long to get from the trailhead to where the backpack had been found. It's not far off the hiking path on the other side of a large, fallen tree that looked to have been hit by lightning.

"Can you hold her?" Sloane asks, dismounting and handing over Pudding's reins.

Then she slips the small backpack from her shoulders and digs out a digital camera.

"What direction is the ledge you found her on?"

I point northeast, past the exposed clump of roots to where the first of the orange marks we left is visible. When tracking in these mountains, we always carry a can or two of spray paint to mark our way. It has a dual purpose, it eliminates the risk of going around in circles, and it makes retracing our steps a piece of cake.

"What made you head in that direction?" she wants to know.

"See the snapped branch on that young pine? JD found a few strands of hair snagged on it."

She slowly walks toward the tree I indicate, scanning the ground around her. She's clearly looking for something. When she gets to the broken branch, she starts snapping pictures. Then she swings around.

"I have to look up to see the hair and I'm five seven. Chelsea is only five foot one. Also, her hair is medium blond, this is dark brown."

Taken aback, I loop Pudding's lead around my saddle horn and dismount Will.

"Stay," I tell him as I walk over to Sloane.

I glance at the lock of hair, which is at about eye level for me. She's right, even if the color wasn't off, there's no way the little girl I plucked off that ledge could've gotten her hair tangled on a branch that would've been about a foot over her head.

When we look for clues when we're tracking, we look for anything that stands out. The hair on that branch pointed us in a certain direction. I realize it carries a different value for Sloane. To her, it's evidence.

"Could you take a few pictures of me collecting this?" she asks, handing me the camera. "Just point and click."

I start taking pictures as she unzips her backpack and removes a black plastic bin. When she opens the lid, it looks like an evidence collection kit. She pulls on a pair of blue gloves and grabs a small brown evidence envelope as well as a pair of disposable tweezers.

I keep snapping until she's collected the hair from the branch, and signed and dated the small, brown envelope.

"You're thinking someone was after her?"

Sloane nods as she tucks the envelope away and snaps off the gloves.

"Yes. The girl's been talking in her sleep and it seems she may be starting to remember things."

She slips the backpack over her shoulders. When she holds out her hand, I return the camera, which she loops around her neck.

"How far are we from the location?"

"Knowing where we're going, I'd say twenty minutes, half an hour."

"Okay, don't go too fast, I want to keep an eye out for possible evidence."

I nod and walk back to where Will is still waiting patiently, Pudding by his side. I hold on to Sloane's mount as she grabs on to the horn, puts her left foot in the stirrup, and swings up in the saddle. Then I mount up as well, and lead us through the trees.

For a while there's only the sounds of the woods and, normally, I would enjoy the quiet ride, but knowing Sloane is behind me, the silence has my thoughts spinning.

Then suddenly I find myself asking, "What happened in Billings?"

The pause drags on so long, I resist turning around.

"I fucked up," she finally responds in a soft voice.

I have to strain to hear and I'm about to prompt her for more when she starts talking again.

"There's really nothing else to say. I messed up, trusted

the wrong person, and was left holding the bag. Trying to work a job that sometimes requires fourteen- or sixteen-hour days while single-handedly taking care of a baby, who wakes up at all hours of the night, is impossible."

It's been on my tongue a few times, and I've resisted asking Ama or even Sully what the deal is, but I feel I can finally justify asking the question.

"Where is Aspen's father?"

She waits a beat and then answers, "Did I mention I fucked up?"

At that, I glance over my shoulder and catch her shrug, but she doesn't look away.

"Let's just say he's not in the picture. Not anymore. It took him a month to figure out he wasn't cut out for parent-hood and took off."

"What a fucking loser," I burst out.

What piece of shit man walks away from his child?

I mean, my own parents weren't exactly perfect, I didn't even know my father existed until I was almost thirty and he showed up on my doorstep. Although, in his defense, he didn't actually know of my existence either. My mother had kept that a secret from both of us for as long as she was alive.

But walking away from a little baby?

"I sure know how to pick 'em, don't I?" Sloane scoffs.

Frankly, I don't really know much about her life. At least, not the one she led in Billings. I don't have any idea who she was seeing, but there's one thing I do know.

"It's his loss."

There is no more conversation until we reach the rockier terrain leading to the edge of the gorge. I dismount and encourage Sloane to do the same. Then I tie the horses to a tree so they have some shade, before leading Sloane to the edge of the drop off.

The narrow ledge is visible below and beyond that, the sheer rock face continues down until it reaches the tops of the trees in the valley below. It's an absolute miracle that girl managed to cling on to that barely three-inch ridge for however long she was there.

"Did you see anything when you were down there?" Sloane asks, peering over the edge.

"See anything...on the ledge? Like what?"

She lifts the camera and as she begins to take pictures of the gorge below, she inches a little too close to the edge to my liking. To anchor her, I hook a finger in a loop on the waistband of her jeans and use my weight to balance her.

"I don't know. The girl mentioned dead eyes staring up in her sleep and, apparently, repeated it after she woke up."

I tug her back from the edge and take her place to get a better look. It's a fair way down and, other than an occasional silver glimmer of the creek through the canopy of the trees, it's virtually impossible to distinguish any details.

"Didn't notice anything at the time, I was focused on the girl, and I can't really see much of anything now."

"Do you think you can get me down there?"

"To the bottom of the gorge? Not easily. We'd have to follow the creek upriver from where it merges into the Fisher River, which is miles north of where we crossed. I'd have to look at satellite images, but finding our way to this spot could take the better part of a day, if not more."

I don't miss the muffled curse under her breath.

"What about to the ledge?"

I swing around, my eyebrows raised.

"That ledge?" I point back to the narrow ridge that somehow saved that girl's life. "Hell no," I tell her emphatically. "Even if we had the team here and all the proper gear, it would be a hell no. This isn't some recreational rock wall for amateurs to play around on."

She narrows her eyes on me and jerks that stubborn chin up.

"Amateur? I'm here investigating the possible abduction of and sexual assault on a young girl. I'm hardly playing."

Sexual assault?

A sick feeling twists in my stomach at the memory of her small body trembling uncontrollably against me. The thought of someone violating her like that has me see red.

I take her point, she's doing her job, but that still doesn't mean I'm going to play fast and loose with her safety. Even if I had the proper equipment with me, letting someone without experience rappel down that cliff would be irresponsible.

"Do you have a long lens for that camera?" I ask her. "If she saw something with the naked eye from that ledge, you should be able to pick it up from up here with a zoom."

It takes her a moment to react, but then she dives into her backpack and triumphantly pulls out a padded pouch. While she changes out the lens on her camera, I grab a spray can from my saddle bag. Then I walk back to the spot directly above where we first spotted the girl clinging to the cliff, and drop down to my stomach, inching part of my upper body out over the edge.

"What the hell are you doing?" I hear Sloane behind me.

Instead of answering, I give the can a few shakes before aiming it at the rock face below and marking it with a downward arrow.

"Making sure we can find the spot from below, if need be," I tell her as I scramble back and get to my feet. "Start taking your pictures."

She rewards me with the flash of a smile before lifting her camera.

Six

SLOANE

"Oh my God. Did you see that?"

I look up from my computer screen to glance at Carmi, who is doing homework at the kitchen island. Sully is at the ranch, and Pippa had some work to do at her auto shop.

"See what?"

She points at the play mat on the floor where I put Aspen down for some tummy time.

"She rolled over."

Sure enough, my daughter is now lying on her back, little legs kicking and her hand firmly clasped around one of the toys hanging down from the mobile of her play mat.

I groan, digging my fingers into my eyes. They're gritty from intensely staring at the screen for the better part of two days.

I snapped well over two-hundred pictures at the gorge on Kenelty Mountain on Friday. We were out there for several hours, but weren't able to spot anything with the naked eye.

My hopes are fixed on the images I took, but it's taking a lot longer to zoom in as close as I can and scan every inch of every image. A bit like looking for Waldo, except I have no idea what exactly it is I'm looking for, or if anything is even there.

Yesterday, Chelsea was released and she and her mom went back home. Unfortunately, the girl wasn't able to provide me with anything new. According to her mother, the doctor suggested Chelsea's disconnected state is a result of the severe psychological trauma she endured and referred them to a psychiatrist in Kalispell.

So, as of right now, the only leads I have are the hairs—which were sent to the State Crime Lab in Missoula—Chelsea's minimal recollections, and piles of images. Sadly, those are what have demanded my attention, and made me miss this milestone in my child's development.

I suddenly find myself blinking against emotion, and slap my laptop shut before sliding off the chair onto the floor to join my daughter.

"Did you just roll over?" I coo at her upturned face. Drool is covering her little fist as she tries to shove her hand —toy and all—in her mouth. "Are you feeling pretty pleased with yourself?"

"Mm-gah."

"Is that so?"

I smile through my tears as she launches into an animated litany of garbled sounds only she understands.

"You know what?" I announce as I get to my feet and pick my baby up. "We're stuck inside while it's a beautiful day out. Wanna go for a walk?"

"Sure!" Carmi agrees enthusiastically.

Anything to get out of the homework she already left to the last day of the weekend. As I've learned in the short time

I've been here, my little cousin is not a fan of school, reminding me a lot of myself at that age.

"Can we go check out the new house?" she asks.

Sully mentioned the influx of trucks rumbling past the house are heading for the property in the back, which apparently belongs to Dan. I had no idea, but my uncle told me he's building a house along the river.

For some reason, I'd always pictured Dan living at High Meadow forever. So hearing he's building a place of his own immediately piqued my curiosity. Uncle Sully lived in one of the cabins at the ranch until he had a family and then he built this place, needing more room. I never really stopped to think maybe Dan has found someone he wants to start a family with.

There was no way I was going to ask Sully, but the first chance I had, I cornered Pippa. I tried to be casual about it, but I think she saw right through me. She mentioned he may have been seeing Shelby Vandermeer at some point—I remember her parents; they own the feedstore—but didn't believe it was anything serious. I have to admit, that didn't feel very good.

Still, I'm curious by nature—hence my chosen profession—so I take Carmi up on her suggestion.

"Sure, why not?"

It's warm out, so I leave Aspen in her romper when I fit her into the baby sling, but I do rub some sunscreen on her legs and arms, and fit the little sun bonnet on her head for protection. She likes facing outward so she can kick her legs and wave her arms.

My daughter is a mover, even before she was born, she seemed to be in constant motion. She's already rolling over and before you know it, she'll be crawling all over the place.

I get the feeling I'll be having a hell of a time keeping her contained.

"Do you like fishing?" Carmi asks as we walk around the house to the back.

"Sure. Your dad used to take me all the time when I was younger. Taught me how to clean fish too."

Carmi exaggerates a mock shudder and kicks at a small stone in her path.

"Why? You don't like fishing?" I probe.

"Fishing's fine, but not the cleaning part. Yuck."

I grin as I let my eyes drift over the river. "Gotta clean 'em if you wanna eat them."

"But doesn't the blood bother you?"

I focus on my cousin.

"Not really. I mean, I don't think about it, but I remember a friend in high school who would faint if she got a paper cut." I veer into Carmi and bump her lightly. "What made you ask?"

"I dunno. I was thinking you probably can't be a detective if blood bothers you."

"Does it bother you?"

She makes a gagging sound that more than conveys her answer, and I wonder if perhaps she'd thought about becoming an investigator one day. In which case, I'd better not inform her there are much worse things than blood you can be confronted with. My mind is briefly transported back to the first autopsy I attended. Not a pleasant experience, and it doesn't really get easier with time.

I hook my arm through hers as the sounds of construction get louder. The house can't be too far.

"You know, I remember you used to hate broccoli when you were little, but you sure seemed to like it last night." I give her a little squeeze. "We grow out of stuff when we get older. Who knows? Ten years from now the sight of blood may not bother you anymore."

"I hope so."

It's hot out and there isn't a lot of tree cover, so by the time we walk around the first truck parked along the side of the dirt road, Aspen is literally plastered against my front, and I am sweaty and gross. I'm tempted to turn around, but curiosity, as well as Carmi's determined pace a few steps in front of me, drives me forward.

Until my young cousin stops abruptly and I almost bump into her.

"*Wow,*" she breathes.

When I follow her line of sight, I have to agree.

"Holy hotness."

The house is not much of a house yet. The foundation is obviously in, but they've just begun to stack the giant logs that are apparently to make up the outside walls. A large crane sits beside the stack of lumber for the heavy lifting. The walls are two high and it looks like they're in the process of adding the third layer of logs.

They, being five healthy, wide-shouldered, and shirtless men.

JD is the first one I pick out, he's closest and has his back toward us, his dark, gleaming braid reaching below his shoulder blades. Wolff is easy to spot, since he's facing our way and lifts a hand in greeting. I don't know who the two guys in the baseball hats are, but I have no trouble identifying Dan. Even without his distinctive white cowboy hat, I'd like to think I could've picked him out based on physique alone. I've spent plenty of time fantasizing about that man's body.

Then I watch as he pulls a rag from his back pocket,

removes his hat, and wipes the sweat off his face and from his neck.

I tell myself it's the heat making my knees buckle.

～

Dan

"Are you going to have a porch swing?"

"Maybe," I mutter, fielding Carmi's nonstop chatter.

But most of my attention is on Sloane, who is sitting on one of the logs, her arm protectively around the baby strapped to her chest. She throws her head back, laughing at something JD said, and I shove down a jab of jealousy at the uninhibited way she is around my friend, when around me I can sense her reservation.

When she picks up the bottle of water JD handed her and puts it to her lips, I can't take my eyes off the long lines of her exposed neck. A thin layer of sweat makes her skin glisten and I imagine my tongue stroking up the slim column, tasting her.

Her throat moves as she swallows the water, and a drop clings to her plump bottom lip when she lifts the bottle away. I almost groan out loud when her tongue darts out, catching it right before it rolls down her chin.

Maybe I did make a sound, because suddenly she turns her head my way, her eyes wide and questioning.

"...Can I come pick it out?"

Carmi's voice penetrates my real-time fantasy and acts like a cold shower. I force myself to tear my eyes from Sloane and look at the teenager.

"Pick what out?"

I've clearly missed some of what she said when she rolls her eyes at me.

"Your dog, silly."

A dog?

"First let me finish building this house," I tell the girl. "Then we'll worry about whether or not I should get a dog."

She shoves out her bottom lip in an impressive pout that does not go unnoticed by Sloane.

"All right, Carmi," she intervenes as she gets to her feet. "This little one needs her nap, you and I both have work waiting, and I think it's time for us to let these guys get back to building a house."

I shove away from where I was leaning against my truck's rear fender. I haven't really had a chance to talk to Sloane since we got back on Friday. A lot has happened since then and I'm thankful I have the damn house to keep me busy, but I'm curious to know if she was able to see anything interesting on all those pictures she took.

Or so I tell myself.

"You guys get started," I call out to the crew. "I'll be there shortly."

Sloane lifts her hand to the guys and starts walking. I fall into step beside her as Carmi skips ahead. I can feel Sloane's glance in my direction and turn my head to look at her.

"Your house is going to be beautiful," she shares.

"Thanks. I hope so."

She beams a smile, and I have to shove my hands in my back pockets to resist the urge to touch her.

"How are you making out with those pictures? Find anything?"

I immediately regret changing the subject when her face falls.

"No. Nothing yet. I took so many, I'm only about two-thirds through."

She did spend a lot of time making sure to get every possible angle, even going down on her stomach, hanging over the edge, while I held on to her ankles.

It would be too bad if her efforts didn't net her something useful.

"Frustrating," I commiserate.

Suddenly she stops in her tracks.

"You don't have to walk me all the way back, you know."

I open my mouth and immediately close it again, letting my eyes drift to Carmi, who is crouched at the edge of the river up ahead, poking a stick in the water.

"I didn't mean—" she starts what I know is going to be some kind of apology, but I don't let her finish.

"Jackson is in intensive care," I find myself saying, giving voice to the dark cloud that's been following me all weekend.

Yeah, if I didn't have something to keep me physically busy, I think I would've come out of my skin.

I got the news Friday night when I found Thomas out on the porch again on my way to my cabin. He called me over and I could tell the old man was shaken. No sooner had I joined him when Ama came outside with a drink for him and a beer for me. I knew something bad had happened when she took a seat next to me.

"Jackson? What happened?"

Sloane grabs hold of my arm, and my eyes find hers. She knows he's a friend.

"Saved up his meds and took 'em all at once Thursday night," I bite off, still angry as hell.

She clamps a hand over her mouth and whispers, "Oh no..." before she seems lost for words.

Yeah, me too.

Over the years, since his mother and Jonas became an item, he and I had become friends. The first time I met him he was getting ready to start his special ops training. The unit he was assigned to was stationed at Fort Bragg, but he'd come to spend time at the ranch whenever he could.

Sloane isn't pumping me for information, which tells me she'd probably already heard about Jackson's medical discharge last year.

It was last December—two weeks before Christmas—we got word he'd been hurt while conducting an operation overseas. Jackson lost his right leg from right above the knee. I don't think any of us know the details surrounding his injury, and it's not likely we ever will, but after his release from the Womack Army Medical Center, Jackson went to a dark place.

For a while, he was in an inpatient, physical rehabilitation program at the Veterans Medical Center in Fort Harrison, right here in Montana. I visited him a couple of times but he made it clear he'd just as soon I didn't come. I know both his mom and Jonas tried to get him to come back to the ranch, but he basically blew them off and ended up renting an apartment a few blocks from the medical center.

We'd all been worried about him, and as it turns out, with good reason.

"How is he?" she inquires

I shrug. "Alive. That's as much as I know for now."

Sloane gives my arm a squeeze before dropping her hand. I already miss the connection.

"Uncle Sully never mentioned anything, or I would've checked in with you."

Ama pointed out it's not common knowledge yet, mainly because his condition is uncertain at this time. They'd wanted me to know so I could keep an eye on Thomas during the night since Jonas and Alex were still in Helena, staying close to the hospital. I don't think JD or even Wolff know yet. I ended up spending the past few nights in the spare bedroom at the ranch.

"It's not really something that's easy to talk about without feeling like you're betraying a trust," I point out.

She tilts her head and scrutinizes me.

"And yet *you're* telling me?"

I shrug.

"You were always easy to talk to."

About most things.

Seven

"This is new."

I take in what used to be an old, ramshackle house in downtown Libby, which now has been converted into a quaint restaurant.

Wild Bites is the name on a sign hanging in the front yard.

"Hope you still like game?"

I grin at Dan who offered to carry Aspen in her car seat. When he asked if I would have dinner with him, I told him that would be contingent on whether or not I could bring my daughter. It's still Sunday, and unless there is a work-related emergency, I don't want to leave her with a babysitter on the weekend.

To be honest, I was a little ambivalent about sharing a meal with him—especially now I see what a nice restaurant he's taking me to—but I didn't have the heart to say no right after he told me about Jackson. He seemed to have been hit hard with that news and, frankly, I was flattered he felt comfortable talking to me. It almost felt like it used to be between us before I tried to turn us into something else.

And ruined it all.

When I told Pippa why I wouldn't be around for dinner, her eyebrows disappeared into her hairline but, to her credit, she didn't pry.

We ended up taking my Jeep because of Aspen's car seat, but Dan insisted on driving. It's funny, that would've been something I'd have been offended by eight years ago—interpreting it as overbearing and even misogynistic—but it didn't bother me today.

Mind you, I wouldn't have taken it well had I been on the job, but it seemed to be just old-fashioned chivalry. Kind of sweet, actually.

As is him carrying Aspen and holding open the door to the restaurant for me with his free hand.

"Reservation for Blakely," his mellow voice sounds behind me as he addresses the restaurant hostess.

"Of course. Right this way."

I follow her into what, at some point, must have been the living and dining rooms, but is now a large open space with a beautiful stone fireplace centered on the front wall and large windows on either end. I feel the heat of Dan's hand in the small of my back as I navigate through the tables to one by the window the woman leads us to.

"You're kidding me, right?"

Dan abruptly drops his hand from my back at the comment. When I turn around to see who the voice belongs to, he's already facing off with two women sitting a couple of tables away from us.

One of them has a curious expression on her face but the other one looks like she could spit nails. *Yikes.* I'm going to take a wild guess the grumpy one is the Vandermeers' daughter, Shelby. She looks like she's pretty serious to me, despite what Pippa told me.

I don't want my child to be in the middle should liquid, china, or utensils start flying, so I reach around Dan to grab the car seat.

"I've got her," I mumble, and rush to join the woman waiting with the menus at our table.

Behind me I can hear a shrill, "Does she know?"

I try not to listen to Dan's voice, his reply just too low for me to hear, and focus on the hostess. She tells me our waitress's name is Natalie, who will be with us shortly. Then I set Aspen's seat on one of the chairs so she's facing the table. I take the seat next to her, making sure my back is toward what sounds like it may be turning into a bit of a scene.

Perhaps the better move is to cut my losses, grab my daughter, and bail, but I don't want to create more of a scene. Despite the slightly sick feeling in my stomach, this may actually be for the best. It certainly is a good reminder, anything more than friendship between Dan and me is a bad idea.

"Sorry about that."

I note he pulls out the chair on the other side of me, instead of the one across the table. I guess, like me, he'd prefer to look out the window over facing the other diners.

"No worries," I assure him.

"I should probably—"

"Hi, I'm Natalie." The server cuts Dan off as she pours ice water in the glasses on the table. "I'll be looking after you tonight. Can I start you off with a drink?"

Then she catches sight of Aspen, whose eyes barely poke out over the table.

"Oh, my goodness, is she ever cute! Is there anything I can get for her?"

"Thank you, that's nice of you, but she should be fine. I actually have a bottle with me."

"Well, just let me know if you need me to warm it up," she offers before repeating, "Would you like something to drink?"

I order a Big Sky IPA when I see the local Montana beer listed on the drink menu.

"We'll probably need a few more minutes with the menu," Dan tells her after ordering a beer as well.

"Take your time. I'll be right back with your drinks."

The moment she walks away, Dan leans over.

"I want to explain what happened earlier."

I hold up my hand to stop him. "Really, there's no need."

He grabs my hand, places it on the table, and covers it with his.

"But I want to. That was Shelby Vandermeer, from the feedstore? She moved back to town in the spring, newly divorced, and we hooked up from time to time. Keeping it casual was something we agreed on or else it would never have happened."

"Let me guess, somewhere along the way she changed her mind? I've been told it's a woman's prerogative," I point out. "Did you ghost her?"

He lets go of my hand and uses both of his to rub his face.

"I can't believe you'd think that of me. No, I did not. I met up with her, told her I was sorry but was not in the market for anything more serious, and I ended things."

"A Big Sky for you, and one for you," Natalie leans in,

placing the beers in front of us. "Do you need a little more time?"

"Yes, please."

The server makes a face at Aspen, who rewards her with a big, toothless grin.

"Oh my, you look just like your daddy, don't you?" Before I can correct her, she straightens up and announces, "I'll give you a few more minutes."

I glance at Dan, and notice him staring at my daughter.

"She doesn't really look like me, does she?"

"You carried her in, you both have dark hair, and I'm blond. People make assumptions."

"Yeah, no kidding. Shelby jumped to the same conclusion."

I think that much was obvious and I can't help feel a little sorry for her. We're not that different. Glancing over my shoulder, I notice the table she was sitting at is empty. When I turn back, I find Dan staring at me.

"We should probably figure out what we want to eat," I suggest self-consciously, and start scanning the menu.

"Yeah," he agrees.

But I can still feel his eyes on me, until he finally opens his menu.

Dan

I feel one side of my mouth pull up as I watch those pretty blue eyes drift shut.

The food was great, as usual, and the conversation pretty

easygoing. She shared a bit about her job in Billings, and I filled her in on life at the ranch and told her about my fairly newfound father and half sister. All relatively safe topics, providing me with zero answers for the list of questions churning in my gut.

And now I'm watching as she slips the bottle from the baby's lips and eases her back in her car seat.

"Here you are."

The waitress slides a discreet leather folder on the table, and I use the fact Sloane has her hands full with Aspen to claim the bill. Ignoring her glare, I pull a few bills from my wallet and get to my feet.

"Ready?"

She nods and swings the diaper bag over her shoulder, as I reach for the baby seat.

Weaving through the restaurant to the exit, I notice there's a family sitting at the table Shelby and her friend vacated. I didn't see them leave, but I knew she was gone when I no longer felt her eyes burning holes in my back.

What a clusterfuck. She'd been primed to make a scene, and if not for her friend unexpectedly jumping to my aid, I don't think I could've done anything to stop it. It was a good reminder why I don't do relationships, especially in a small town like Libby. It gets messy.

"What do I owe you?" Sloane asks when we get to her Jeep.

I don't bother responding and shoot her a look instead. Her lips press together in a thin line intended to show me her displeasure. Like water off a duck's back to me. I may not have had my father around to teach me to be a gentleman, but my mother made sure certain values were instilled in me.

Aspen remains sleeping as I place her in the car.

"Are you gonna have to wake her up to get her ready for bed?" I ask when I get behind the wheel.

"No, that's why I put on her pajamas when I changed her diaper earlier. I can slip her right in her crib."

"Will she wake up during the night?"

"Once or twice. If I'm lucky."

I glance over and for the first time notice the lines of fatigue in her face.

"Which means you're not getting a whole lot of rest," I observe out loud.

She simply shrugs.

"Goes with the job."

"Speaking of which," I latch on right away. "I know you mentioned the sperm donor bailing, but why did you leave Billings? I got the impression from Sully you loved your job."

"You asked Sully about me?"

Just like that, the tables are turned and I find myself on the spot.

"Not sure how we got on the subject, but he must've mentioned it at some point."

It's a blatant lie. I hounded him for information, especially the first months after she left. After that I grabbed any opportunity I could get to find out how she was doing.

"But you're avoiding my question," I point out.

"Fine," she concedes after a lengthy pause, during which I'm sure she hoped I'd back off.

Fat chance.

"Jeff was an aspiring musician working as a bartender at a bar not far from the precinct. It was nothing serious." She turns and throws me a pointed look. "Much like your arrangement with Shelby. No strings, occasional. Anyway..." She waves her hand. "Long story short, I was already in my fourth month when I found out I was pregnant with Aspen. I'd been too busy to pay much attention to what should've been signs. I informed Jeff, he seemed excited at the prospect, and we actually tried to make something of the relationship. Reality was not so fun, I guess, and as I mentioned, he bailed a month after I went back to work. I tried for a couple of weeks with the help of babysitters while I worked, but my focus wasn't where it should've been. After having a bit of a public meltdown that almost blew a case my partner and I had been working on for nearly a year, I realized I couldn't do it on my own."

"So you came here? Isn't your mom somewhere in Utah?" I probe.

"Actually, Mom and Steve moved to Panama last year, and until last week she didn't know."

I glance over at her and catch a sheepish look on her face. "Didn't know what?"

Then she blows me away with the answer.

"About Aspen. Nobody here knew either."

"What?" I react a little sharply. "Why would you not share that with your family?"

She faces away from me and stares out the side window, and for a few moments I think perhaps this conversation is done.

"Too many reasons and, in hindsight, all of them stupid," she finally admits. "Just another mistake to compound all the mistakes that got me there in the first place. I guess I wanted to prove—to them, or maybe to myself—I wasn't that reckless, impulsive, problem-child anymore. That I didn't need rescuing and could handle my own problems like any normal functioning adult."

I don't bother pointing out that a normal functioning

adult wouldn't have kept a child a secret, since I get the sense she's already come to that conclusion on her own.

It explains why Sully never mentioned anything about Sloane becoming a parent. He didn't know. I imagine talking to her uncle and her mother cannot have been easy conversations. There's no need for me to add to that. If anything, she could probably do with a bit of support.

"You know, I think it took a whole lot of strength to recognize you needed help, and even more guts to return home to find it."

From the corner of my eye, I catch her nodding as she swallows hard.

"You do realize I wasn't born here, and lived here less time than I have anywhere else, right?"

I grin. Sloane was never good at taking compliments.

"Doesn't matter," I counter. "You and I both know Libby is home."

She doesn't say anything to that, but a faint smile touches her lips when she closes her eyes and leans her head back against the seat.

It's a twenty-five minute drive from the restaurant home, and by the time we drive through White Haven, just south of Libby, Sloane is asleep in the passenger seat. Already sleep-deprived, I'm sure the full stomach and the two beers she had at dinner helped knock her out.

She needs the sleep, so I take the next exit off the highway. Using the backroads past the regional airport will force me to go slow and add some much-needed time to our drive home. It also gives me a chance to process what she told me.

Her choices wouldn't have been mine, but I can see how she came to make them. Sometimes when you try so hard to do the right thing, you end up making the wrong decisions. I might know a thing or two about that.

Hell, life might look a whole lot different now, had I done things differently all those years ago. At the time I was overwhelmed trying to take care of my mother, it sucked up every bit of free time I had. Not that I'm complaining, I feel lucky I was able to do that much for her. However, medical bills were piling up and I was losing the battle to keep my head above water. I had less than nothing to offer someone else.

I always thought, once Mom died, I'd be in a better place to start something. But I never got the chance, because by the time I buried my mother and started getting my life together, Sloane was already gone.

I glance in the rearview mirror to check on Aspen. Her seat faces backward, but a mirror installed against the back-rest allows me a view of her sleeping face. Then I look at her mother beside me, her soft mouth slightly open, and my chest gets tight.

For just a moment, I allow myself to imagine they belong to me.

Eight

SLOANE

It's much tougher going this time.

Clearly the department ATV isn't as suited to the some-times dense tree growth, and I end up having to find alter-nate routes to get where I want to go.

After almost getting lost twice when I veered away from the trail, I end up abandoning the vehicle and continuing on foot. It's a rough trek, but at least I can follow the fading paint marks the HMT team left behind.

I suppose I could've gone back to the ranch to see if I could borrow Pudding, but that would've meant likely bumping into Dan, again. I'm pretty sure he would've insisted on coming with me, and I've decided it's safer for me to avoid the high frequency he seems to emit that I find myself drawn to.

Dan is one of those people who seems clear on who he is, and what he wants. He's stable, grounded, and a genuinely good person. He's everything I'm not and, therefore, is on an entirely different wavelength.

I didn't see it years ago, but it is obvious to me now.

Anyway, I'm up here by myself because I need to double-check on something.

Last night after Dan brought me home, I put Aspen to bed and lay down myself, but after that nap in the car, sleep wouldn't come. I ended up opening my laptop to work on the photos. It was almost three this morning when I spotted something that looked out of place. I couldn't distinguish what exactly I was looking at—I enlarged it to the point the picture became grainy—but the contrast of the bright yellow color stood out.

This morning, I tried running it through several filters at the office, but couldn't get the image any clearer. I knew I had to go back up there, see if I could get a visual. So I asked Betty if the Sheriff's Office happened to have high-powered binoculars I could use. Jason Heany, one of the deputies, overheard me and loaned me a pair he uses for hunting. Nice guy, he also helped me hook the trailer with the ATV up to one of the department's Ford F-150 crew cabs.

I'm not going to lie, it's a bit creepy up here by myself. No one was parked at the trailhead but since I abandoned the ATV, I've occasionally heard these noises. Sounds of something other than me moving in the forest.

Of course, there's plenty of large wildlife up in these mountains. Elk, moose, mountain lions, and black as well as grizzly bears. I don't particularly want a close encounter with any of those.

There it is again; this time it sounded like a branch snapping.

My hand automatically goes to my hip, where I carry my service weapon as I slowly spin around and scan the woods around me. I stare into the trees for a good minute or two before I resume my hike. I'm starting to second-guess coming out here on my own.

It's Jason's fault I'm freaking myself out. He mentioned the fall black bear hunting season opening in two weeks and asked for me to keep an eye out for fresh scat. I spotted some when I got off the ATV. I'm pretty sure they're black bear droppings, they were mostly berries. Now that I think about it, I started hearing stuff after that.

Pissed at myself for letting some poop rattle me, I pick up the pace.

When I finally get to the gorge, I take off my backpack and first fish my cell phone from the side pouch to check for a signal. I have two bars, which is better than nothing. I leave the camera and the extra lenses in the backpack for now, but grab the binoculars and take my phone. Then I move to the edge.

I transferred several copies of the image in question to my phone so I have the original picture but also a few cropped close-ups to help me locate the actual spot. I pull the full image up on my phone, take a good look, and start walking along the edge to find the right angle.

Of course, I keep a safe distance from the drop, I have no desire to end up at the bottom of the gorge, but when I think I've found the location, I drop down to my stomach and inch closer to the edge. In the picture, the yellow blob appears right at the base of the cliff, so I have to get close to the edge if I want to pinpoint it with the binoculars.

Ignoring the sudden wave of vertigo when I first glance down, I scan the drop below. Nothing really jumps out at me. On my phone I flip through the close-ups, comparing the rock formations with what I can see with the naked eye.

Then I see it—not right below me, but about fifty feet

to my right—a flat boulder leaning upright against the base of the rock wall. A small glimpse of yellow appears to be stuck at the top. Keeping my focus firmly fixed on the spot, I slip my phone in my back pocket, and lift the binoculars to my eyes.

At first the view through the lenses is blurry, and I'm momentarily disoriented. Luckily, Jason showed me how to adjust the focus, and I manage to get the image to clear. I've lost my spot, but it doesn't take me long to find the tall, flat rock again.

Then I pan up a tad and refocus on the splash of color. It's a coat, at least, that's what it looks like. One of those puffy winter coats. One of its sleeves appears to be caught on something and the rest of the coat is hanging from it. I follow the streak of canary yellow down to where the second sleeve dangles what is probably a few feet off the ground.

It isn't until I zoom out a little that I see it; a hand, reaching up.

The sight startles me so hard; the binoculars slip from my hands as I scramble back from the edge. Luckily, I have them on a strap around my neck, or they would've ended up down below.

Like that body.

I need my camera.

Getting to my feet, I walk over to my backpack and pull out the Canon. I don't think the larger lens I brought will do the trick but I'll give it a shot. Otherwise, I can try using the binoculars as magnification for the camera. It'll require some dexterity, but I'm determined to bring back photographic evidence.

My mind is already spinning with the measures that will have to be taken to retrieve that body. But the first step would be for me to get down there and gather whatever evidence I can. For that I need my boss's support—hence the photographic evidence—and a tracker to guide me.

I lie back down on my belly and first try with the lens mounted on the camera, but I can't zoom in close enough to see the hand. It's also impossible to see through the small viewfinder, and the digital screen isn't much better. Still, I shoot a number of pictures before I remove the lens and try taking a few shots through the binoculars. That looks more successful in terms of magnification, but the quality may have suffered.

Next, I'd like to see if I can't view a bit more of the body if I look down from above. There's a bit of a rock outcropping directly overhead, creating a shelf jutting out over the drop. A tree is perched right on the edge, its roots spreading wide as they cling onto the rocky surface. I'll have to watch where I put my feet, I don't want to trip and lose my balance.

No sooner am I stepping over the first obstacle, when I hear a loud grunt behind me. Unfortunately, in my haste to spin around at the sound, my left foot gets hung up on a protruding root, and I feel myself going down. I barely manage to prevent doing a full face plant by catching the brunt of the impact on my forearms. Ignoring the jab of pain, I snap my head around to see if whatever made that sound is getting ready to jump me.

Yikes. It's a black bear, but it appears to be more interested in my backpack than it is in me. It looks young. I wince when I hear a loud rip and watch the content spill on the ground. Extra lenses, my crime scene kit, a box of gloves, and a couple of granola bars, which is apparently what it was after.

I stay as still as I can until the animal is done eating and rummaging through my things, and—with a nerve-wracking long look in my direction—takes off into the trees. Then I drop my head down on my forearms and take a deep, shaky breath, blowing it out slowly.

I give myself a minute, scanning my suddenly aching body for serious injury—I don't think I broke anything, but I'll probably have a few scrapes and bruises—before I carefully push myself up to sitting. Next, I check the equipment. Both the camera and binoculars are still around my neck and show some scratches, but appear intact. Thank God for that; my sparse savings wouldn't be able to take the hit if I had to replace either or both.

Since I'm already on the ground, and only a foot or two from the edge of the rock shelf, I inch my way closer until I can only just peek over the side. From up here the yellow fabric is not hard to spot, but it's too high up to see much else. Once again, I lift the binoculars to my face and adjust the focus, zooming in closer.

The hair on my neck stands on end and goosebumps break out all over my skin when I see what is below.

Staring up at me is a face, with just a pair of black holes where the eyes used to be.

Dead eyes.

Dan

"How is he?"

Jonas looks up from his desk.

I noticed he was back earlier this morning, but the new vet had just rolled up. Old Doc Evans finally hung up his hat two months ago, at six months shy of his seventy-eighth birthday, and his practice was taken over by Janey Richards, a new transplant from the Eureka area.

Doc Evans did the rounds introducing her before he took off on a South American cruise to celebrate his retirement, but we haven't had reason to call her in yet. Most of the minor stuff we can handle ourselves. Today she was here to administer booster vaccines for equine influenza and equine herpesvirus. It's always a significant job, given the number of horses we have, and normally requires quite a few of us to facilitate.

We do two of these a year—the spring vaccinations and the fall boosters—so we had a routine going with Doc Evans. But since this was the first time with Doc Richards, and she had a few of her own preferences, it took us a little more time.

I just saw her off before I came inside.

"He'll live. He's alert but not happy about it. I'm not sure what to do with that, he's a mess. Won't talk to anyone, but Alex is still there; sitting, waiting, until the nurses tell her visiting hours are over. Then she moves to the waiting room. I swear, she's got the fucking patience of a saint."

He rubs his face with his hands before sighing deeply.

"Any idea when they're going to let him go?"

"Probably tomorrow he'll be moved to the psychiatric ward for a twenty-four-hour assessment. Depends on his cooperation what'll happen after that."

"Jesus."

"Yeah. Hope he smartens up and lets us bring him back here, where he can learn to feel useful again."

Jonas slaps his hands on the desk before he changes the topic. "How did it go with the new doc?"

"Fine. We're all done."

The phone on his desk starts ringing.

"Good. Go grab some lunch. I'm just gonna take this and will join you in a minute."

Exiting the office, I head toward the kitchen where Thomas and Sully are already eating at the long kitchen island. But my attention is drawn to the playpen in front of the large sliding glass doors.

"Hey, pretty girl," I mumble, leaning over the side to find Aspen looking up at me, shoving some kind of plastic ring in her mouth.

Her little fist is drool-covered, and the bottom of her sleeve is soaked. Sloane had mentioned she was teething. Poor thing. Doesn't stop her from flashing me a big smile though. I can't help smiling back.

"You having fun?"

In response she purses her lips and starts blowing raspberries, her little legs kicking excitedly.

"Could you grab her for me?" Ama calls out behind me. "I've got her bottle ready."

As soon as I reach down, both her little arms come up.

She weighs next to nothing as I settle her in the crook of my arm and turn around. Three pairs of eyes are on me, two of them grinning, and a set of blue ones glaring. I ignore them all as I reach for the bottle on the counter. I shake a drop on my hand, testing the temperature like I saw Sloane do at dinner last night. Aspen's lips automatically open when I offer her the bottle.

Then I slide my ass on the nearest stool and settle the baby on my thigh.

"What's for lunch?"

Ama shakes her head, turns to the stove where she loads a couple of quesadillas on a plate, and sets it in front of me. Feeding Aspen with one hand, I start eating with the other.

When Jonas walks in a few minutes later, Ama is

burping the baby, and I'm diving into my second serving. I was hungry.

"That was Junior Ewing," Jonas directs at me. "Looks like you're taking Sloane up Pointer's Creek in the morning."

My quesadilla freezes halfway to my mouth before I lower it back to my plate.

"She found something?"

Jonas nods. "A body at the bottom of the gorge."

"No shit?" That comes from Sully. "Do we know who?"

"The sheriff's looking into it. The body looks like it's been there a while though."

"Then why does Sloane have to go? If it's just a recovery, our guys can go," Sully suggests.

"Because it's her job," I remind him. "She'll need to process the scene for evidence before we can recover the body."

My comments earn me a glare, but I don't give a damn. It's about time people start treating her like the adult she is. Starting with her uncle.

"And once she's done, we can have a team with a basket up top to haul the remains out that way," Jonas adds.

"Then isn't it faster just to rappel down the gorge?"

"Your niece has no experience," I point out.

"Yeah, but you're not gonna be able to make it in and out in one day if you follow the creek," Sully counters.

Yeah, I'm pretty sure he's feeling a little protective of her.

Jonas saves me from a response.

"Exactly, which is why I need Dan to pack gear so they can set up camp."

Nine

DAN

I strap the bedroll holding a mat and sleeping bag behind Pudding's saddle.

Both horses have been outfitted with saddlebags holding a few basic supplies for us and the horses, a set of dry clothes and shoes, an emergency kit, and everything Sloane will need to process the scene, including a few high-powered flashlights and a machete. My bedroll includes one of the lightweight pop-up tents the team uses when we're on longer trips, and as an afterthought, I also loop a lightweight sleep-hammock around the horn of Will's saddle.

I turn my head when I hear the storm door slam shut and just catch Sloane coming down the porch steps. Biting off a grin, I watch her walk toward me, a little bow-legged, as she tries to navigate Alex's borrowed leather chaps. It had been Jonas's suggestion—a good one—since we'll be going through some rough terrain. This won't be an easy trail ride.

"Shut your mouth," she grumbles when she reaches me.

"I didn't say a word," I point out.

I notice she opted out of a western hat and chose a Tilley hat instead, which is better than the ball cap she was wearing when she showed up. At least the floppy hat will give her better coverage from the sun.

"You didn't have to," she mutters. "I could read you loud and clear."

I guess being a single mother does little to improve one's morning mood. Sloane never was a morning person, to my recollection.

"Did you manage to have a coffee this morning?" I carefully inquire.

"Barely half a cup."

I hand her the thermos I prepped earlier and point at the neoprene sleeve I fit over her saddle horn.

"It stays pretty hot."

I get a mumbled thanks as she fits the thermos into the sleeve.

"Are you ready to roll?"

"Yep. Let's get this over with," is her reply.

I give her a hand mounting Pudding, which can be a bit tricky with all the extra gear, and then I grab my saddle horn and swing up on Will.

"Show-off," she mutters under her breath before clucking her tongue to prompt Pudding into motion.

I follow closely behind as we make our way past the ranch house. We'll take the trail to the river, but this time we'll stay to this side of the water. I looked over some satellite images with Sully last night, and it's easier to cross a bit farther north, where we're closer to the mouth of Pointer Creek and the vegetation on that side of the river is a bit less dense.

It's early and the sun is still coming up. The golden light

hits the mist rising off the river and makes the dew covering the grass sparkle. It's a pretty picture, one I catch Sloane capturing with her phone.

I can tell from the chill in the air, we're getting closer to fall. The nights are cooler and the days are definitely getting shorter. Some of the trees are even starting to turn and pretty soon the endless green of the mountains will be filling with deep reds and rich golds. Fall is my favorite time of year. Mother Nature's last colorful abundance before winter turns the mountains dull.

I have a two-way radio—a Motorola Talkabout—with a thirty-five-mile radius, which does double duty as an off-grid locator if something happens. It should also allow for Sully to track us on satellite from the computer at the office, and he'll be able to alert us to any obstacles ahead and suggest alternate routes.

The plan is for us to call in around noon to check in with the rest of the team and strategize based on our progress. We're hoping to make it to the location sometime midafternoon, in which case Sloane has several hours of daylight to do what she needs to. We'll then camp down and the team will set up at the top of the rock face in the morning, so they can bring up the body. Sheriff Ewing will be with them, as will the county coroner to take possession of the remains.

Will is used to riding up front so he passed Pudding and took the lead a while back. I check over my shoulder to make sure Sloane is still behind me. She hasn't said a word since we left the ranch, and I let her be, giving her a chance to get a bit more caffeine in her system. Pudding is just a few paces behind, and I hold Will back to allow her to pull up beside me.

"We should probably cross here," I suggest, pointing at a sandbar in the middle of the river. "Pointer Creek is not far up ahead, but the river is deeper there. This is easier."

"Okay."

"We can probably stay dry from here to the bank, but if you look on the other side, the water moves faster and is therefore likely deeper, so there's a small chance we'll get wet."

"I'm not scared of a bit of water."

I'm not sure she realizes how uncomfortable it can be, spending a day in the saddle in damp clothes, but I don't think it would stop her if she knew.

"I'm sure you're not. Which reminds me, going back out on that cliff by yourself wasn't exactly a smart move. You should've let me know."

Her eyes spark fire and two red spots form high on her cheeks.

"This again? I was doing my job and can take care of myself."

This is Sloane's stubborn streak coming out, and I can't let it go. I know she has a chip on her shoulder, and I get where it comes from, but it's time to let it go.

"Policing and investigating is. Wilderness tracking and search and rescue is mine," I point out. "I'm happy to let you do yours, if you'll let me do mine."

With that, I nudge Will into the river, listening for the splash of Pudding's hooves following.

Sloane

96

. . .

Dear God, if I get attacked by one more mosquito I'm going to scream.

What's even worse, they don't appear to affect Dan. I swear they're devoting their full and undivided attention on me alone.

"How in tarnation is it they do not bother you?" I question for the umpteenth time.

Dan grins and shakes his head, annoying me even more.

"Where do they all come from anyway? I didn't notice any up on the trail."

"We're next to a creek, in a gorge where the sun only reaches a couple of hours a day. This is mosquito heaven."

I swat at another persistent swarm clouding around my head, and dig my bottle of Skin So Soft out of the saddlebag.

I notice Dan watching with a smirk on his face.

"What?"

"I told you; you need DEET."

I angrily spray myself before twisting my body to face him.

"I will have you know that studies have shown Skin So Soft is eighty-five-percent effective."

My ass is sore, I have bug bites covering every inch of exposed skin, and my feet are still wet in my damn boots. To top it off, I've needed to pee for the past two hours but am afraid if I pull down my pants, I'll only create a fresh new target for the freaking skeeters.

I'm not in the mood, but that doesn't appear to deter Dan. He once again seems to have an answer ready.

"You mean eighty-five-percent as effective *as* DEET, which makes DEET still the better choice. I've read the study."

He reaches back to pull his own can of bug repellant from his bag and leans over.

My glare has zero impact on him as he patiently waits me out, making me feel like a petulant child. Of course I give in, I don't really have a choice or I'll look like an even bigger ass.

I'm just so damn miserable and the thought of spending the night away from my baby isn't helping.

"This stuff stinks," I can't resist pointing out.

It's the main reason I didn't want to use it in the first place.

"The mosquitos think so too."

"Are you making fun of me?"

Instead of answering, Dan suddenly tilts his head back and seems to be peering up through the trees. Abruptly he pulls back on his reins, bringing Will to a halt. Then he looks back at me with a grin, and points up.

"Look up. Remember the arrow I painted? We're here."

The first thing I do when we dismount is run into the bushes and shove down my pants.

At this point, I have zero inhibitions.

Relieved beyond belief, I join Dan, who has removed the gear and the saddles from the horses, and is spanning a rope between two trees.

The spot he chose to set up camp is a small clearing at the edge of the creek. I remember seeing it from above.

"What can I do?"

"Get out of those wet boots. You brought dry socks and running shoes, right?"

"Yes, I packed everything Sully told me to."

"Let me finish getting the horses settled and I'll do the same. Then let's go to work."

I glance in the approximate direction I believe the body to be and suppress a shudder. As much as I'm eager to get some answers, I'm not looking forward to it.

Ten minutes later, I follow Dan's broad back into the trees. My feet are dry, my bladder is blissfully empty, and—although I hate to admit it—the bugs are finally leaving me alone. I try to keep my eyes fixed somewhere between his shoulder blades, but it's a bit of a challenge since his ass is a sight to behold in those well-ridden Wranglers.

Heck, my own jeans are molded to my butt in a way that feels like they're tattooed on. Not a surprise after being in the saddle for almost nine hours. I'm feeling it too and it'll probably feel worse in the morning, but for now, I'm glad to be walking.

When we reach the base of the rock wall, I tilt my head back and spot the arrow up above. That means the body is somewhere to our left. When I glance in that direction, my view is blocked by a large boulder.

I tentatively sniff the air, but I can't smell much beyond the aroma of damp earth and pine. No scent of decay, which confirms what I already suspected; the body has been down here for a while, which is easier to deal with. Still, I feel a bit guilty at the surge of relief. It doesn't matter how long the body has been down here, it was a person once.

"You lead," Dan says, gesturing for me to pass him.

As soon as I find my way to the other side of the boulder, I spot the flat rock, and the yellow coat caught on it. I stop and lift my camera, snapping pictures as I slowly move toward it.

"Look up there," Dan says, tapping on my shoulder as

he points at a jagged rock jutting out from the wall about fifteen feet up.

A little strip of yellow fabric is stuck to the end. I lift my camera and take a few shots.

Because of the position of the body, my assumption had been that they came from above—either fallen or pushed—but this is actual evidence in support of that theory.

"I can get up there and collect it, if you want," he offers.

"That would be helpful after I'm done processing."

Which will never happen if I don't get my ass in gear. Snapping pictures to avoid what is the most important piece of evidence is not moving things along. I take in a fortifying breath and finally focus my attention on the body.

From this distance, I can see the hand is almost skeletonized, but I can't see much of the rest of the body. I keep snapping pictures as I approach, creating an artificial barrier from the horrific vision through my viewfinder.

I'm pretty sure the body is female from the clumps of long hair that cling to the skull, but also the clothing still covering parts of her. That is, the parts that remain. One of her legs looks to be wedged between the boulder and the rock face, but the other leg is missing. Her head is actually separated from the rest of her body. It's clear at some point animals were at her.

"Jesus," I hear Dan mumble behind me.

I swallow the bile down and grit my teeth as I force my mind to focus on details and not the horror of the whole picture. I need to be as meticulous as I can in processing the evidence so I don't miss anything.

Even though I've had some training, the occasions where I've had to use my acquired skills were far and few between. I'm not a crime scene, or forensics tech, and neither am I a coroner, but we don't have the luxury of a team with all those specialties at our fingertips here.

Speed is of the essence in collecting and preserving the body and any related evidence, when a scene is exposed to outside elements. Hell, even a late summer rain or a good stiff wind could wash away something that might've been key evidence in solving this case.

So, although it's not ideal, the job is on me and I have to do the best I can.

For the next while, I forget time and any signals my body is sending. I'm so immersed in the work, I don't notice we're losing daylight until Dan turns on one of the flashlights to help me see what I'm doing.

"Thank you," I mumble.

"How much longer do you figure?" he asks. "It won't take long to get completely dark down here and these lights may not be enough. We also still have to set up camp."

Shit. I'd forgotten about that.

"Okay, okay. I'd like to get her into the body bag, along with the evidence bags, but I'll need your help for that."

I've taken pictures of every conceivable angle, I've collected every little scrap of what looked like it might be evidence I could find, and there really isn't much more I can do.

The task of getting the remains in the body bag is by far the most unpleasant one. There isn't a whole lot holding her together, other than perhaps connective tissues and her clothes, but we manage to get the job done.

"Any idea how long she's been down here?" Dan wants to know when I zip her securely inside the bag.

"It'll take the coroner to figure that one out more accurately, but given she was wearing a winter jacket, I'd guess at least five or six months. I found a receipt in the jacket pocket dated January twenty-first of this year, so some time after that."

"Nothing else to identify her?"

"Only the receipt, which is from a gas station in Pablo."

Pablo is a small town with a largely Native American population near the Pablo National Wildlife Refuge. It's also the seat of government for the Flathead Indian Reservation.

The girl's hair is very dark, she could be Native American, but Pablo is a good two-and-a-half to three-hour drive from here. How would she have ended up here?

"I want to get a call in to Junior," I mention. "See if there are any young girls reported missing from that area."

"You're sure she's young?"

"Pretty sure. Based on her clothes and the unicorn charm she had clipped to the zipper of her jacket. Probably not much older than Chelsea Littleton."

"Fuck," he curses. "That can't be a coincidence."

Nope. I'd bet my life coincidence doesn't play into it. Chelsea and this girl may not be the only victims either.

I glance around at the deepening shadows and shiver involuntarily.

Who knows what else is hiding out there?

Ten

DAN

I can see the tension etched on her face.

It's a heavy load to carry, stumbling on a case like this fresh on the job. Especially since I know Sloane is eager to show her mettle.

"Want more coffee?" I hold up the kettle.

She shakes her head. "I won't sleep." Then she changes her mind. "Oh, what the hell, hit me up. I'm so exhausted, I don't think there's anything that can keep me awake once I go horizontal."

We just had dinner, although I don't think Sloane ate much. A couple of MREs that only required hot water, and I always pack a small tin of coffee and my camping percolator with my gear when we head into the mountains.

We're sitting on a couple of logs I dragged to the small fire I built to boil the water. Not the most comfortable seats but they'll do. At least the radiant heat from the fire is welcome since, now the sun is down, the chill is starting to set back in.

Sloane gives me her thermos and I top up her coffee before handing it back.

"Sorry, I know you normally take cream and sugar. Didn't think to bring it."

She waves me off. "This is fine. I'm grateful you thought to bring coffee." Then she takes a sip and chuckles at herself. "Actually, you'll probably be the grateful one tomorrow morning. I'm a bit of a bear without my morning coffee."

"You don't say," I mumble under my breath, as I get up to toss the last log on. "Which reminds me, I should probably chop some more wood now so we have enough to boil water tomorrow morning."

"Are you being a smart-ass?"

I glance over and grin at her, before grabbing the small hatchet and one of the flashlights. Then I move around the tent to the edge of the clearing to a couple of dead trees I've been able to get dry wood from. I lay the flashlight on the trunk of one so I can see what I'm doing, when the light catches the plastic of the body bag twenty feet back.

Sloane didn't feel right leaving the body behind, despite the fact we'll have to haul it right back to the rock wall tomorrow morning. She claims it's because she doesn't want to leave what is now considered evidence unguarded. I think in handling the remains, what was the abstract concept of a body became what was once a living, breathing, young girl.

The glimpse of the black bag is a stark reminder of our purpose here.

Glancing over my shoulder, I can still see Sloane sitting in the glow of the fire, her hands wrapped around the thermos of coffee, staring into space.

I built the firepit in front of the tent which we set up to

face the creek. The hammock is secured between two trees, close to where the horses are tied down but set back a bit so I can keep an eye on things with one side and the front of the tent in view.

Not that I think there's anything to worry about—other than perhaps inquisitive wildlife—but it gives me peace of mind.

It doesn't take me long to have enough wood chopped for tomorrow morning. When I return to the fire with my arms full of wood, Sloane barely acknowledges me. She's either deep in thought or half asleep. After I stack the logs beside the pit, we sit in silence for a while, with only the sounds of the babbling creek, the woods around us, and the occasional snap of a hot coal.

Every so often I glance over at her, but she seems mesmerized by the dying flames. I can't help wonder what is going on in her mind, which is really no different from any other day. I'd love to have a glimpse inside, maybe get some answers to questions that have been pestering me.

What the hell, I might as well. It's not like she can walk away now.

"Why did you leave?"

It takes a moment for my question to register, but when it does, she turns to me with her mouth hanging open. She doesn't look confused, she looks incredulous.

"Are you seriously asking me that now?"

I note she doesn't seem to have any trouble knowing exactly what I'm referring to.

"Yeah, I am. And for the record, I tried to contact you for weeks after to get that answer, but you ignored me, so I eventually gave up. I may not have been too quick on the uptake, but even for me that was a bit more rejection than I was willing to take."

The last thing I expect is for her to burst out laughing, but that's exactly what she does. Literally bending over laughing.

I was curious before, but now I'm pissed, and suddenly the feelings of anger I carried around for far too many years are back. I'm about to let it all out but I don't get the chance.

"That's hilarious," she sneers. "You being rejected? I think you've got it backward. Aging clearly has affected your memory."

"Nothing wrong with my memory," I scoff.

"No? So you remember you were the one telling me to go in the first place?"

Now I'm the one with my mouth open, except I'm genuinely confused.

"Bullshit. When did I do that?"

"After your mother's funeral. You had too much to drink and I walked you back to the cabin."

"I remember that, but I don't remember telling you to go anywhere. I just remember you were suddenly gone without explanation."

"Yeah, because you told me to take the job. That was after you kicked me out of your bed, buck naked," she snarls.

I am literally dumbfounded. Mute, unable to form words, let alone speak them.

Surely, I would remember Sloane in my bed, naked. Christ, I'm getting a hard-on just at the visual image that creates.

"Wait," I wrestle from my vocal cords when it looks like she might get up. "All I remember from that night is you walking me back and tucking me into bed."

The reflection of the few flames remaining is visible in her glistening eyes, revealing a darkness I don't recognize.

"I did," she answers in a soft voice, lowering her gaze. "And the timing was probably off, but I needed to know if there was any chance before I accepted the job in Billings."

It's like a fist squeezing my chest as I try to process what she's saying.

"Any chance of what?"

Her eyes lift and she studies me for a beat before sharing, "Any chance for you and me."

What the fuck?

That fist tightens, making me want to hurl so bad I have to swallow down the bile.

"You asked me that?" I ask, my voice hoarse.

She shrugs. "Well, technically, after telling you about the job offer, I wanted to know if there was any reason for me to stay."

"That's not exactly the same."

I must've been drunker than I recall, because I can't for the life of me remember any such conversation.

"It was pretty obvious," she counters. "Since I was not wearing any clothes when I asked you."

"If that was the case, I must've been comatose because, even with a single functioning brain cell, there is no way in hell I'd ever kick you out of my bed."

I lean forward with my forearms on my knees to make sure she hears me loud and clear.

"Naked or otherwise."

~

Sloane

. . .

What just happened?

I scramble to my feet, moaning at the tight pinch of muscles all over my damn body. My heart is hammering in my chest. I need some air, some distance, so I can gather my thoughts.

Could it be...?

I give myself a mental shake; don't go there.

Right now, I don't trust myself to read his comments correctly. I'm too frazzled. If I let myself go there it would create a seismic shift, which would have me questioning everything. It would mean bitter regret, and eight years wasted.

No, I can't think like that. How can there be any regret when I have a beautiful daughter I wouldn't trade for anyone or anything?

Space. I need a little space.

"I think I'm going to wash up a little before I turn in," I announce, trying not to look at him.

"Take the flashlight."

His voice is soft, and I wonder whether these revelations shook him as much as they've shaken me.

I nod in response, and dart into the tent to grab my bar of biodegradable soap, a clean shirt and underwear, and my microfiber towel.

While Dan was hanging his hammock earlier, I explored a bit and discovered a large flat rock in the water a little upriver, just around the bend. I thought I'd get up early tomorrow morning to have a quick dip and a wash, but now is as good a time as any.

I need a few minutes alone to collect myself.

"Don't go too far," Dan calls after me.

"I won't," I promise.

Even with a flashlight, it's a little creepy walking into the dark alone, but I don't have far to go. As soon as I clear the tree cover on the other side of the bend, I notice it's much lighter. When I look up to the sky, I see the clouds which gathered late this afternoon have cleared, giving the nearly full moon a chance to reflect off the water.

The rock I found earlier protrudes from the bank into the middle of the creek, which creates a bit of a shelter from view. I walk out onto the flat surface and drop my stuff, before quickly stripping down and slipping into the shallow water.

Holy fucking hell, that water's cold.

My whole body puckers up, but it's nice to be able to wash the worst of the sweat and the grime off me. Ducking my head under, I use the soap to give my hair a quick rinse. By the time that's done, my body seems to have adjusted to the temperature and I let myself enjoy the buoyancy of the water for a bit. It feels good, soothes my tight muscles.

I'm leaning with my head back against the rock, my eyes closed, when a loud crash behind me has me surge up out of the water.

I scramble to my feet and blindly grab for the towel to cover myself, my eyes scanning the shore. The shadows are so dark, I can't see shit beyond the tree line so I reach for the flashlight with my free hand. Of course I left my damn sidearm in the tent.

Some detective I am.

My only—rather weak—excuse is my discussion with Dan rattled me enough to forget.

"Sloane! Are you okay?" I hear him bellow. *"Fuck. Sloane!"*

Then I hear movement on the shore and aim the flashlight to find the source of the sound, only to see Dan's large form burst from the trees. He has a gun in one hand and lifts his other hand to protect his eyes from the flashlight as he steps onto the rock. I immediately lower the beam and rush toward him.

"What was that?"

"I don't know yet, I had to make sure you were all right."

It's not until his hand squeezes my very naked shoulder, I realize my state of undress. Nothing but a thin towel haphazardly held up in front of me in one clenched fist, barely covering my bits.

Wonderful.

Apparently, I haven't lost the knack to embarrass myself in front of this man.

"I'm fine, but what was that crash?" I ask, eager to distract him.

My attempt is only partially successful as his eyes scan down my body. Then he clears his throat.

"Could be wildlife, could be anything." His gaze comes up to meet mine. "Why don't you put some clothes on and we can check it out."

I suppress a shiver I'm not sure is from his scrutiny, or the chilled air. Either way, I should probably get dressed.

"Turn your back," I tell him, because if I turn mine first, my ass is going to be on display.

He does as I ask immediately—always the gentleman—and I swing around, reaching for the pile of clothes. As I rush to get dressed, I feel a tingle of awareness running down my spine, and I wonder if he's peeking.

The idea is tempting; Dan as a gentleman in public, but a beast in bed.

~

The crash turned out to be nothing more than a large, dead branch coming down, partly on the girl in the body bag.

It was sobering, a reminder someone died here, someone's daughter. It certainly pushed all earlier thoughts from my mind.

So when I finally duck into the tent—by myself—it's with the full weight of responsibility to find the person or persons responsible for whatever happened to this girl and to Chelsea Littleton. Because there's no doubt in my mind the two are connected.

Exhausted, I crawl into the sleeping bag, noting the mat underneath isn't exactly comfortable, but it'll have to do for one night. I use the saddlebags as a lumpy pillow and pull the sleeping bag up under my chin. I close my eyes, and try not to think of my baby.

"Night, Sloane."

His voice startles me, and I catch his shadow moving outside the tent in the lingering glow of the fire. It looks like he's heading for the hammock, only twenty feet or so away.

"Night," I call back.

Then I close my eyes again, and try not to think of Dan.

Eleven

Dan

I already have the coffee percolating on the fire when I hear the tent zipper.

I hear her footsteps moving away and glance over my shoulder to see her slip into the woods. Answering the call of nature, I assume. She's gone a bit longer than I would've thought, and I'm contemplating looking for her, when she reappears closer to the creek. Her hair is wet.

"I was about to go in search of you."

I fill her thermal mug and hand it to her when she joins me by the fire. She takes a deep swig that has to be burning her mouth before answering.

"Had to dunk my head in the water to wake up." Then she holds up the mug. "This will hopefully clear the cobwebs. I slept hard."

Shit, I wish I could say I slept at all, but other than dozing off for a few minutes a couple of times, I was awake all damn night. My eyes are gritty but my mind is clear this morning. I had a lot of time to think.

Sloane cups the thermos in both hands, holding it in front of her like some kind of shield she can hide behind. But there's no hiding the frown on her forehead or the tension around her eyes. She may have slept hard, but it wasn't restful.

I fucked up.

I have no idea what went through my alcohol-pickled brain eight years ago, but it's clear I broke something that night.

How ironic, when I distinctly remember deciding, once the dust had settled on Mom's funeral, I would finally ask Sloane out on a proper date. See if she was interested in something more than the friendship we had, because I sure as hell was.

I'd been biding my time, my life being what it was at the time, I didn't think I could give her what she deserved. I was afraid she'd reject me right off the bat. So, I waited, and then when she apparently served herself up on a platter, I blew her off.

Unreal.

Of course, now that I know, I'm not going to leave a stone unturned until I have her naked in my bed again. Except this time, I'm gonna make sure she stays. For good.

It's going to take work though. I've got a lot of ground to cover, a lot of time to make up for, and a lot of hurt to set right. But the very first thing I have to do is make sure there is no miscommunication whatsoever about what my objective is.

Starting with this...

I step into her and cup her face in my hands. Her eyes widen, but since I've effectively trapped her hands between

116

us, she can't push me away, and I don't give her a chance to object because my mouth is already on hers.

My heart is hammering in my chest, too cognizant of everything I could be doing wrong right at this moment. It's out of character for me to be so forward—I'm generally the cautious and predictable one—but I'm going with my gut on this, and my gut tells me to be bold in my approach.

It's a risk that could earn me outright rejection.

Sloane freezes under my touch, but only for a moment. Then her body seems to relax into mine, her arms find their way around my waist, and her lips open to the coaxing of my tongue.

Her taste...*damn*...it's as new as it is familiar. A taste I already know I'll never tire of.

When her tongue slides along mine, goosebumps break out all over my skin. She moans in my mouth, and I feel the soft vibration down to my bones.

Talking about bones...there is no way she doesn't feel my painfully hard cock pressing into her stomach.

I'm about to end the kiss before I lose all control, when a metallic clang sounds right behind me, startling both of us.

"Sorry," Sloane mumbles, as she slips around me and bends down to retrieve the thermos she dropped.

"That's my line," I tell her, reaching over to grab her wrist to prevent her from putting the distance back between us.

She keeps her eyes aimed at my chest as I turn her to face me.

"I'm the one who's sorry. I can't explain what happened that night, and it doesn't even matter if I could. Nothing I can say now is going to take away the fact I hurt you, and no amount of sorry is going to fix that."

117

That earns me her eyes, but they're hard and narrowed, and her voice has a definite edge.

"So you decided to kiss it better?"

I don't hesitate with my response. "No. The kiss was to make it clear where I stand."

She lowers her eyes to the ground between us and says, in a soft voice, "Too bad it's eight years too late."

Well, I didn't expect it to be easy.

"We will see about that."

~

Sloane

I am petrified.

It took me a long time to get over Dan, and it terrifies me how little control I had over my response to him. My mind was screaming no, but my traitorous body was all over that kiss.

That kiss.

I can't tell you how often I fantasized about kissing him, imagined being in his arms, our bodies pressed close together. This was so much more, and not just because of the impressive boner I could feel every inch of. I've never been this conflicted over a kiss.

It's not that I don't believe him—I don't think he could've faked his shock—but for the past eight years I lived with the pain of rejection as truth. It's become part of me and isn't so easy to switch off. In fact, I'm not sure I'll ever be rid of it.

I top up my coffee from the pot still sitting on the small

fire. I spilled most of what was in my mug when I dropped it.

"We should probably eat something," he interrupts my thoughts. "It's ten to seven, those guys should be here soon."

Right, there's a girl who I need to identify and return to her family. Someone is missing their daughter, and here I am, worrying about a silly kiss. Clearly, Dan already put it behind him.

I take the granola bar he offers me.

"Thanks." I peel the wrapper back and take a bite. Still chewing, I ask, "Should we break up camp now?"

He shakes his head. "Let's do it after, we can take our time." Then he leaves me standing by the fire.

Not sure what he wants to take his time for, but I want to get out of here as soon as possible. Call me crazy, but I feel responsible for the girl's remains.

I turn around at the sound of a soft hiss and find him spraying himself with bug spray. When he catches me looking, he raises a questioning eyebrow and holds up the can of DEET. Even a whiff of the stuff in the air makes me want to gag, let alone when I spray it all over my skin. But, since I already have an impressive collection of bug bites I have no desire to add to, I concede and take the offered can.

I'm just handing the can back to Dan when his radio crackles alive.

"Tracker Three for Tracker Six. Rise and shine, kids. Over"

I recognize Bo's distinct deep rumble.

"This is Tracker Six. Morning. You guys here already? Over," Dan responds

"Had to wait for the sheriff at the trailhead. About to ride out now. Over"

Dan checks his watch.

"Roger. We'll be ready. Out."

Five minutes later we each pick up one end of the black, heavy-duty bag we left just inside the tree line, and start walking toward the rock wall. We try to keep the surprisingly heavy bag as level as we can to avoid jostling the remains inside too much, but it means the going is slow.

When we get to the large boulder we have to circumvent, my pack starts sliding off my shoulder. It holds my crime scene kit but also, and more importantly, my camera. I was hoping to properly record securing the remains in the basket, and take some pictures as well as it's being hauled up to the edge of the cliff, into the hands of the sheriff waiting up there.

"Hold up," I warn Dan, who is leading the way. "Can we put her down for a sec?"

After carefully lowering her to the ground, I hoist the strap back up my shoulder and start looping my arm through the other one.

"Want me to take that?" he offers, holding out a hand.

I shrug and slip the backpack off again, handing it to him. Who am I to argue if he wants to carry the extra weight?

"Where are they going to lower the basket?" I want to know.

The area right above where we found her is probably not the best location. Dan tilts his hat back, rubbing his hand over his chin as he looks up to scan the ridge.

"Probably best if we wait for the guys to get there. We'll figure it out then. But for now, let's move the body to level ground on the other side."

Once we have that done, I get a little restless just standing around, waiting. So, I grab my camera and go exploring along the base of the cliff, walking toward the flat rock where we found the girl's remains. I snap a few more shots of the location, as well as up to the ledge above.

As I'm shooting, I move around the rock to the other side. I looked around here yesterday, but with a focus on the body. Now, I pan my camera around, away from the wall and toward where the creek runs, clicking the shutter, until something catches my eye.

I lower the camera and squint, but all I can make out is something light in color against the trunk of a tree. Not quite sure what I'm looking at, I move closer.

When I recognize it, I immediately jump into action, snapping away furiously.

"Dan! I need my kit!"

I probably startled him because in no time at all I hear steps running toward me.

"What is it?" he pants.

Lowering the camera, I point out the bones I spotted.

"I think maybe it's part of her missing leg."

I could see how an animal might have dragged off the leg to feed in the shelter of the trees.

"I'm going to need my pack," I mention to Dan over my shoulder as I approach the bones.

Crouching down, I notice the foot appears to be missing and the lower leg is separated from the upper leg at the knee joint. I quickly take a few close-ups.

"Here."

Dan hands me my backpack, and I retrieve a pair of gloves and a large evidence bag. Then I carefully collect the bones.

"These should probably go with the body."

As I get to my feet, I cradle the evidence bag in my arms. When I swing around to return to where we left the body bag, my foot slips on a root. If not for Dan's steadying hand on my elbow, I might've lost my balance, or worse, dropped the remains. As if burned, I surge forward and out of his reach.

This is nuts. Here I am, holding a body part, and yet my body virtually sizzles at his touch.

A sharp, high frequency whistle echoes through the gorge.

"They're here," Dan announces.

While he gets his team on the radio to determine the best location, I head over to the black bag and unzip it, placing the missing bones in with the rest of her. I wish I'd found her foot as well, but who knows where that was dragged. I would love to spend some time looking for it, but the foot holds twenty-six bones, most of them small, and they could be spread out anywhere by now.

At this point, I think it's more important to find out who this girl is.

I slowly zip the bag back up, taking one last look at her remains. Something seems off, but I can't quite put my finger on it. When I catch sight of Dan approaching, I quickly close it all the way and get to my feet.

"I warned them about the leg bones. They're lowering the basket over there."

He indicates a spot halfway between the arrow he painted and the rock plateau where I nearly fell on my face. I see someone leaning over the edge, it looks like Bo. The next moment the basket is tilted over the edge and is lowered slowly.

Once the basket is on even ground, I help Dan lift the bag in, but I leave strapping the remains in tightly to him.

When a few moments later, the basket is pulled up, I feel

restless. But I force myself to watch until I see her disappear out of sight at the top. Then I resolutely turn to Dan.

"Let's pack up and get going."

We're silent as we break up camp, saddle and load up the horses, and start heading back downstream. I try to enjoy the ride but my ass hurts and my mind is still trying to figure out what it was that seemed off about the remains.

We're a little over an hour into our return trip when a lightbulb goes off.

"Which leg was missing?" I ask Dan.

He has a puzzled look on his face but answers anyway.

"Left. Why?"

My stomach shoots up in my throat.

"Because I'm pretty sure the remains I collected this morning were from a right leg."

Twelve

DAN

It's been forty-eight hours since I've been here, but the change is pretty dramatic.

The log shell was stacked and we'd almost been done putting up the trusses, but I didn't expect the roof to be up in just a couple of days.

It's nice. It cost a whack, but I'm really digging how the slate gray steel panels look against the rugged logs.

I opted for a simple two-level design, mainly because it was the most economic use of space without taking up too much land. It was important to me to leave enough room for a small paddock and a barn without taking down too many trees. The second floor has three large dormers, and the windows on the front—main and second floor—will be large to allow a clear view of the Fisher River and the mountains beyond.

It already looks like a proper house on the outside, even though we haven't yet started on the inside.

"That's a nice-looking house."

I turn around to find Sully walking up the driveway.

I saw him briefly late yesterday afternoon when Sloane and I got back to the ranch, but we didn't really talk. I have a feeling that's about to change. Sully is not the type to drop in to be neighborly.

"Thanks. I'm surprised they got the roof up so fast. Turned out good."

He steps up beside me and takes a long, hard look at the house.

"How many bedrooms?" he finally asks after a lengthy silence I just let play out.

"Four."

I can feel him turning his eyes on me, but I keep mine fixed on the house. If he has something he wants to talk about he's gonna have to come out and say it.

"You planning for a big family?"

"I'd like a family, eventually, yes."

Another pause.

"With Sloane."

It was more of a statement than a question, but it definitely requires a response. I turn to face him.

"In an ideal world."

Sully frowns. "I don't even know what the fuck that means."

"It means I would like to think it's possible, but it'll take a bit of convincing to get Sloane to believe it is."

He's still frowning at me, so I decide to elaborate a bit.

"I fucked up."

Sully snorts. "That's a given."

"Eight years ago, I had no idea. Had no clue why she took off, and up 'til the day before yesterday, I still had no clue."

"I assume you have a clue now."

"Yup."

"You plan to fix it?"

"Already working on it."

Sully turns back to the house, tilts his hat back a little, and scratches his forehead.

"She's stubborn."

"I know," I confirm.

"She's not gonna make it easy, especially if she's been hurt by you."

"Know that too."

He adjusts his hat, shoves a hand in his pocket, and turns to me.

"Well, best of luck with that."

Then he starts walking back down the drive.

"Hey!" I call after him. "You're not gonna try and scare me off?"

I'm not sure I like the grin he throws me.

"Nah. My sister's gonna be here in a few days. Trust me, she'll take care of that."

I watch him casually stroll back toward his house, not quite sure whether he just cursed me or gave me his blessing. Not that it makes a lick of difference, it won't stop me from going after Sloane either way.

I haven't seen Sloane since yesterday. I offered to look after the horses when we got back since I knew she was eager to get home to see Aspen, and her Jeep was gone by the time I walked out of the barn. As soon as she had cell phone reception, she'd contacted Junior Ewing to find out the remains were safely at the Medical Examiner's office—which is housed in the same building as the Sheriff's Office—and would not be looked at until this morning. I also heard her request a cadaver dog team be sent into the gorge to look for additional remains, and she was upset when Ewing suggested they wait until the ME had a chance to look at the remains.

I'm sure she knows more by now, and I have to admit, I'm curious, but I'm not about to bother her with questions about her case. When I call—which I hope to do tonight when I think the baby is sleeping—I'm going to be focusing on Sloane.

But first I want to check out my house.

There is no door yet, nor are any of the windows installed. The stonework for the fireplace also still has to be done, but all of those things will happen once the interior framing is up, which I'm going to start tomorrow. I've taken tomorrow and Monday off, which gives me four straight days. JD said he'd help, and both Fletch and Wolff mentioned they'd drop by if they had time.

Daylight is waning outside, but the first thing I notice when I walk in is the amount of light still coming in through the window openings in the front. I move to what will be the living room window and look out at the river. It would be so nice if I could move in before winter hits.

It's the beginning of September, which will give us this month and October—hopefully—before the snow starts flying. Let's say eight weeks. If we could get the framing up, windows and plumbing and electrical done, I can work on things like flooring, drywall, kitchen, and paint over the winter while already living here.

From the corner of my eye, I notice movement as a large bull elk walks along the shallow bank of the river into view. A magnificent animal, proud and majestic, as it stops and raises its head, appearing to scan the other side of the river in the setting sun.

It's rutting season, when the male elk is at its most

aggressive, vying for any and every female crossing his path, and confronting any competitors, but this guy looks relaxed, almost peaceful as he calmly checks out his surroundings.

Taking my phone from my pocket, I pull up the camera app and shoot a couple of pictures. The light is just right, deepening the contrasts and the colors.

I think I'm going to enjoy sitting out on my porch at dawn or dusk, having a coffee or a beer, just watching all this beauty play out in front of me. Better yet if I had someone special beside me.

Mom would've loved this. She really took to country living after we moved from town to the ranch. At the time, I would have given her no more than a few months left to live, but the fresh mountain air seemed to give her a boost. In the end, she was with me for almost five more years before the cancer finally won.

I wonder if the elk is catching a scent when he stretches his neck and lifts his chin up in the air. But then he lets out a distinct loud, wailing bugle. A pitched sound that carries far on high frequency waves, serving as both a mating call and a communication of dominance.

Steam is rising from his flared nostrils as he tests the air. But just when he sets up for another call, his head lifts high as something appears to draw his attention downriver. I can see the tension ripple through his muscles, moments before he abruptly swings around and lopes off in the opposite direction, disappearing from sight.

Something spooked him.

It's probably time I head back to the ranch anyway, it's getting dark out and I don't want to miss out on the enchiladas Ama promised for dinner.

As I swing my leg over the ATV I grabbed to come over here, I feel a prickle between my shoulder blades. I turn to look down the drive behind me but there's nothing to be seen.

Then I start the engine, turn on the headlights, and aim for the trail back to the ranch.

~

Sloane

"I'm not sure that's such a good idea."

Sully raises his head and the expression on his face tells me my objections are going to go nowhere. Which really sucks, because in my situation—being at the mercy of someone else's kindness—I really don't have a voice.

"What do you mean?" he returns. "It makes perfect sense. I mean, you can stay here, of course, but I would think you'd welcome a place of your own."

He's right, I would. Don't get me wrong, I love my uncle and his family—especially my little cousin—but it's hard to find a peaceful moment in a busy household like this. I wouldn't mind being able to put my feet up on my own table, picking my own TV shows, getting my morning coffee without needing to get dressed first.

However, moving into the vacant cabin at the ranch—two doors down from Dan—may not be a wise decision. I lived there before and the close proximity got me in trouble the first time.

"What about Mom?" I throw out in a last-ditch effort, even though I know it's a losing battle.

"That's the beauty of it," my uncle points out. "The place has a spare bedroom. Aspen's crib can fit into the primary one while Isobel is here. You wouldn't have to worry about the little one if you had to work late or got called out in the middle of the night."

"Only while Mom's here though."

"Right. But that gives you at least two more weeks to figure out a more permanent solution. Although, knowing your mother, I wouldn't be surprised if she ended up staying longer."

Yikes. I'm not sure I'm ready for that.

The last time Mom and I lived together was before I went to college and that was tumultuous, to say the least. Of course, I was barely out of my rebellious teens back then, but I've also lived on my own for about thirteen years now, and Mom and I both have strong personalities.

I foresee fireworks, but to be fair, I don't think those can be avoided anyway. Such is the nature of my relationship with my mother. I know I used to balk at anyone comparing us, but the reality is, we are very much alike.

"Whose idea was this anyway?" I'm curious to know.

"Ama actually suggested it when I picked Aspen up from the ranch earlier this week," Pippa contributes.

That makes me feel a little better. I was afraid my uncle might've brought it up at the ranch, which would've been a bit embarrassing. To be able to go into an arrangement like that, I would insist on a proper rental agreement. I'll get my first paycheck at the end of next week, but I still have savings that will cover me for first and last month's rent.

"I have to drop by the ranch tomorrow anyway, I'll chat with her, find out what the terms are," I concede.

I was hoping to talk logistics with Jonas tomorrow, but that's related to this case.

This morning I was in the medical examiner's office, witnessing the examination of the remains we found in the gorge. In his estimation, the bulk of the remains belonged to a young female between the ages of twelve and sixteen. She had some bone fractures, and her skull showed evidence of blunt force trauma, but the ME wasn't comfortable drawing a conclusion as to whether the injuries indicated accidental or inflicted.

He felt she'd likely been down in the gorge for anywhere from six to nine months, but admitted most of that was based on what she was wearing. He explained the complexity of putting together all the different factors that go into determining an actual timeline is only compounded by the fact animals clearly had been at her body.

Her ethnicity was another thing he brought up, pointing out some of the facial bone structure, as well as some remnants of skin, which he felt might suggest a Native American ancestry.

The leg was a different matter altogether. According to the ME, it looked to be male; something about the femur being thicker, or wider. He also felt it had probably been down there longer. That information threw me for a loop. It doesn't really fit the pattern I thought we might've bumped into.

Not that there is any concrete evidence at this point to even connect the girl's remains to whatever happened with Chelsea, but I'm still going to proceed as if it does.

The ME wanted to consult with a forensic anthropologist. To have them take a look at all the remains and get their input on his findings before he makes up an official report. In the meantime, the sheriff felt there was enough cause to call in assistance from a dog team to see if there are more remains to be found in that gorge. He's taking care of that, while I'm using what I learned from the autopsy to narrow down the long list of missing persons.

This girl, in particular, must have family still actively

looking for her. So, I plan to dive back into the list of filed cases of the past twelve months I downloaded onto the department's server after we finish dinner.

Aspen is already asleep, and should be good until about eleven when she usually wakes up for a feeding. That gives me about four hours of uninterrupted work.

"I'll clean up," I offer when I've finished most of my dinner and get to my feet.

I did my share of cooking in the days before I started my job, but I haven't contributed a whole lot since. Doing after dinner cleanup is the least I can do.

It doesn't take me long to rinse and load the dishes into the dishwasher. I'm just making a quick cup of tea to take upstairs when my phone rings.

Before I give myself a chance to consider if it's wise, I pluck it off the charger on the counter and answer Dan's call.

"Hey, sorry I ran off yesterday," I start apologizing, as I slip out the back door for some privacy.

"No need. Did you get the picture I just sent you?"

"Picture? I don't know, my phone was charging, let me see."

I put the phone on speaker and open my messages. There's a new one from Dan.

"Oh wow, look at him. He's beautiful."

The image is of an elk standing on the edge of the river, bathed in the orange hues of the sunset.

"That was not even an hour ago in front of my house up the road from you," he informs me.

"For real? That's amazing."

"Yeah. I was looking at him, thinking I can't wait to be sitting out on the porch, drinking a beer after work, and having this for a view."

I find myself smiling because that sounds pretty amazing. I turn to my right, where the river is but I can't see much of the view now, it's pretty dark. Sully and Pippa opted to build their house perpendicular to the river, but Dan's place is built parallel to the water.

"I bet," I affirm. "How is the house coming along?"

"Roof is on, believe it or not, and I'm hoping to get the bulk of the interior framing done over the next four days. I took a few days off."

"That sounds like a lot of work for four days."

"Some of the guys are coming out to give me a hand. Still, it's a tall order to get it all done. We'll be able to put a decent dent in the work though."

"That's good. Talking about work..."

It's tempting to stay out here, talking to him, but I really want to try and find the girl's family.

"I hear you. Maybe sometime over the weekend, when you have a moment, pop up the road and share a beer and a sunset with me on the porch."

I feel myself flush at his invitation but don't allow myself to think too long before I answer.

"I think I'd like that."

"Good. Night, Sloane."

I can hear the smile in his voice and wonder if he can hear mine as well.

"Night."

Ending the call, I save the image of the elk as wallpaper on my phone.

Thirteen

SLOANE

"Nita Isadore."

I slide the missing person's file from the Lake County Sheriff's Office I printed off across Junior's desk. A measly one-page report.

"Check the description of what she was last seen wearing," I point out.

"That's the jacket," he observes.

The yellow winter jacket was described in great detail, including the unicorn zipper tab. The rest of her clothing matches what we found with the body. Even the long sleek hair as seen in the snapshot of the pretty, smiling girl matches. As soon as I looked at that picture, I knew the remains we found belong to Nita Isadore.

The single sheet of information lists the particulars on Nita, and the report made by the girl's mother that her fifteen-year-old daughter had gone to the Quicksilver

Express at the Exxon gas station in Pablo to pick up some milk and was never seen again.

A note at the bottom of the report stood out. One word; runaway, followed by a question mark.

"Now look at this one."

The second report I hand over is the original, taken by the Confederated Tribal Police in Pablo. It is several pages long and far more detailed. Nita and her mom live in a trailer home only two blocks from the gas station. According to these additional notes, Nita was a good student, worked part time on Friday nights and Saturdays at the hair salon in town where her mother works. According to the woman, her daughter had ambitions to become a beautician.

A few handwritten notes show the few steps tribal police took to find the girl, but not much appears to have come of it. There were no official searches done.

"They wrote her off," my boss observes.

The same thing I was thinking. She was labeled a runaway, despite anything even remotely suggesting that might've been the case. It doesn't even look like they talked to anyone but the mother and the clerk at the gas station store.

The tribal police did go through the steps of sharing the report with not only the Lake County Sheriff's Office, but neighboring Ronan and Polson Police Departments as well. It was the Sheriff's Office that uploaded the information to the Montana Department of Justice Missing Persons Database, which is where I found the one-page report.

"I called Lake County, talked to the current sheriff, who's only been in office since the spring after his predecessor died of a heart attack. He wasn't aware of the case until I told him. Long story short, he was able to locate the original full report sent to them by the tribal police and faxed it to me."

"They had some major changes in Lake County late last year," Ewing shares as he flips through the pages. "The county withdrew from Public Law 280, and therefore the responsibility for funding and policing tribal lands fell squarely back on the shoulders of tribal police. I think this file may have fallen through the cracks during that transition."

Although, I appreciate the background, the fact remains the report of a missing girl was basically filed away without a second look. Call me a cynic, but I suspect the fact she happened to be Native American may have played into that.

"Yup. Sheriff Lee promised to email me a link to the files with the security camera feed from the Exxon station. It's a miracle they actually obtained that evidence, let alone saved it on their server. Although, I'm not sure how helpful it's going to be. There's a note in the report saying nothing notable was found, but I plan to check for myself."

"Good. Let me see what I can do to get a hold of the girl's dental records," Junior offers. "I have a contact with the CSKT who might be able to help."

The CSKT stands for Confederated Salish and Kootenai Tribes, which governs the Flathead Reservation. Tribal police would fall under that umbrella as well, and would be more appropriate for them to pay the mother a visit, rather than having me call her out of the blue.

I'm instantly relieved, although it does make me feel like a bit of a coward. Calling family members wouldn't be my choice—especially with potentially devastating news—but driving to Pablo and back would've cost me a whole day.

"Thank you."

As I walk out the door, he calls me back.

"Sloane? Before I forget, I've got a cadaver dog team coming in after the weekend. Jillian Lederman is also an experienced rock climber and specializes in searching rough terrain, but it still wouldn't be a bad idea to loop the HMT boys in. At least let them know what's going on in their backyard."

"I already talked to Jonas this morning," I inform him. "He's offering to go over location and terrain with the cadaver team."

I get a thumbs-up and duck down the hall.

I also addressed the issue of a written arrangement regarding the cabin, which was met with some resistance. Jonas insisted he wasn't going to take rent from me, and I was equally firm when I told him I would find another place where I'd be allowed to pay my own way. Jonas seemed a bit taken aback, and old Mr. Harvey—who'd been listening in on our conversation—cackled heartily at the expense of his son.

We did end up coming to an agreement, which was basically a month-to-month arrangement, with thirty days' notice, and a rent of seven-hundred dollars a month. It took a while to get to that amount since Jonas started off countering my suggestion of fifteen hundred—which is an average rent in Libby—with the ridiculous offer of fifty bucks a week.

We hammered it out in the end and shook on it. The handshake was my concession when Jonas balked at official paperwork. The move is supposed to take place this weekend before Mom gets here on Sunday, which means I'll have my hands full this weekend.

On my way to my cubicle, I bump into Frank Schmidt and Jason Heany, two of our deputies.

"Didn't take you long to weasel your way into the boss's

good graces, did it?" Frank challenges me. "What was it...all of a week? You may wanna wipe the dirt off your knees."

I was prepared to ignore him. It's nothing new and ignoring it is more effective than any reaction. I got this kind of stuff in Billings when I first joined the PD, and aside from that, I remember Frank from my time as a deputy here. He didn't particularly like me then and made it known.

But Jason seems offended on my behalf and feels the need to intervene, throwing Frank an elbow.

"Cut it out with that bullshit. And you know that's exactly what it is—bullshit. If Ewing hears you, he'll have your ass."

"What the fuck is the matter with you?" Frank swings on him. "She's got you pussy-whipped already too?"

"Schmidt. My office," I hear Ewing bark behind me.

This is going from bad to worse. None of this is going to help me deal with the likes of Frank Schmidt. In fact, this will only serve to make him hate me more. From what I understand, he had his eye on the new position I was hired for, and feels passed over by someone with less years on the job and a female to boot.

I'm pretty sure he's not the only one whose nose is out of joint. After all, this is rural Montana and it's still mostly a good-old-boys' club out here.

Frank shoots me a dirty look and purposely brushes my shoulder as he passes me.

"Sorry about that," Jason apologizes when the other deputy disappears into the sheriff's office.

"Not your problem," I assure him. "Nor is it mine. The fact he's a misogynistic asshole is all on him."

With that I head to my desk, stuff my copies of the missing persons file in my backpack, and head for the door.

"Heading home?" Betty calls out when I pass the open door to her office.

"Yeah, but I'm around, I'll be working from home, so call if you need me."

I'll be working, but I'll also be packing up Aspen and my things. I'll be moving to the ranch this weekend and Mom is getting in on Sunday. I've got a lot going on, but hopefully after the weekend things will settle down a bit.

When I get behind the wheel of the Jeep, I quickly call Pippa.

"I'm on my way. Do you need anything from town?"

"No. I was just about to call you to see how long you'd be. We're heading over to Nella and Fletch's for dinner. Do you want to come?"

"Thanks for the invite, but I think I'm going to pass. I'll quickly pick up something for myself and be home shortly. I've got some stuff to do tonight."

"No rush. See you in a bit."

I'm thinking pizza.

Maybe I'll get an extra-large one, pick up some beers as well.

~

Dan

Not bad for two guys putting in a day's work.

We've got the mudroom and the downstairs full bathroom right next to it framed in. We were also able to get a head start on the small walk-in pantry on the opposite side of the kitchen. If we can get up the two walls of the family room at the back of the house tomorrow, I'll be a happy camper. It'll leave two days to make a dent in the upstairs. I have three bedrooms, one bath on the left, and then the primary suite to the right of the stairway to frame. That's never gonna get done in two days, but there's always next weekend.

That reminds me, I need to confirm with the window contractor to see if he has all my windows and doors. He's scheduled to be here on Monday, but he was supposed to confirm. Once he's done and the house is sealed, I can get the electrician in here. The sooner the better. I'm limited to working during daylight, but once I have electricity, I'll be able to work at night as well.

"Looks pretty good," JD shares when he walks in.

He's been helping me load the power tools in the back of my pickup truck, which is, unfortunately, something we'll have to do until I can store them here safely.

"Yeah, we made good time."

I pick up one side of the compressor while he lifts the other end, and we carry it outside. Once loaded, I close the tailgate and close and click down the cover.

"Is that all?"

"You left your cooler on the porch," JD points out.

Right. Ama had it ready and packed with food and drinks this morning when I was heading out. I brought a couple of camping chairs and we sat out on the porch for our lunch break.

"I'll grab it."

I start heading up the porch steps when I hear JD behind me.

"Looks like you've got company."

I swing around and see a familiar Jeep coming up the driveway.

I watch as Sloane pulls up next to my pickup and gets out. I notice her cheeks look a little flushed.

"Hey."

"Hi. I took a chance and brought pizza and beer. But both will keep if I'm interrupting something," she quickly adds.

"No interruption," JD answers for me. "I've got plans tonight, so I was on my way out."

He doesn't mention those plans are with his couch and a baseball game on TV, like he told me earlier, but I'm not about to out him. Not when he's doing me a favor by making himself scarce. Any of the other guys might've stuck around on purpose, just to piss me off.

"If you're sure...there's plenty for everyone," Sloane assures him, grabbing a large pizza box and a six-pack of beer from the passenger seat.

"Nope, I'm outta here." Then he turns to me. "I'll be here at eight tomorrow morning. I'll grab us some breakfast."

I clap him on the shoulder.

"Thanks, man. Appreciated."

As JD heads for his truck, a loud wail comes from the Jeep's back seat. She brought Aspen.

Sloane has her hands full, so I pull open the back door, finding the little one with her face scrunched up, loudly voicing her displeasure.

"What's going on in here? Momma put you in the car and then forgot about you?" I spout nonsense at her as I struggle to get the damn seat belts off her. "Well, we're gonna fix that, aren't we?"

When I'm finally able to lift her out of the car and settle her against my shoulder, her crying stops immediately. Sloane is standing by the stairs, a grin on her face.

144

"Hope you don't mind I brought her."

"Why would I mind?" I pass her and carry Aspen up the steps to the porch, where I sit down in one of the camping chairs, rearranging the baby on my lap.

Sloane joins me, setting the pizza box on the cooler between the two chairs. Then she peels a beer from the six-pack and offers it to me, before placing the remaining ones by my feet.

"The family is over at Fletch and Nella's, but I didn't feel up to it. It's more of a beer and pizza night with my feet up."

"So sit," I prompt her.

"Just let me grab her stuff from the car."

I watch as she pauses by the front door opening, leaning inside.

"Oh wow, I can't believe how much of a house it already is. It went up so much faster than I thought it would."

"It's because it comes like a building kit. It's just a matter of following the instructions and fitting the right pieces together. Still, it's only a shell—walls and a roof—which looks good from a distance, but it's a far cry from being habitable. There's a ton of work left to be done before you can call it a house."

"Be that as it may," she returns with a smile over her shoulder as she continues to her vehicle. "What is here is already stunning. I can only imagine what it'll look like when it's finished."

I like that she likes it. I like it a lot, even though I force myself not to get carried away.

She returns a moment later with Aspen's car seat and a diaper bag. Then she plucks the baby off my lap and lifts her over her head, smiling at her as tiny hands grab for her face.

"You can sit with us while we eat, okay, Nugget? Mommy brought you a nice cold ring to chew on."

She blows a raspberry in the baby's neck that has the little one smiling wide, before plopping her in her seat. The promised ring is quickly produced and Aspen grabs for it with both hands, shoving it in her drooling mouth.

"Teething?"

"Is she ever," Sloane acknowledges, dropping down in the other chair with a deep sigh. "Well, we should probably eat before she gets fussy again."

The pizza is good, loaded with protein and other great stuff. We talk while we eat. Mostly I ask questions and Sloane tells me about her case. The little one eventually falls asleep in her seat around the time she apparently goes to bed normally.

It's nice, sharing some food and a beer, talking effortlessly about random stuff, and even the silences are comfortable with Sloane. If you ask me, this date beats sitting at a fancy restaurant or going to a movie. I'm relaxed, she's relaxed, and nothing beats this view.

With only two slices left in the box, I slide down in my chair, full and sated, as I stretch my legs in front of me and watch as the setting sun gives the river and the mountains a deep golden hue.

"Gorgeous," she whispers beside me.

"Yes," I agree, as I glance over and catch her eyes.

When I reach out to her, she places her hand in mine without hesitation. I close my fingers around hers.

"Thank you for this. It's a perfect way to end an exhausting but productive day."

"Yeah," she returns as her eyes drift back to the view, but her hand stays clasped in mine. "It's just what I needed. I haven't felt this relaxed in months."

There's a lot to be read in that statement, but for now I'm content taking it as a compliment.

When darkness finally wins, she slips her hand from mine and pushes up out of her chair.

"I should get going. Get this little monkey tucked into bed."

"I'll take her," I offer, when she reaches for the car seat.

I carry Aspen to the Jeep and secure her seat in the back. I leave the buckling in to her mother and wait for her to be done. Instead of opening the driver's door for Sloane, I box her in against the car, bracing my arms on either side of her and leaning my body close.

She doesn't resist, in fact, her eyes almost hold a challenge.

Well, I've never been the type to back down from one.

When I kiss her this time, I'm not trying to make a point, I'm staking a claim. My lips bruise and my tongue takes charge, as I pin her against the side of the car using only my body.

She moans down my throat when I force my leg between hers and roll my hips. I can feel her heat through my jeans and enjoy a moment of triumph when she rocks her hips, rubbing her core against my thigh.

This.

There is nothing like the feeling of exhilaration when dominance is willingly conceded. All the more meaningful from someone as strong and powerful as Sloane.

The reason I keep my hands from touching her is because I know the moment I do, the balance of power shifts. For now, I prefer holding on to it.

Which is why I let her ride my thigh until I can feel her body tense as her fingers dig into my ass. Then I abruptly end the kiss and remove my leg from between hers. Her eyes are glassy and her cheeks are flushed, but she doesn't look happy I left her hanging.

"Drive safe," I tell her, before she has a chance to gather herself.

"Fine," is her short answer.

I open the door and wait for her to get in behind the wheel before closing it. Then I step back as she starts the Jeep. She backs up a few feet and then stops, rolling down her window.

"I forgot to mention," she calls out. "We're going to be neighbors. I'm moving into Fletch's old cabin on Sunday." She smiles. "I'll be right next door."

Shit. It'll be impossible for me to resist her when I know she's only a few feet away.

I watch her taillights disappear and wonder who's actually in control here.

Fourteen

SLOANE

I lean back in my chair, close my eyes, and listen to Carmi and her friend's chatter outside.

It's disturbing to think those girls are not much younger than Chelsea or Nita.

I rub my burning eyes, the result of staring at my laptop, trying to decipher what is poor quality security video from inside the gas station store. There's about two hours' worth of footage from about seven to nine on the night Nita went missing.

Her mother informed police her daughter had forgotten to grab milk when she picked up a few things at the store before dinner. So at seven thirty, right after she'd finished watching an episode of *Friends,* she sent her back there.

That poor woman. I can't imagine what she is feeling.

I've watched the full footage twice now, fast forwarding through parts where no activity was noted, and replaying sections where customers were coming into the store. From seven twenty-five through eight o'clock—which is the most plausible time window for Nita to walk in—there were a total of five customers in the small store. From what I could tell, three were male, two female. None of them bought milk, and none of them were Nita.

The second time I watched the whole thing through, I tried to focus on what was happening outside the store. The camera angle is such, at the top of the screen, you can partially see through the store's front windows. You can't see the pumps, only a portion of the parking spots right in front of the store. I've written down the specifics of every vehicle pulling up during that two-hour stretch.

Frustrated, I close the screen with the video feed, and pull up the email from the Lake County sheriff so I can reply and thank him for his assistance. I scroll down the original email to see how he signed off so I can properly address him, when I notice a second link. I guess I was so eager to pull up the feed, I didn't look any farther.

When I click on it, another online folder appears, this one is titled "northeast corner." Inside is another video file for the same time period, which looks to be of the outside. This camera has both the gas pumps and the front of the convenience store in view, as well as the two car-wash bays. At this angle, I can even see a part of the side street.

Before I can hit start though, Aspen makes herself known. She had another restless night, had developed a fever, and at Pippa's suggestion, I ended up giving her some medication, which seemed to help. She was fine earlier this morning, has been taking her bottle just fine, and went down for her morning nap without issue, but that didn't last too long. She's only been down for forty-five minutes.

"Hey, sweet girl," I coo, approaching the crib.

Yeah, her cries sound like she's in pain. Even when I pick

her up—which would normally settle her down some—she continues to cry.

It's funny, I can barely remember who I was before I became a mother, and yet I still feel so new at this at times. I try rocking her for a bit, bouncing her on my shoulder as I walk around our bedroom, but to no avail. Her little head feels warm against mine.

"Let's get you a clean diaper first, okay?" I suggest.

Maybe I can check her temperature while I do that.

I grab what I need from the dresser and put her down on the bed. She doesn't like that and lets me know. I'm not sure what happened to my sweet, happy child.

"Awww, poor kiddo," Pippa commiserates as she slips into the room, waving the bottle of infant Tylenol and one of the frozen teething rings.

"Good call," I tell her. "I think her fever is back."

"She can have a dose every four to six hours, it's been over eight."

While I struggle with Aspen's flailing limbs, trying to get a clean diaper on her, Pippa gives her another dose of Tylenol.

"Were you trying to work?" she asks, eyeing the laptop I left open on the bed.

I nod, close the last snap on Aspen's romper, pick her up, and shove my face in her little neck as tears burn. My God, maybe it's just lack of sleep, but I feel so damn overwhelmed. Single parenthood, moving here, a new job, teething, demanding case, and tomorrow moving again.

I thought I'd be able to do this, but right now—Aspen's woeful cries muffled against me—I feel like an utter failure.

"All right, then." Pippa plucks the baby from my hands and bounces her on her shoulder. "Go splash some water on your face, grab your laptop, and go work in Sully's office.

He's taking the girls to the ranch for a ride." Then she presses a kiss to my baby's downy head. "I've got this little one."

The mirror in the bathroom shows my pitiful state. Swollen, red eyes, tear streaks down my face, my hair sticking out every which way. I'm a fucking mess. Instead of splashing water, I shove my whole head under the faucet.

When I walk into the bedroom a few minutes later, it's empty. Pippa must've taken Aspen downstairs. I feel an immediate surge of guilt. What kind of mother leaves her sick child for someone else to deal with?

Then I catch sight of my laptop, and am reminded there is a mother in Pablo who may just have found out the daughter she's been looking for is likely no longer alive, or Chelsea's mom, who to this day doesn't know what her daughter endured and how she ended up clinging to a cliff, a hundred or so miles away from home.

My child is taken care of, she's loved and safe. Those mothers don't have that luxury, which is why I have to at least find them answers.

Grabbing my laptop, I head downstairs and duck into my uncle's office.

Ten minutes later, I'm watching the outside security feed from the gas station on the large screen of his iMac. Sully's twenty-seven inches is loads better than my measly fourteen-inch screen.

Reviewing this feed is much slower going because I can't fast forward. In fact, I have to stop and rewind regularly. There is more happening on the screen; vehicles pulling in and out, people pumping gas, pedestrians walking by, and you can even see part of the street Nita would have walked down to get to the store.

I'm writing notes as I go, jotting down little things that

stand out and time stamps I want to revisit. It's not until my second run-through something jumps out at me at the seven thirty-four time stamp.

There's an entrance/exit into the gas station from US-93, and a second entrance/exit around the corner on 2nd Street North, the street Nita would probably have walked down. Most vehicles seem to come in off the highway, and exit the same way. Only a few seem to use the one around the corner.

At seven twenty-nine, a delivery truck turns into the Exxon off the highway and pulls up to the second pump closest to the road. I can see the driver, wearing a dark-colored ball cap, get out, but then lose sight of him as he presumably fills his tank.

Then at seven thirty-four, he gets back in his truck, but instead of looping around to get back onto the highway—like most do—he goes the other way. He passes the front of the car wash, and parks his truck around the far corner, parallel to the side street Nita would be coming down at about that time.

The next thing I see is the driver walking back around to the front of the building and entering the convenience store.

As soon as he disappears inside, I pause the video and open a second window. Then I pull up the feed from inside the store again and fast forward to where I can see him coming in. He walks to the cooler and appears to grab a few drinks before approaching the counter.

Now I can see his ball cap is green and he's wearing what looks like a dark navy padded jacket, but I can't really make out his face. I only see the bottom half, he's keeping the bill of his cap low, and from this angle, it obscures his eyes and nose.

He seems to order a pack of smokes, and pulls a few bills from his pockets, paying in cash.

At seven thirty-eight he moves to the door to head back outside.

I pause the feed and return my attention to the outside view. Instead of play, I hit fast-forward to get to seven thirty-eight.

I watch as the man walks out and immediately turns right toward the car wash. Instead of going back to his truck around the outside of the car wash, he abruptly appears to dart into the second empty bay. Something clearly drew his attention.

When I catch a quick flash of yellow coming into view at the back of the first empty bay, disappearing again almost instantly, I shoot up straight in my chair. My heart is racing and my breath shallow, as I rewind to the point where the man exits the store. Instead of focusing on him this time, I zoom in on the first bay of the car wash and play it in slow motion.

There she is, the yellow coat is unmistakable; Nita. She appears to use the empty bay as a shortcut to get to the front door of the convenience store. I'm so focused on her, I don't even see the guy coming up behind her until I see her suddenly lifted off her feet, a hand coming around to clasp over her mouth, and an arm grabbing her around the waist.

The next moment she's gone, and so is the man with the green hat.

It's a full five minutes before the truck moves.

"Take your time, sweetheart."

The poor girl is fidgeting in her seat as she seems to mull

156

over my question if she remembers hitching a ride, maybe getting into a truck.

For a moment I wonder if FaceTiming her was the right decision, but I wasn't going to be able to drive out to Columbia Falls until after the weekend. I would really love to make a firm connection between the two girls.

If our perp is indeed this truck driver, Nita and Chelsea may not have been the only victims. There may have been more girls he picked up along his route.

"I...I'm not sure."

I'm not sure is not no, but it still doesn't really help me. I'm going to have to approach this another way.

"Chelsea, do you remember having a big argument with your parents?" I probe. "You were upset and left the house."

Her eyes dart off-camera and she appears a little sheepish. I assume she's looking at her mother or both her parents.

"I remember."

Her voice is soft, but I'm hopeful when her response is sure.

"That's good. So, you were upset and walked out the door. Did you turn right or left?"

"Right," is her immediate answer.

"Why did you turn right?"

Something in her face changes. She seems to become more alert.

"Because of the Mountain Climber, the stop is up a few blocks."

"The Mountain Climber?"

"The county bus," she explains.

I send her a little encouraging smile.

"And you were planning to take the bus?"

"Yes, to the movies in Kalispell," she says, more

animated now as she appears to remember a bit more. "I thought I had money in my backpack, but I forgot I spent it on Subway for lunch the day before."

That was more words strung together than I'd heard her speak before.

A deep frown appears between her eyebrows as she falls silent again.

"Chelsea? What happened when you discovered you had no money for the bus?"

She darts a glance away from the camera again. I get the sense she remembers more but doesn't want to speak in front of her parents, there's not much I can do about that.

I suspect she probably wasn't ready to return home after discovering she didn't have bus fare and maybe tried to hitchhike into Kalispell. Something I would assume her parents have clear rules about.

"Did someone stop to give you a ride?" I ask, trying to take a bit of the responsibility away from the girl.

We're back to nodding.

"Was it a car or a truck?"

I'm sitting on the edge of my seat, almost willing her to give the answer I can feel in my bones is coming.

She tucks her long hair behind one ear and bites her lip.

"Car," she finally says, deflating my balloon.

I was so sure.

It's hard not to feel a little deflated, but I can't lose sight of the fact the girl is finally starting to remember, giving me information I didn't have before.

"But I changed my mind and ended up not getting in," she adds, much to my surprise. "I thought maybe I could walk over to visit with Jessie for a bit before going back home."

Off-camera I hear a sharp inhale of breath and Chelsea turns her head in that direction.

"Who is Jessie?" I ask quickly, to get the girl's attention back. "Is she a friend?"

"She's Tessa's sister, she works at the Pizza Hut. Tessa is my friend."

"Okay, so you went and saw Jessie at the Pizza Hut," I prompt her.

This time she shakes her head, looking confused.

"I don't think I did. I remember seeing the Pizza Hut sign when I cut through the gas station, but I don't recall going inside."

"Gas station?" I echo, all my senses on full alert.

"Yeah, the Exxon. It's right across the street. The last thing I remember is passing the ice cooler on the side of the gas station when this white truck pulled up and blocked my path, so I had to go around it."

I can barely contain my excitement, but I want to make sure. "A white truck, like a pickup truck?"

"No. Bigger. Like one of those delivery trucks."

Bingo.

Fifteen

DAN

"Looking good."

Thomas hands back my phone.

I'd taken a few pictures of the progress at the house so he could see. Once I have water and electricity up and going, I'll have to take him over to watch a sunset with me.

That's one thing I'm definitely going to miss about living here, sharing an after-dinner drink on the porch with the old man.

It's a habit we got into after Mom passed away. After years of looking after my mother, suddenly the nights became lonely. One night I was wandering around the ranch, looking for something to do, rather than spending another evening in deafening silence, when Thomas called me over. He'd been watching me, sitting on the porch, smoking his clandestine cigar and sipping his daily glass of whiskey.

I joined him that night, listening to his stories about

growing up in Texas, meeting his deceased wife, Mary, and dating back to his own ranching days. I returned the next night, and the one after that, slowly getting pulled into the fabric of his family after losing mine.

He's also the person I turned to when, out of the blue, this guy David Zimmerman showed up claiming to be my biological father. Then again, a couple of years ago, when I found out I had a half sister living in Durango, Colorado.

Discovering a father and sister I didn't know I had took a bit of getting used to. I'd been feeling pretty pissed with my mom at first but Thomas talked me through that as well.

These days I'm in regular contact with both. I don't see Lindsey—my sister—as much as I'd like to. She's married with two little ones and her husband is the president of a motorcycle club that owns several businesses in town, so it isn't that easy for them to get away. I've been to see her once, but I'm probably due for another trip out there at some point.

When my father learned of my existence after Mom died, he actually moved to Kalispell, so he and I catch up fairly regularly. He actually may get a kick out of these progress pictures; I should probably send him a couple.

"When are your windows coming?" Thomas asks.

"Tuesday. He was supposed to be here tomorrow, but something came up. Won't really set us back though. We only got the primary bedroom, closet, and bathroom done today. That was a lot more work than I thought. The one-day delay on the windows means I can focus on the other rooms upstairs I haven't even touched yet."

"Boys coming out to help again?"

Most of the guys were over at the house helping at some point this weekend. Even Jonas showed up yesterday after-noon, but he left to head back to Fort Harrison this morn-

162

ing. Apparently, Jackson is going to be released tomorrow and Alex and Jonas are bringing him back here.

"JD and James."

"Good." He holds up his hands, gnarled with arthritis. "If not for these useless paws, I'd be over there in a heartbeat, giving you a hand. Been known to build a thing or two in my day."

I suppress a grin. Ninety-two-years old, he can barely lift his tumbler of whiskey, so I can't really see him wielding a hammer, but I have no problem believing there wasn't much he couldn't do at one point in time.

"I'm surprised she's back already," he mumbles under his breath.

I turn to see what he's talking about, when I catch sight of Sloane's dark red Jeep coming up the driveway and turning toward the cabins. I haven't seen her since Friday, but I know she was supposed to move into the cabin today. Her Jeep wasn't here when I got back from the house.

"Wasn't she picking up her mom?"

Thomas glances at his watch. "Yeah, but her plane was supposed to land at seven ten. It's seven forty-five now. It's an hour-and-a-half drive."

Good point.

I push up to my feet. "I'm just gonna go...check."

"You do that," he calls after me, snickering.

I catch her just as she lifts Aspen's seat out of the car.

"I can take her."

I'm already reaching for the baby seat when Sloane's head swings around at the sound of my voice.

"Jesus, you startled me."

But she lets me take charge of Aspen, who looks to be fast asleep.

"Where's your mother?" I ask as I follow her to her front door.

"Ugh," she groans as she steps inside. "She's stuck in Denver for the night. She'd boarded her flight to Kalispell, but apparently there was an issue with the plane. They were sitting on the tarmac for over an hour before they were told to get off the plane. Anyway, the flight was cancelled and they put her on another one tomorrow."

"Oh no," I commiserate, setting the car seat on the couch, as Sloane dumps her keys and the diaper bag on the small kitchen island.

"Yeah, it sucked. I didn't get her message until I stopped for gas just outside Kalispell, and I turned right back around."

"Luckily after a weekend of keeping me awake and on my toes, Aspen decided to finally sleep. She was out the whole time."

She moves to the baby and, with gentle hands, peels her out of the seat.

"I'm just going to put her down."

I feel a little awkward standing in the middle of her living room. It's eight o'clock at night and it sounds like she hasn't had much sleep this weekend, so making a pot of coffee is probably not a good idea. A beer or a glass of wine might be a better option.

Peeking into her fridge I notice it's full of all the necessities—Ama's handiwork, I'm sure—but other than milk and bottled water, there isn't anything to drink. My fridge is only two doors down though, and it's well-stocked with beer.

"Are you leaving?"

I let go of the door and turn around. It could be my imagination, but she actually looks a bit disappointed.

164

"I was just going to grab us a couple of beers from my fridge."

"Ohh, I would kill for a beer."

I grin at her. "No need to resort to violence. Give me one minute."

When I return a few moments later, Sloane is standing in the kitchen, leaning on the counter with her head hanging down. From the bedroom I hear the baby's soft cries.

Walking up behind her, I set down the beers and lift my hands to her shoulders, massaging them gently. Next thing I know, she spins around, burying her hands and her face in my shirt. Circling her with my arms, I pull her in tight. Her body shudders as she cries silently, drowned out by her daughter's increasing complaints.

"I need t...to get her."

Pressing a kiss to the top of her head, I gently set her back.

"I've got it. You sit down and have your beer."

She must be at the end of her rope, because this is not like her. Tears rolling unchecked down her face, she looks worn to a thread. I bend down and kiss her wet cheek.

"Go on, sit down."

Then I head for the bedroom where Aspen is now wailing in earnest. I duck in and close the door behind me.

"Hey, you...what's with all the ruckus?" I babble as I walk up to her crib.

Her face is scrunched up and she's trying hard to shove her little fist into her wide-open mouth. I pick her up and lift her against my shoulder, holding her with a hand under her little butt. A very wet butt.

I spot a towel on the dresser I spread on the bed, and when I check the top drawer, I find a bunch of baby clothes and diapers. I pull out something that looks similar to what she's wearing and a clean diaper. Then I lay her on the towel and quickly strip her down.

As soon as I remove her wet diaper, the wailing eases up, and the next moment she's trying to stuff her foot in her mouth. Undressing her turns out to be far easier than trying to get a diaper and clothes back on her. I'm sure the snaps on her pj's aren't exactly lined up, but she doesn't seem to care.

She's not crying when I pick her up again. In fact, she appears to be quite happy in my arms, listening to me hum. I briefly contemplate taking her out to her mom, but then I see her eyes growing heavy, so I start rocking her instead.

I'm hoping to win myself some major brownie points if I can get her to sleep again.

～

Sloane

Nothing has gone as planned this weekend.

Not a single thing, not even Dan showing up at the end of it all.

To start with, I did more work than I'd planned to, thanks to Pippa stepping in on Saturday and taking care of Aspen. She didn't sleep much again that night.

I wasn't able to get a hold of the sheriff until this morning, so I took my daughter and drove into town to meet up with him at the office. I was able to show him what I found on the videotapes, and told him about my conversation with Chelsea. Of course, Aspen decided to start crying, making conversation really difficult.

Junior indicated it was probably time for him to get in touch with Sheriff Lee, as well as the Columbia Falls Police Department, to coordinate efforts now that we've been able to confirm these two cases definitely appear to be related. He also suggested I look into other missing persons cases that could fit similar parameters tomorrow.

Then I had to run back to Sully and Pippa's to move my things into the cabin, only to find my uncle had already moved everything. A good thing, since all I had time for was putting a few things away in the new digs before I left to pick Mom up at the airport. Clearly, we know how that turned out.

My plan had been to go home, put Aspen down, and roll into bed myself—I need the sleep—but instead I end up having a meltdown in Dan's arms.

I guess there's worse things.

"I heard you singing to her," I share when I hear him come out of the bedroom.

"Me? Singing? You're hallucinating."

He plops down on the couch beside where I'm sitting with my legs folded under me, and twists the top off the beer I left for him on the coffee table. He puts the bottle to his mouth, but I can see a smile crinkle the corners of his eyes.

"I'm pretty sure," I insist. "I could swear I heard you sing, *Ain't No Sunshine,* in there."

He puts his bottle down and rolls his head to the side so he's looking at me, a grin on his lips.

"Cowboys don't sing."

It could be those dark eyes, dancing with humor and a hint of heat, or maybe it's sheer gratitude that has me climb right on his lap. Straddling him, I slide a hand on either side of his face and tilt his head back.

"I'll have you know I have excellent hearing," I whisper, my nose touching his.

"Yeah?"

His voice is growly as his fingers dig into my hip. Then he hooks me around the neck with his other hand and pulls me down to his lips.

I may have made the first move this time, but there's absolutely no question who's kissing who. It's all I can do to keep up with the sensations his mouth and tongue are stirring up.

My body—aside from childbirth, mostly dormant this past year—wakes up under his touch. It's like the pins and needles of fingers and toes defrosting, except it's every single nerve ending coming alive. Pain and pleasure are only a hairbreadth apart.

His hand slides down the back of my pants, squeezing one of my generous ass cheeks before slipping between my legs. He finds me already wet and without preamble fills me with his fingers. My entire body convulses around the intrusion. I let my head fall back as my hands curl into the longer hair at his collar.

"Okay?" he rumbles, his lips sliding down my neck.

"Mmmm," is the best I can manage as I rock myself on his fingers.

"Fuck, Sloane, I want inside you so bad, but I don't wanna—"

So, I grab his face with both hands, kiss him hard, and look him in the eyes.

"Yes. I want that too."

I'm not sure if I'm going to regret this tomorrow, but there's no way I want to stop now.

Apparently, I'm not the only one who feels that way because suddenly Dan surges to his feet, his hands under my ass. I wrap my legs around him as he carries me into the spare bedroom where he tosses me onto the bed. For a second, I watch as he kicks off his boots, but when he starts stripping off his shirt, my hands get busy getting naked as well, tackling my own top.

My heart is bouncing around my chest wildly, and I'm almost hyperventilating when Dan shoves his jeans down his legs and kicks them off. I'd seen and admired his chest, but the rest of him is equally impressive. He doesn't give me much of a chance to ogle him, when he puts a knee on the mattress.

"You're running behind," he grumbles, grabbing the waistband of the pants I was about to remove, and stripping them right off me, underwear and all.

Then he sits back on his knees between my legs, his hands loosely around each of my ankles. He looks his fill, to the point I get a little uneasy and automatically cover my mommy-pouch. My body changed a lot during my pregnancy with Aspen. It never bothered me, but I find myself suddenly aware.

Until he mumbles, "Jesus, you're so gorgeous I don't even know where to start."

"Inside me," I suggest, dropping my legs open.

"Fuck me. Hold that thought."

He reaches over the edge of the bed and comes up with a wallet he likely fished from his jeans. From it, he produces a foil packet.

"Aren't you the Boy Scout," I tease him, mostly to keep from whimpering at the sight of him rolling on the condom.

He puts his hands back on my ankles and slides them all the way up my body, mapping my curves. Then he braces himself on either side of me and leans down, closing his mouth on a nipple. I can feel the pull of his hot mouth all the way down to my pussy.

Slowly he lowers his hips in the cradle of mine, and I feel the crown of his cock brush me, as he makes room for himself. Then he moves my arms above my head and holds them pinned there.

"Wrap your legs around me, and hold on. This'll be fast and furious," he grumbles.

The next moment he steals all my air as he aims true and fills my body.

"You gotta breathe, baby," he reminds me.

I take in a deep breath, and—as if he was waiting for my cue—Dan starts moving. As promised, it's fast, and it's furious. His strong legs power him deeper than I thought possible.

My senses are overwhelmed in so many ways as my body is driven to new levels of pleasure. I am not in command of anything, and it feels amazing.

Dan starts to grunt with the effort to hang on to control as his rhythm begins to falter. I can feel the tension vibrate in his muscles, even as my legs begin to tremble.

"That's it. Come for me, baby."

It's not an easy slide into bliss, this is like being hurled off a precipice. I don't recognize the sounds coming from me as my body flies apart.

I barely notice Dan planting his cock deep, and shoving his face in my neck to stifle a yell when he comes. All I can do is try to breathe, my body limp and boneless as he covers it with his. I welcome his weight, it's secure, otherwise I'm afraid I might float away.

I moan my displeasure when he eventually moves, but all he does is roll us, so he's on his back and I'm half draped over him.

I feel his lips brush my forehead.

"Rest," he whispers.

Sixteen

DAN

"No, I'll figure it out."

I expected her to say that, but that won't deter me.

"It's already settled. Ama is looking after Aspen, JD and James can get started at the house without me, and I was going to have to go into Kalispell at some point this week anyway to grab some supplies at The Home Depot. I might as well do it today and pick up your mom at the same time."

She looks like she's not done objecting so I bring up the one thing she won't have an argument against.

"Besides, isn't the dog team arriving this morning? Who better to brief them, show them around? This is your case."

Her eyes narrow to slits before she turns her back on me and returns her attention to getting Aspen dressed.

Coming out of the bedroom this morning, she was clearly surprised to find me on the couch. She probably thought I'd snuck out like a thief in the night. I hadn't, but she'd been sleeping hard and after the baby woke me up around eleven thirty last night, I didn't want to risk waking her.

Aspen had been hungry and I had to google how much formula to feed her. That little thing has a good set of lungs, I was surprised she didn't wake her mother. Luckily, she settled down quickly after I fed her. I guess I could've gone home then, but I ended up crashing on the couch instead, where Sloane found me fifteen minutes ago.

She looks pretty cute straight out of bed, with squinty eyes and her hair poking every which way, but her mood first thing in the morning is a little scary. I know I'm risking bodily harm when I ease up behind her and press a kiss to the nape of her neck, but she only grunts in response.

"Why don't you hop in the shower?" I suggest, pushing my luck. "I can take her over to the ranch. I'm heading there anyway."

I step back when she picks up Aspen and turns around, kissing and snuggling her daughter for a moment—her eyes closed—before handing her to me.

"Let me grab her bag. I'll text you Mom's flight number."

A few moments later I'm walking toward the ranch, the diaper bag slung over my shoulder and the baby in my arms. It's a pretty safe bet I'm going to draw some comments when I walk into breakfast, but I don't give a flying fuck.

The world is my fucking oyster today.

Last night was a surprise. I'm a patient man, I'd been fully prepared to take whatever time needed to show Sloane how things could be between us. But then she made the first move, climbed on my lap, and kissed me in a way I wasn't left wondering whether she was into it. Sure, part of it may have been stress release, but it was my touch she responded to.

So, yeah, I'm feeling pretty great today.

I smell the bacon when I come in the front door. Ama is by the stove, and Wolff, Thomas, JD, and James are already eating at the table.

Thomas is the first one to see me. "Well, butter my butt and call me a biscuit."

Of course that has everyone looking up.

"That didn't take long," JD comments before shoving a piece of bacon in his mouth.

James—who never talks much—raises an eyebrow before he returns to his breakfast as well. Wolff does the same with a grin and a shake of his head, as Ama makes a beeline for me. Or rather, Aspen, who is rather abruptly plucked from my hold.

"I'll take that baby and you sit your ass down before breakfast is all gone."

I do as I'm told since I'm pretty damn hungry, and load up a plate.

"There's been a small change in plans," I inform James and JD. "I have to run into Kalispell. I've got to hit up The Home Depot for a few things and I'm picking up Sloane's mom from the airport."

"*You* are?" Thomas inquires.

My response is a simple, "Yep."

Then I dig into my breakfast.

I met Isobel, Sloane's mother a couple of times, years ago, but I have no trouble picking her out of the crowd disembarking the plane.

For one thing, the family resemblance is impossible to miss, and for another, she has me pinned with a look the moment she walks into the terminal. There's no doubt she knows who I am too.

"Here," she says by way of greeting when she reaches me and hands me her carry-on.

Then she marches right past me to the baggage carousel, leaving me no choice but to follow.

"How was your flight?" I ask when I catch up with her.

It earns me a flash of familiar-looking blue eyes. "A day too long."

I try to be sympathetic. "Yeah, that was unfortunate."

"A pain in my ass is what it was," she counters, turning to me. "What was unfortunate was finding out I have a granddaughter when she's already four-and-a-half fucking months old."

A few heads turn at her raised voice and probably the swearing. I catch a few looks myself, quickly identified as a guilty party by some. If only they knew how much I wish I could make that claim.

"And then I get a text message this morning, saying my daughter can't even be bothered picking me up." She quickly turns her head away, but I still catch a shine in her eyes. "Now I have to wait even longer to see my grandbaby."

I don't have to be a mind reader to know there's a lot going on below her angry surface. I even get Sloane carries responsibility for that, but she doesn't need to have more blame than she deserves piled on her shoulders.

I send a quick text to let Sloane know her mother arrived. Then I wait until we have collected her suitcase and are on the road back to the ranch before I speak.

"In all fairness, Sloane planned to come to the airport but I talked her out of it."

"What the blazes for?"

I can feel her glaring at me, but I keep my eyes fixed on the road.

"Has she told you about the case she's working on?"

"What case?"

I tell her about the girl we rescued from the gorge, and the remains of the other girl we found. She doesn't interrupt and seems to be listening intently as I explain how her daughter is working her butt off to find whoever did this before he gets a chance to do it again. All while she's trying to get her feet back under her.

"To top it off, she hasn't had a whole lot of sleep."

Isobel snorts.

"Because Aspen is teething," I clarify, setting straight whatever assumption she made.

"So, it sounds like you two have reconnected."

"We have."

She's quiet for a while, and I'm good with the silence. It lasts until we're coming up on Happys Inn, a small hamlet maybe twenty miles from the ranch.

"I still don't get why she left in the first place," Isobel muses. "She loved it here. I really thought she was getting her shit together. She had a thing for you, you know?"

"Had a thing for her too," I admit.

I glance over and catch her eye.

"Still do."

Sloane

Jillian Lederman is not at all what I expected.

I guess I had a picture in my mind of someone more seasoned, a bit more rugged, and definitely bigger than the petite redhead. I swear, she can't be more than five foot two at most, and with a bit of effort, I could probably lift her right off her feet. She's tiny and I feel like a freaking Amazon standing next to her.

"Nice place."

She swirls around, checking out the ranch house and the grounds.

I met up with her at the office for a short briefing with Sheriff Ewing. He'd already told me he's been in touch with the FBI and law enforcement agencies in Flathead County and Lake County, and has their cooperation in this investigation. But in the actual briefing there wasn't a whole lot to discuss, since we don't really know what—if anything—we might encounter. We will try to stay in constant communication.

The meeting here at the ranch will be more important, which is why we drove here in tandem.

"Are there dogs around?" she asks. "Emo was cooped up in the back of the vehicle all day yesterday, and then all night in the motel room. She needs to stretch her legs."

"No, no dogs at the moment. Just horses."

"She won't pay them any mind."

I can hear the dog whine and whimper as Jillian opens the gate of her SUV.

"Come on, girl, go do your business."

"That's an unusual color," I observe as the gray dog jumps down and immediately starts sniffing for a patch of grass to do her business.

"She's called a silver/gray sable."

She's gorgeous, the dark face and paws contrasting with the gray coat. I watch as the sleek animal explores the grounds, not straying very far as she continuously turns her head to check in with her handler.

"Beautiful."

"I know. I got her from the shelter, believe it or not. The people who owned her gave her up, claiming she was too hard to handle, but they wanted a family dog. They should've gotten a golden retriever, not a Malinois," she derides, clearly with strong feelings on the subject. "These dogs are active; they are happiest when they have a job to do."

"Was she trained already?"

"No. I trained her. She's not my only dog, I actually have five. A couple of search-and-rescue dogs, and two more I trained as therapy dogs. In an ideal world where I would have the space, I'd love to be training shelter dogs exclusively. It's true certain breeds make for good working dogs, but I believe most dogs can be given a purpose."

She darts me a glance, a bit of a blush on her face.

"Sorry. I get a little carried away."

I grin at her. "Not at all."

Emo saunters up to me, nudging my hand with her nose.

"Is it okay if I pet her?"

"Oh yeah, she's very social. Loves people."

"How is she with babies?" I ask. "I have a little one inside."

"She's fine with kids. How old?"

"Almost five months already."

Behind me I hear the door open and someone step out on the porch.

"Do I need to move shit out here, or are you coming in?" Sully wants to know.

"Coming in."

I quickly make the introductions before we follow him inside. He walks straight through to the kitchen where Wolff and Bo are seated at the big table. I don't see Ama or my daughter.

Sully catches me looking. "She just went up to put Aspen down for a nap. You can probably still catch her. I'll do the introductions."

"Be right back," I tell Jillian, before darting down the hall and up the stairs.

I find them in the spare bedroom where Ama is just putting her down in the Pack 'n Play we set up for her.

"She was nodding off when I fed her," Ama informs me in a low voice. "And fell asleep while I was still changing her diaper."

I peek into the travel bed where my little girl is sleeping peacefully, a little flushed and her pink little mouth partially open.

"She looks out," I observe. "I'm glad at least one of us is catching up on some sleep."

"Hmmm. Busy night?" Ama teases me with an eyebrow raised.

Not much at High Meadow goes unnoticed, especially by Ama.

"No, actually," I rush to inform her. "Last night was the first night in many I slept well."

No need for her to know it was the stupendous orgasm Dan gave me that knocked me out, and the care he gave Aspen all night that allowed me to sleep through.

I'm not really sure how I'm supposed to view what happened. I have a tendency to want to put things in well-defined boxes, but I don't know where to place this. I want to keep an open mind, but it's not easy when you try to protect your heart at the same time.

I was surprisingly unmoved by Jeff walking out, but the consequences when he bailed were painful. Dan, however, has the ability to really hurt me.

With one last look at my daughter, I head back downstairs and join the group in the kitchen.

Several maps and printouts cover the surface of the table.

"Bo and Wolff will go with you. They'll help you set up the ascent/descent system. Have you worked with one before?" Sully asks Jillian.

"Yeah, I have."

"Are you going down with her?"

This question is aimed at me but Jillian answers.

"Actually, I would suggest to hold off until I actually find something. The more we can minimize scent pollution, the easier it'll be for Emo to pick something up."

"Fair enough," I agree, a little too eagerly.

Being lowered down the side of a cliff isn't my idea of fun. I'd rather not if I don't have to. Of course, if the dog finds remains, I won't have a choice.

Other than to indicate on the satellite images approximately where we found the remains, I mostly listen. Jillian and the team divide the area along the creek into three search grids, starting today with the area I indicated, and moving farther out from there.

Wolff and Bo head to the barn to get their horses saddled and the climbing gear packed up, while Sully outfits Jillian and me with two-way radios so we can stay in touch while she's searching the gorge.

Jillian wants to drive her SUV to the trailhead, and I'm towing the trailer with the ATV up the mountain. She and I will ride the ATV as close as I can get and walk the few minutes it takes to get to the ledge.

We're just stepping out the door when Ama stops us, carrying over a large cooler.

"Water and sandwiches," she states gruffly and turns back inside before I have a chance to thank her.

Sully walks us to the vehicles.

"Dan is picking up your mom?" he asks as he holds the truck door for me.

"He offered," I reply a bit defensively.

"I'm not saying it like it's a bad thing," he quickly clarifies. "It was the best solution, given you have your hands full and Fletch and I are the only ones left to run the ranch with Jonas picking up Alex and Jackson."

I almost forgot about Jackson coming home today.

"Shit, is Aspen going to be in the way?"

My uncle gives me a look like that's the stupidest question ever asked.

"She could never be in the way, and besides, Bo told me earlier Jackson will be staying with him and Lucy at the horse rescue."

That's actually a pretty good idea. The ranch can be a bit overwhelming with the sheer number of people around almost all the time. I imagine the last thing he would want is being watched or hovered over all day long.

Their place is pretty quiet in comparison, just Lucy and Bo, and of course, the animals. Lucy runs an equine therapy program at the horse rescue which, now that I think about it, might benefit Jackson as well.

As I pull away from the ranch with Jillian's SUV in my rearview mirror, I wonder if Jillian's work with rescue dogs would interest him.

My phone on the center console pings with an incoming message.

She's here. Waiting for bags.
Good luck today. I'll check in later.
XOX

XOX.
  I'm grinning all the way up Kenelty Mountain.

Seventeen

DAN

"Did she get in okay?"

The question comes from the office when I pass by. I backtrack and poke my head around the door. Ama is sitting behind the desk, working on the computer. Sully is nowhere to be seen. He's probably in the stables or the breeding barn.

"She did. She's putting her stuff away."

Since we used that room last night, Sloane and I ended up quickly changing the sheets and opening the window to get some fresh air in there this morning. There was no lingering evidence of what went on in there when I carried in Isobel's bags earlier.

"So what are you doing here? Aren't you supposed to be working on your house?"

"I'll head over there shortly, but first I was hoping to pick Aspen up."

Ideally, Sloane would introduce the baby to her mother, and I'm probably way out of line, but the woman has traveled a long way. I'm not sure if she's aware the baby is here at the ranch right now, but even if she's not, it doesn't seem right for someone else to be looking after the child.

"You were, huh?"

"I think there's some time to make up for," I reason. "Isobel is Aspen's grandmother, she came here to look after her, and the sooner she can start doing that the better it is for everyone."

Ama regards me with her head slightly tilted, making me wait.

"You may have a point," she finally concedes. "She's been down for almost two hours, I was gonna wake her up soon anyway. Don't forget to change her diaper, and she should eat soon," she yells after me when I duck back down the hallway.

Aspen sure is a sunny baby. She definitely wakes up in a better mood than her mother, even with a full diaper. She's happily babbling, her little fist tugging on my beard as I carry her back to Sloane's cabin.

Isobel must've heard me come in because no sooner have I put down the diaper bag on the couch, when she walks out of the bedroom. Then she freezes on the spot, her hands covering her mouth, and her eyes wide and shimmering with tears.

Before the waterworks are released, I quickly cross the room with the intention of handing Aspen over, but the baby holds on to my facial hair for dear life.

"Hey, Peanut, you need to let go so I can hand you to your grandma," I mumble, trying to dislodge those little digits from my beard.

"Come here, beautiful girl," Isobel coos, carefully taking her from my hands.

"Clothes and diapers for her in the top drawer.

There's a can of formula, bottles, and some other baby stuff in the top cupboard to the right of the sink, and I'm sure there's stuff in the diaper bag I put here." I point at the couch.

Isobel's eyes narrow over Aspen's downy head.

"You seem quite at home here," she observes.

And there's my cue to leave, before the statement turns into an inquisition.

"I'm sorry, I've gotta run. I've got work to do."

"What the hell? What happened here?"

I can't find a single spot to focus on, there are bright red streaks wherever I look.

Fucking spray paint on my beautiful logs.

James drops the brush he's holding in the bucket, just as JD comes around the corner.

"It's coming off," the older man assures me as I try to take stock of the damage. "Takes a little elbow grease, that's all."

"You didn't call me."

"To what end?" JD pipes up. "We handled it. Called the sheriff's office, waited for the deputy to stop by to take a report and some pictures, and now we're cleaning."

He's probably right but I'm still taking it all in, trying to wrap my head around it. My eyes catch on something through the door opening.

"Inside?"

I'm already rushing up the porch steps and through the door.

Fuck.

"Most of it's going to be covered with either drywall or

flooring," James points out behind me, clapping a hand on my shoulder. "What's left we can fix."

"Did you piss anyone off recently?" I hear JD ask.

"Probably, but I can't imagine anyone who'd do something like this. I mean, why?"

"Vandals? Bored teenagers blowing off steam?" James suggests.

"I'm a bit off the beaten track here though. At the end of a dirt road. Not like I get traffic."

"You had trucks coming in here with the lumber though. Big-ass trucks with those logs would've drawn attention."

I guess that's true, but this doesn't feel like teenagers tagging a place and snickering about it later. For one, there's nothing recognizable in the angry red slashes, other than perhaps rage. This is someone conveying a message.

My mind keeps wanting to go to the one person I know has strong negative feelings toward me, but I simply can't see Shelby sneaking out here in the dark of night, wielding a spray can. That said, she threw me for a loop before, and I'd be a fool not to at least consider the possibility she had something to do with this.

"Did you guys happen to check with Sully, see if he noticed anything?"

When James shakes his head, I grab my phone out of my pocket and dial.

"Yeah." Sully sounds preoccupied.

"You busy?"

"Why? What's up?"

"Someone spray-painted my house last night or overnight."

"You're shitting me."

188

"Nope. You wouldn't have seen or heard anything would you?"

"Last night? I don't think so. I'm in the barn right now, but when I get back to the office, I can pull up the feed from the security camera I have on the front of the house. Maybe it picked up something."

"I appreciate it."

"Who'd do something like that?" Sully wants to know.

"That's what I'm trying to find out."

"Well, until you do, I have a couple of GoPro cameras here we can put up for the time being. I can pop over on my way home."

"That'd be great."

Tomorrow the windows and doors arrive. They probably won't be able to get them installed in one day, but the downstairs should be possible. At least I'll be able to lock it.

In the meantime, I guess I'll be setting up camp here tonight.

As shock wears off and anger takes its place, I take another look around. *Fuck*, they really did a number on the place. So much for finishing the framing today. That's not going to happen.

"Do you have an extra brush?" I ask James.

"Back of JD's truck. He picked up a bunch of cleaning stuff in town."

The next few hours I take my frustrations out on the red paint inside while JD and his dad are scrubbing outside. By the time I hear someone drive up outside, I have blisters from scrubbing so damn hard. Tossing my brush in the bucket, I head out to see who it is.

I walk over to Sully, who is standing by his truck, chatting with James. When he sees me approach, he lifts his chin in greeting.

"I got something on the camera, but it's not much. At two forty-seven in the morning there's a glimpse of what looks like a pickup passing our house. No headlights, nothing that stands out."

Since two-thirds of this county drives a damn pickup, unfortunately, that doesn't help me narrow down who it might have been.

One person I know who definitely does not drive a truck is Shelby Vandermeer. Of course, that leaves the rest of the population, but it still is a bit of a relief.

~

Sloane

Today's search was frustrating.

Of course we got a bit of a late start, plus we had to wait for the pulley system to be secured and tested before Jillian went down. Then we were supposed to lower Emo, but the poor dog was frantic the moment she lost sight of her handler, so Jillian had to come back up and a second line had to be secured so the dog could be lowered along with Jillian.

All that took a decent chunk of time, leaving us with just a small window of searching before we had to pack it up for the day. Hopefully tomorrow—with an early start and the logistics already in place—will be a bit more productive.

You'd think we should be able to find the rest of the two sets of remains. Although, Jillian pointed out, it's not that unusual to find parts of the same body spread out over a large area if wildlife gets a hold of it. She also warned that in cases like that, more often than not, some parts stay permanently lost.

My hope is we'll at least find something more of the man's body. Anything that could identify him, but best-case scenario would be his skull, which would give us the option of comparing dental records, and be an alternative method of identification to just DNA.

It's not until I turn onto the driveway to High Meadow, the realization my mother is waiting at the cabin hits me full force.

Yikes.

I'd fantasized about having a soak in the tub once I put Aspen to bed, but I doubt I'll have a chance, given the big talk I know is waiting for me at home.

Blowing out a big breath, I park my Jeep, grab my bag, and head inside.

I don't see anyone when I walk in, but I can hear splashing and my mom's voice coming from the bathroom. She must've picked up Aspen from the big house. I really wanted to be there when she met my daughter for the first time, but I guess it wouldn't have been fair to keep her waiting even longer.

I drop my bag and take off my hiking boots before I poke my head into the bathroom.

Mom is sitting on her knees on the floor next to the tub, focused on Aspen who is sitting in the bath insert, kicking her little legs in the water and having a good time. She loves her bath time and, frankly, so do I, and I feel I've already missed too many.

"Hey."

I'm greeted by my daughter's wide smile when she spots me.

Then my mother turns her head, and I'm treated to one

of her mom-stares. I remember it well, the kind that tells you your life is hanging in a precarious balance. It immediately launches me into a nervous damage control mode.

"I'm sorry I didn't come to pick you up, but I had a cadaver dog team come in from Missoula today and I had to go out to the search area with them to—"

"You not picking me up doesn't even register on the list of things I'm upset with you about," she cuts me off. Then she barks out a harsh laugh. "Although, *upset* seems too benign a word for the storm of emotions I feel."

Yeah, I wasn't really expecting Mom to go easy on me, but one can hope.

"Fair enough," I concede. "Why don't I get her bottle ready and throw something easy together for dinner while you finish up her bath."

I only have the basics in the fridge, I haven't had a chance to do groceries yet so it's slim pickings, but I can always whip up an omelet.

"Ama brought over a lasagna earlier. It's in the fridge, it just needs to be heated," she says, her back already turned.

Ama has her shit together, that woman deserves an award. I should probably take notes because I want to be like her when I grow up. Talk about capable. She raised two kids, juggles two households, works in the High Meadow office, offers babysitting services, *and* manages to make sure everyone is fed.

I only have my job and one child to worry about, and I have trouble doing that.

Aspen's bottle takes me a few minutes to get warmed up, and by the time I have the lasagna in the oven, Mom already has her out of the tub. I look in the fridge for something to drink and wish I'd had the foresight to make a stop for some beer and wine. I have a feeling I might need it.

"Here we are," Mom announces. "All clean and nice and drowsy."

She has Aspen propped up on one arm, the baby looking up at her grandmother with sleepy adoration. It's such a sweet image, it hits me right in the feels, and when Mom hands her to me, it takes me a moment to react.

"Hey, baby girl," I mumble, burying my face in her little neck for a moment as I compose myself. "Are you ready for your bottle?"

I sit down on the couch and feed her while listening to my mother clean up the bathroom. Aspen falls asleep about halfway through her bottle and I carry her to the bedroom, easing her down in her crib. Then I turn on the noise machine I borrowed off Pippa, which helps her stay asleep. Unless, of course, her incoming teeth bother her again.

Like a coward, I linger in the bedroom, picking out a change of clothes, and wishing I could access the bathroom from here so I could hop in the shower without having to face Mom. Instead, I remind myself I'm a thirty-three-year-old woman and not a teenager, leave my clothes on the bed, and walk inside to face the music.

"Did you see Sully yet?"

Mom is in the kitchen doing a few dishes, and only quickly glances over her shoulder before answering.

"Briefly, yes. I went over to the house earlier to say hello to Thomas and Ama."

"Did you see Jonas or Alex?"

I'm curious to know if they made it home yet.

"They weren't there."

She turns and dries her hands on the kitchen towel, then she dives into the fridge and digs a bottle of champagne out of the vegetable drawer.

"Steve got this bottle for us. He suggested we needed a

good bottle so we could celebrate and hash it out at the same time."

She sets it on the kitchen counter and starts digging through the cupboards for glasses.

These cabins are just the basics so it's safe to say this kitchen isn't exactly outfitted to serve Dom Perignon. I think we're lucky Mom finds two wineglasses. While she tackles the champagne, I set two places at the table and grab our dinner from the oven.

A few minutes later we're seated across from each other, and Mom raises her glass. I follow suit.

"To Aspen," she toasts.

"To Aspen," I echo, and we clink glasses.

"She is absolutely the most beautiful baby I've ever laid eyes on."

I smile at Mom's words. Of course, I agree wholeheartedly, but it's nice to hear someone else say it.

Except, it shouldn't come as a surprise my mother would think that. In fact, I bet Mom loved her even before she laid eyes on her.

I feel so stupid.

"Mom, I'm so sorry."

She nods. "I know, but damn, it hurts. You're gonna have to give me some time."

Nothing for me to say to that, really, so I stay silent.

"What happened to us, Sloane? I remember a time we were like peas in a pod. We did everything together."

The question is rhetorical. We both know damn well what happened.

I was sixteen, I found my mother beaten to within an inch of her life, and my dad with his brains blown out. My dad could never quite settle at home after he returned from his last deployment. He never wanted to acknowledge he likely suffered from PTSD, and it was a source of friction between my parents. His outbursts of anger became more volatile until one day the darkness took over. When he saw what he'd done to Mom, he killed himself.

The years after, I struggled with anger. I guess most of it I took out on Mom—who'd been lucky to have survived—but it was aimed at my father. Mom and I both went through counseling, both individually and together, but we never really got back to where we were before.

Any bumps we hit in our relationship took a lot of work to overcome, and I guess at some point it was just easier to minimize interaction. Mom was building a new life with Steve, my stepdad, and I was setting my own course.

"He's been gone for seventeen years," I point out.

There's no need for me to explain who I'm referring to.

"I know," she acknowledges. "And it would kill him to know after all this time we still carry the marks he left on us."

She's right. "We need to let him go, let the anger go."

"Yeah," Mom agrees. "That beautiful child of yours deserves a loving family."

She gets up and rounds the table, where I'm already on my feet, waiting.

It's been years since I've cried in my mother's arms.

But this time the tears are healing.

Eighteen

SLOANE

I haven't seen Dan since yesterday morning.

I sent him a message last night when I was in bed, thanking him for picking up Mom, but as of earlier this morning, I haven't heard anything either.

I'm sure he has his hands full at the house, after all, he took out part of his day to drive to Kalispell. Although, I have to admit, I had my eyes peeled this morning when I was leaving the ranch.

"Eckhart! In here," Ewing calls when I walk by his office on my way out the door.

I left early to check in at the office to see if anything new had come in, before heading back out to Kenelty Mountain. Jillian is probably already on her way, so I'm eager to get out of here.

"Morning," I say as I poke my head around his door.

"Are you on your way out?" Junior asks.

"I am. Back to the search today. I checked my emails,

nothing from the lab, not that I was really expecting anything yet anyway," I update him. "Any luck with the security feed from the Columbia Falls gas station?"

Ewing asked the local PD to look into obtaining a copy from the Exxon Chelsea was taken from.

"Yes, actually. They're supposed to be sending through a copy today. I've got some meetings today, but I'll see if I can get one of the deputies to have a look at it when it comes in."

"If you do get it, can you forward the copy to me?"

"Will do. And keep me informed."

I pop my head into Betty's office to let her know where I'm going to be, before heading out. I'm about to get behind the wheel of the department truck with the ATV on the trailer still hitched, when I notice Deputy Schmidt pulling his cruiser into an empty space two parking spots down.

This is probably the end of his shift. I already saw Jason inside, finishing up his reports before going home. Those two are on the same shift.

Frank clearly sees me and shoots me a dirty look, which I pretend not to see as I lift my hand in a friendly wave. I'll kill him with kindness.

On my drive to the trailhead, I replay my talk with Mom last night, which actually was quite cathartic. We remembered some good times, prior to Dad's passing, and tackled a few major stumbling blocks we'd encountered since.

It's funny what a difference it makes communicating when you're not always in defensive mode. When you're not working from the assumption the person across from you is your opponent. It's not that I wasn't aware of the chip on my shoulder, it's that I felt it was justified.

But in talking with Mom last night, I realized each of us fed into the negative expectations the other had of us. I would blame the breakdown of communication on Mom, and she'd blame me for the same. In the end, it was both of us who were responsible for the erosion of our relationship.

When I finally hopped in the shower—right before bed —I felt wrung out, but a weight had definitely been lifted. Despite Aspen waking up twice, I felt like a new person this morning.

Jillian and Emo are waiting along with Bo, but I don't see Wolff.

"Sorry I'm late. Hope you weren't waiting too long."

"We just got here a few minutes ago," Jillian assures me.

"Wolff not with us today?" I ask Bo.

"No. Apparently there was some trouble at Dan's new house yesterday and he is heading over this morning."

My attention is piqued. "What trouble?"

"Some vandalism. Dan spent the night there and they're trying to rig up some kind of security today."

I guess that explains why I haven't seen or heard from him.

I'm tempted to call and find out more, but I'm sure he has his hands full.

I'm actually bored.

Jillian and Emo have been down in the gorge for almost three hours and other than to check in over the radio from time to time, there hasn't been much action.

I'm starting to worry this may have been a waste of time when the radio crackles to life.

"Slo...in......thing. Over."

All I hear is half words and a lot of static.

"Jillian? Say again. Over"

For a moment there is nothing and when I glance over at Bo, I see he's watching intently.

"Sloane? I found something. Over."

My heart jumps in my chest as I shoot to my feet, and I immediately join Bo, who is already bent over the grid map we have spread out on a tree stump.

"What'd you find? Over."

"Remains. More than one body. They've been here a while. I think you should come down. The area is surrounded by rock walls on three sides. I had to walk back to get through on the radio. Over."

Jesus. More than one? How many bodies are down here?

"Can you give us a location on the grid? Over."

"Northeast corner of the third grid. On the satellite image it should look almost like a tributary, an arm off the gorge itself. From what I can see at the base of it, most of the top is tree-covered, but there looks to be a small section where the rock is exposed at the top. Maybe that's visible on satellite. Over."

Bo marks the approximate location she indicated on the map with a small stone. Then he unfolds the printout of the satellite image and places it beside the map. It's a printout, so the resolution isn't great, but it's easy to locate the branch of the gorge on the image, and a sliver of white is visible through the trees. That must be the top of the cliff she's referring to. Bo places a pebble on the satellite image as well.

"Jillian, where are you now? Over."

"Back at the southwest corner of the grid where I started. Over."

I blow out a sharp breath through pursed lips. I'm not sure if it's adrenaline or fear—perhaps a combination of both—but my body feels like it's vibrating.

"Wait for me there. I'm on my way. Over and out."

Bo is looking at me with a dubious look on his face.

"What?"

He shakes his head. "I'm not sure that's a good idea."

"I have to go down there. It's my job," I remind him.

"I know it is, but I'd feel a lot better if you could wait until we got some backup here," he insists.

"You don't need backup to lower me, do you?" I challenge him, stuffing a couple of water bottles along with my camera in my backpack.

"No. But we might to get you and Jillian back up here."

"Plenty of time for backup to get here then."

Before he throws more objections my way, I pull out my cell phone. I only have one bar of reception, but it's enough to get Ewing on the phone.

"Boss, the dog found remains."

"Good news," he responds. "Hopefully there's enough to help us identify the guy."

"It may actually be more than one set. I'm heading down there to get eyes on it, but communication may be an issue. You may want to see about organizing a forensic recovery team," I suggest. "And the other thing, once I can confirm it's more than one body, we should probably put a call in to the feds."

"Shit. Just what I fucking need," he grumbles.

"Let's wait and make sure first, but in the meantime, we could probably use some extra hands up here."

"Leave it with me."

As I tuck away my phone, I notice Bo does the same. He must've sent a text because I didn't hear him talk.

Either way, there are no more objections from him. Only basic instructions on the mechanics of my imminent descent as he helps me into the harness.

Fear is definitely setting in now; the butterflies are

gnawing holes in the lining of my stomach. I just hope to hell I don't make a fool of myself and scream, since I'm the one who insisted on going down there. Knowing Bo, he'd never let me forget.

Five minutes later I'm walking off the edge of a cliff.

Willingly.

~

Dan

"What's her name?"

I look up at him and shake my head.

"Look, I'm not even sure she had anything to do with it," I backtrack.

Wolff showed up earlier to give me a hand putting up GoPro cameras outside the house, and has been asking questions. Being a former FBI agent, he can't seem to help himself. He's pretty good too, since I just finished telling him about my most recent interactions with Shelby—something I've kept to myself—although, I didn't mention her by name.

"Can I point out; you also didn't think she had designs on you that went beyond fuck buddy?"

Right. Point taken.

I step out of the way as he climbs down the ladder I've been holding steady.

"Yeah, but what if I point the finger at her and she turns out to have nothing to do with it? Things can get really fucking awkward when I stop by her family's store to pick up an order, which is about once a month."

I realize I walked right into that one when I see the shit-eating grin on Wolff's face.

"Ah, yes, Shelby Vandermeer," he confirms.

Then he grabs another camera and walks to a tree on the other side of the driveway, leaving me to follow behind with the damn ladder.

Glancing over at the house, I notice the installers are working on the second main window in the front. I was able to get hold of the contractor yesterday afternoon and asked him to bring as big a crew as he could get together. He's got two groups working, the second crew is tackling the rear of the house. It looks like they're making decent tracks, and I'm really hoping we can get the place sealed up for tonight.

I prop the ladder against the tree we picked on this side of the driveway. One camera will be aimed down the driveway and the other toward the house. These will be the last of the GoPros to go up. We'll have five up altogether. I'll be able to remotely control and monitor them from my phone or computer.

As Wolff heads back up the ladder, my mind drifts to Jonas's visit last night.

He dropped by with a couple of beers, wanting to see the progress. We ended up on the porch and watched the sun go down, while he filled me in on Jackson. We talked about getting Jackson out here, see if he could be coaxed into helping out, in hopes it might make him feel useful.

Right before he left, he urged me to take some time off, reminding me I probably have close to six months in vacation time banked. I rarely take time off, aside from the occasional time I join Fletch for a quick hunting trip.

Why would I need to? I love what I do, and I have no desire to go lie on a beach somewhere, or hit up the nightlife in the big city, when my idea of fun is doing exactly what I get to do every day already.

But I wasn't going to say no to a full week of getting this build on track, so I took him up on his offer.

"Okay, those are set to go," Wolff announces, climbing down again. "The batteries have two hours of recording time, so unless you want to run out halfway through the day with all this activity going on, I suggest shutting them down until nighttime. You should actually be able to set a timer."

While he hoists the ladder on his shoulder and makes his way back to his truck, I pull up the app on my phone and make sure the cameras are all powered down.

Wolff is checking his phone by the time I join him, and I just catch him cursing under his breath.

"What is it?"

There's something about the look he shoots me that makes me a little uneasy.

"It's from Bo. He needs a hand up by the gorge."

He cocks his thumb over his shoulder toward Kenelty Mountain across the river. That feeling of unease becomes more of a burn in my gut.

"Why, what's happening up there?"

"The dog team found something and Sloane is rappelling down to join them."

I don't think, I react, and immediately turn on my heel to make my way to my truck.

Dammit, Sloane, what the fuck are you thinking?

"Hold up, Captain America." Wolff claps me firmly on the shoulder. "Where's the emergency?"

"She doesn't know what the fuck she's doing going down that rock wall," I snap.

"She doesn't need to; Bo will do all the work. We have the full pulley system rigged up so he could probably do it with his pinky finger. And other than that, she's doing what she's paid to do."

I flip my hat off with one hand, while running the other through my hair.

"Besides that, you can't leave, you've got issues here you have to deal with," he continues.

Not to mention, if I showed up on the mountain, riding in like the knight in shining armor she probably doesn't need, I'm just going to piss her off. Although, that wouldn't stop me if she really was in any danger.

"Point taken," I concede. "Just keep me in the loop."

Wolff looks at me from under the brim of his hat and grins, shaking his head.

"You've got it bad, brother," he states the obvious.

I don't think there ever was a chance of me being subtle about my feelings for Sloane, so I don't see the point of denying them.

"Trust me, I'm well aware."

I watch as he gets in his truck and heads down the driveway, before turning back to the house.

Most of the paint is gone, but there are still a couple of spots visible, especially in the seams between the logs. I grab the bucket with the rags and the rubbing alcohol—which seems to work best on the wood—and get back to scrubbing.

I've got to keep these hands busy while I wait for news.

Nineteen

SLOANE

I freeze when Jillian steps to the side and reveals what she called me down here for.

Right off the bat, I spot a skull and what looks like a spine with a few rib bones still attached. Another rib cage is visible about six feet away from the first one.

This smaller gorge is so narrow it barely sees any sunlight and a wet, earthy scent hangs in the air. Patches of colorful lichen cling to some of the rocks, and the damp ground is covered in ferns.

There's no noise, other than the sound of my heart beating in my ears. The eerie stillness is only emphasized by the pale bones poking out of the lush green.

It's a cemetery, the dead marking their own graves.

Behind me, Emo begins to whine.

"She's confused," Jillian volunteers. "Usually after she finds remains, she gets a treat and a rest."

"Well, her work *is* done. Why don't you take her back?

I'll be a while, I have to take some preliminary pictures, put together a record of all this, before I call in a team to process the scene."

"Are you sure?"

I smile at her. "Yeah. Like Emo, I work best alone."

It doesn't really matter to me, but I have a feeling Jillian would feel guilty about leaving me here if I didn't give her a reason to go.

"Need me to pass on any messages?"

"Actually..." I turn to look up at the one stretch of the ledge that looked to be bare rock from the top. "See that section of the ledge where nothing is growing?" I point out. "I called the office for some backup before I came down. When they get here, can you ask whoever shows up to see if there is access up there from the actual hiking trail?"

My guess is, there will be, simply because I don't think these bodies were dragged here. I think they were dropped here.

"Communication will be easier," she points out. "I'll pass it on. Good luck."

With that, Jillian and Emo start walking back to the main gorge, and soon disappear out of sight. Then I ease my backpack from my shoulders and retrieve my camera. Time to go to work.

I start from where I'm standing, taking a few wide-angle shots first, to show the location of the bones in the general lay of the land. Then I start focusing in on more detail, and make my way around in a big circle.

Time passes, I'm sure, but I'm so focused on recording what so far look to be three or maybe four sets of remains, I barely notice. I find scraps of clothing, a ball cap, and even a few shoes and a stray boot. If those are any indication, I think we're dealing with at least one male, and two or more females.

As tempting as it is to get in real close and start moving some of those ferns out of the way to see what else they might be covering, I know we need a real forensic team in here to handle a dumping ground of this size properly. I don't want to mess up the scene.

I grab a quick break and fish a water bottle out of my pack, taking a seat on a boulder. I'm now on the opposite side of the remains, where the rock walls narrow. My guess is in the spring, the winter runoff makes its way down the mountain and through this branch of the gorge to stream into the main creek. I imagine the water would run pretty deep during runoff, and the creek would be more like a river. I'm thinking it's entirely possible some remains may have washed away downstream.

Taking a few deep swigs from my water bottle, I screw the cap on and tuck it back in my pack. The sound of falling stones has me scanning the far rock wall, where it appeared to be coming from. My eyes are immediately drawn to the section of exposed rock, wondering if perhaps backup has arrived.

I'm just getting up when I hear some kind of snap, and the next thing I know, shards of stone fly off the boulder I was sitting on.

My feet are already moving before my mind registers someone is firing at me. My camera is bouncing on my chest, so I grab on to it and tuck it inside my shirt. Then I duck down as low as I can, and run in a zigzag pattern, heading toward the narrowing section. I should have better coverage there.

If I can get there.

Another snap, and this time I can hear the bullet ping

when it hits something. Not me, thank God, but that can change, I still have about a hundred and fifty yards to go. I grind my teeth and keep my legs pumping.

I think the shots are coming from that clearing up above, but I can't be sure, otherwise I maybe could've dropped behind a boulder to find cover. Whoever is up there shooting, clearly doesn't like me roaming around down here.

Still, I make it into the narrow passage, only about four feet wide. I immediately slow down and take stock. I don't think I'm hit, even though the massive rush of adrenaline could make it hard to tell. I don't seem to be bleeding from any holes. Once I've established that, I take a good look at my surroundings. The walls don't seem quite as high here and look to be narrowing even farther at the top. With my back pressed against the rock face, I'm pretty well covered.

But cowering is not my style.

Unfortunately, my pack is still back there, but my walkie-talkie is in my pocket. When I pull it out and try to call in, nothing but heavy static greets me. I'm not getting a proper signal here. Not even the radio's high frequency waves can make it out of this gorge.

Afraid I'll make too much noise if I try again, I tuck it back in my pocket. I'm going to have to find my own way out of here.

When I look to my right, I notice there's a bend in the narrow gorge I can't quite look beyond. Curious to see what potentially lies beyond, I slip my sidearm from its holster and, sticking close to the rock wall, start moving deeper.

I suspect the entire bottom of this gulley is flooded during the winter runoff, since the bottom is rockier here, slippery with moss and lichen. I have to watch my footing. The last thing I want is to slip and mess up an ankle.

Once I reach the bend, I'm able to see where at the end of the winter, the water would start flowing down the mountain. In spring this would be a waterfall, but right now it's not more than a trickle finding its way down the pile of rocks and larger boulders filling the far end of this valley.

A pile of rocks I might be able to climb.

I can't go back the other way and make myself an easy target, when the shooter could still be up there, and I can't count on someone else coming to rescue me. Hell, I don't even know if anyone would've heard those muffled shots. Normally a rifle discharge would make a sharp cracking sound, but these were dull snaps, most likely suppressed. It's more than possible those guys have no idea what's going on, and are on their way to that clearing I asked them to find. I may have lured them right into the sights of that shooter.

I'll have to get myself out of this gorge and then backtrack along the ridge. Hopefully, I can approach whoever is up there without being seen, and keep the element of surprise on my side.

All of that is assuming the shooter is still up there.

Only one way to find out.

The rocks are treacherous, slimy and slick, and I'm having a hard time keeping my footing.

Pausing to catch my breath, I lean back a little to look up the rest of the way. I'm about fifty or sixty feet from the top, but those remaining feet are a lot steeper. I already tucked my gun back in its holster, needing both hands to climb, but I feel like an easy target.

I can do this.

I'm not exactly sure how much time has passed but,

glancing up to the patches of sky visible through the tree cover, I'm guessing it's mid-afternoon. The last thing I want is to still be stuck on this mountain when darkness falls. I have only a general idea of where I am in relation to base camp, or how long it will take me to get back there. Plus, there's the matter of the shooter between me and the others. Unless, of course, he's already gone, but I won't know that until I get to the top.

Determined, I resume my climb, making sure my foothold is solid before shifting my weight. I'm so focused on getting to the top, I don't notice the branch hanging low over the ledge.

Or the owl perched on the tip of it.

But when it suddenly lets go, swooping close before it flies off, it startles me enough to lose my footing. For a moment I'm literally hanging on by my fingertips as my feet try to find purchase, but then they slip and I land hard on the next rock down, twisting my ankle.

I can't hold back the yelp as a sharp pain shoots up my leg, and I sink down on my ass. My eyes sting with tears, but I blink them away. That fucking hurts.

I may well have just royally screwed myself.

Taking in a few deep breaths, I wait until the sharp edge of the pain ebbs to a steady throb. I don't think I broke it, but I don't want to take off my hiking boot to check. I may not be able to get it back on. Grabbing the radio from my pocket, I try to call out again, but the moment I depress the button, all I get is a high-pitched squeal, followed by static.

I'm not going to be able to call for help so it's up to me to get my ass out of here. There's only about twenty feet to go to the edge. Once I'm up there, I hope I'll have more luck here putting out a call, so the sooner I get up there, the better.

Pulling myself up, I tentatively test my ankle, putting a little weight on it. The pain has me grit my teeth, but the ankle itself seems to hold. I don't think I'll be able to walk on it much, but right now my main worry is getting up these last twenty feet.

With my jaw clenched and sweat running down my face and back from the effort, I manage to get up high enough I can almost reach the edge with my fingertips. Almost, but not quite, and the rock up to the ledge is worn smooth by the water, nothing for my hands or feet to grab hold of.

So close, and yet so far.

I sink down on my butt to get off my ankle, and battle tears of frustration. I could head back down a bit and try to follow a different route up. There may be an easier climb to my right. But first I need a break, I'm getting pretty dehydrated. Unfortunately, my water and my granola bars are in my pack down in the gorge.

I'm suddenly not so sure I'll be able to get myself out of this situation. A growing sense of panic has bile surge up from my stomach and I fight to keep it down. Panic is the most unproductive emotion; it paralyzes if you let it.

Desperate for something to do, I pull free my walkie-talkie again. Surely, I'll be able to transmit something from here, I'm almost at the top. But when I depress the button, once again the walkie-talkie makes all kinds of noise. It's not until I try to figure out how to adjust the frequency, I notice the metal casing of the radio has a deep dent I'm pretty sure wasn't there before. It also looks like one of the buttons next to the short antenna is missing. When my hand automatically wanders to the pocket where I'd tucked the radio, I find a hole in the fabric.

That is definitely new.

Holy shit.

I've been in survival mode, not really thinking about the fact someone was taking potshots at me. Of course I never realized how close I came to actually getting hit. I'm thinking about it now.

As I lean my head against the cool rock and close my eyes for a moment, Aspen's beautiful little face pops in my mind. For the first time since the bullets started flying, I allow myself to cry.

I cry until my tears run dry and my eyes feel gritty and swollen. I would kill for a drink of water, but that's not going to happen unless I get moving. I can't sit here all day.

Tilting my head back, I open my eyes and look up at the ridge...

Just as the toe of a boot appears overhead.

Twenty

DAN

I lasted about ten minutes after Wolff drove off.

Then I contacted JD and got him to come over to keep an eye on the progress at the house. I didn't wait for him to get there but set out right away.

My first stop was the ranch to grab a two-way radio and pick up Will. There I ran into Sully, who went to grab me the radio while I saddled my horse. He didn't seem surprised I was heading up the mountain.

I catch up with Wolff at the trailhead after letting Will stretch his legs up the dirt path.

"Why am I not surprised?"

Ignoring his comment, I nudge Will to fall in step behind Wolff's horse as we veer off the trail. Halfway to the gorge, where vegetation is a little denser, we pass what I assume is Sloane's ATV. Not long after, I hear voices.

In the clearing, we find Bo talking to a woman. The redhead has a harnessed dog sitting at her feet, so I assume this is the dog team Sloane has been working with. We dismount and secure the horses before we join the small group.

Wolff greets the woman with a chin lift, I guess they met already yesterday.

"Dan Blakely," I introduce myself.

"Jillian Lederman."

She has a nice smile and a firm handshake.

"And this is Emo." She indicates her dog.

The animal wags his tail at the mention of his name.

"Can I touch him?"

"It's a her," she corrects me. "But yeah, go right ahead."

I let her sniff my hand and scratch her head. That results in the dog rolling on her back with her legs up in the air, begging for a belly rub.

"Emo! Show a little modesty," Jillian admonishes with a shake of her head.

As I'm crouched, doing the dog's bidding, Bo urges the woman to tell us about the message from Sloane.

"What message?" I inquire, alerted by the mention of Sloane's name.

"There's another section like this—a rocky ridge—about half a mile up along the gorge," Jillian responds. "Sloane wanted someone to check to see if there was closer access from the walking trail to that ridge. It's where Emo found the remains, right underneath. Here, I'll show you."

She walks over to where a map is spread out on an old tree stump, and points at a short, narrower branch off the gorge.

"That's where we located the remains, and the ridge I'm talking about is approximately here."

She indicates a small strip on the south side of that branch.

"You can see the lighter rock on the satellite image," Bo fills in.

Wolff walks over and glances at the map. "I'll go check it out."

"I'm coming with you," I announce.

"If you find a more direct access point there, let me know. It may make more sense to move the pulley system right there. Especially if the ledge is closer to the trail," Bo points out. "For now, we'll stick here and wait for the sheriff's guys to show up."

The two of us are quickly mounted up and retrace our steps to the hiking trail, which we then follow farther up the mountain. At one point, Wolff lifts his hand and brings Judge, his mount, to a halt as he appears to be listening. I strain as well and pick up what sounds like a series of snaps. But when seconds later two deer dart across the trail from left to right, I realize that's probably what we heard.

Wolff lowers his hand and clicks his tongue, urging Judge in motion. At the same time, I nudge Will's flank with my heels, which is all he needs to follow the horse in front.

We haven't gone far when the two-way radio on my hip lets out a loud squeal. It startles the horses and I have a hard time getting the normally laid-back Will under control.

"What the fuck was that?" Wolff wants to know.

"Some kind of feedback."

Immediately after, Bo's voice comes in over the radio.

"Yo, did you guys get that high squeak?"

"Yup. Was that you?" I fire back.

"Hell no," is his response.

"Sloane, it's Dan. Come in." I wait a few beats for a response before I repeat it, "Sloane, are you there? Come in."

"Jillian says if she's in that secondary gorge, she's not gonna hear you."

Right.

"Ten-four."

We continue on the trail for a bit when Wolff points out something to his left. It looks like a game trail—a naturally formed path wildlife travels along—but through the trees I can see a bit of a clearing.

"Is that it?"

If that's the edge of the gorge, it literally is only a few hundred feet from the trail.

"One way to find out," Wolff suggests, guiding Judge onto the narrow track.

When we get to the ridge, I dismount and, leaving Will standing at the edge of the trees, make my way to the edge to look down.

It's not nearly as deep as our original entry point into the gorge. This strip of bare rock is significantly smaller than where we left Bo and the woman, but the fact it's closer to the trail and less deep, makes this a better spot. There are certainly plenty of big trees that would allow us to rig up a descent/ascent system that could handle the heavier traffic. The only—but significant—drawback, is that we are right above where I can see remains poking out of the ferns.

What I don't see is any sign of Sloane.

"She's not down there," I tell Wolff.

"Maybe she's on her way back the other way?" he suggests.

I turn away from the edge and kick something on the ground that makes a metallic sound. Scanning the ground in front of me, my eyes catch on a small, shiny cylinder. I bend down and pick it up.

"A shell. Rifle."

Immediately Wolff dismounts and walks over, his hand on his sidearm as he scans our surrounding.

"There's another one. And there..."

He indicates two more shell casings, keeping his voice low as well. He bends down and pulls a tissue from his pocket, picking them up. I walk over and hand him the one I have. He folds it into the tissue with the others and tucks them in his pocket.

"Those sounds we heard...gunfire?" I guess.

"With a suppressor, could be," he concedes, again looking into the trees surrounding us. "Doesn't look like they hung around."

I swing around and once more scan the gorge below, my heart beating in my throat, and anger burning in my gut.

I'm concentrating so hard, it takes me a second to register the sound of some kind of radio feedback coming from down below, but somewhere to my right.

Is that Sloane? Or did the shooter somehow make his way into the gorge? I don't see a safe route down here and there aren't any ropes.

Wolff points in the direction the noise came from.

"On foot. I'll take the lead; you bring the horses."

I shake my head as I walk up to Will to grab my rifle.

"I've got this, you take the horses," I grind out, not giving him a chance to respond as I start walking.

I half-jog, following the ridge into the tree line, as I try to keep an eye on the gulley below, while at the same time staying aware of my surroundings. It's tempting to just yell her name, but if this shooter is still hunting her, I don't want to risk her answering me and giving away her position.

A cracking sound in the trees behind me has me whip my head around, but it's just Wolff following with the horses. He's about thirty yards away from the edge and maybe the same distance behind me. I notice he still has his gun in his hand.

A good prompt for me to stay alert.

I'm having a hard time not imagining Sloane lying down there somewhere, shot and dead or dying. Then I remind myself she's not some clueless desk jockey, this woman is a seasoned law enforcement officer and probably better trained than I am to handle getting shot at.

Still, she bleeds red, just like everyone else.

I stop in my tracks when I hear that screeching sound again, the electronic feedback. Funny thing is, my own radio stayed silent both this time and the last. But this time it seems a lot closer. Glancing over my shoulder, I catch Wolff's eye and tap my ear. He nods in response. He heard it too and waves for me to move forward.

From what I can see, the gorge has narrowed quite substantially. I can clearly see the rim on the other side. Ahead, through the trees, I notice a small rock platform that appears to jut out a bit. That may be a good vantage point to look down the length of this narrow section.

Unsure of the stability of the slab of rock, I brace myself with one foot on the edge as I lean forward and look down.

Only to find a pair of terrified, upside-down, blue eyes staring back at me.

"Oh, Christ, Sloane."

"Dan?"

"Right here, babe. Are you hurt?"

She hesitates a fraction of a second too long and, somehow, I know what comes out of her mouth next is gonna be a lie.

"I'm okay."

Then I catch her wince when she tries to get to her feet. She's okay, my ass. She's clearly in pain.

I scan her for blood, but I can't see anything.

"Don't move," I instruct her. "I'm gonna get you out."

I wait for her to acknowledge, which she does with a nod after rapidly blinking her eyes a few times.

Wolff is already anchoring a climbing rope to the massive trunk of an old cedar when I turn to him. This is what I love about the team, we're so well in tune, no words are necessary.

I walk up to Will and grab my harness and traction grips from the saddlebag. I fit the grips on my boots, but I don't really need the harness, I can lower myself with just the rope. There's no way in hell I'm gonna risk getting Sloane up the ridge without a harness though.

I manually adjust the straps, guessing at the size she needs, because I want to get her off that rock as quickly as possible.

As I turn back to the ledge, I hear the sound of an ATV engine starting up in the distance, but it seems to come from even farther up the mountain. I meet Wolff's eyes and I know we're both thinking the same thing. But when Wolff reaches for Judge's reins, I shake my head.

"Sloane first."

I don't know if she's injured and we can't leave her sitting on that rock. I need Wolff to help me pull her up on the ridge.

Even from here, I can see the man's jaw muscle clench. I'm sure as a former federal agent, it's counter-intuitive for him to let a potential shooter go, but Sloane's rescue has my priority. To his credit, he turns his back on his horse and joins me at the ledge.

"Sloane? I'm coming down. Don't move, please." I hand the harness to Wolff. "Hang on to that for a sec."

When I lower myself, the only tricky part is the slight

overhang, but once I get one foot braced against the wall below, I set the other down on the rock next to Sloane.

"Toss it to me?"

Once I have the harness in hand, I bend down and slip it over her boots. Then I turn my head to look at her.

"What hurts?"

"Right ankle," she admits.

I move to her right side and hook her under her armpit so she can keep the weight off.

"Whenever you're ready."

When she's on her feet, I quickly strap her into the harness and loop the rope through the guide I clipped onto it. Then I toss the remainder of the rope back up at Wolff.

"Turn to face the rock," I tell Sloane. "I'm going to lift you, while Wolff pulls you up, okay? All you have to do is use your hands so you don't get hung up on that overhang."

Not long after that, Wolff pulls her up on the ledge and unclips her rope, tossing it back down to me. Ten seconds later I have her wrapped in my arms and kiss her hard. Wolff wanders off to take care of the rope, giving us a minute.

"Someone was shooting at me," she says, when I have her safely in Will's saddle in front of me.

"I know. We found the shells when we came looking for you."

She twists in the saddle and tilts her head back to look at me.

"Tell me you got them?"

I point at Wolff who is on Judge in front of us. "Three of them. In a tissue in his pocket."

She pulls her walkie-talkie from her pocket and hands it to me.

"Good. The asshole almost got me. Busted the radio instead."

She points out the missing dial and the dent in the metal casing. Then she shows me a hole in her pocket.

I have to swallow down bile as I realize that may well have caused that high frequency squeal over the radio that spooked the horses. I band an arm around her and pull her tighter to me.

"I'm not letting you out of my fucking sight."

She leans into me.

"That may be a problem. I still have a job to do."

Twenty-One

SLOANE

Dan is not happy with me.

He wanted to sweep me off to the hospital to get my ankle checked out, but I flat-out refused. I insisted we return to where Bo and Jillian were waiting for my backup.

As it turns out, Sheriff Ewing and two deputies arrive right behind us on two more ATVs. Unfortunately, one of them is Frank Schmidt. *Ugh.*

"What is wrong with you?" Junior asks when Dan helps me dismount.

"She was fucking shot at," Dan spits out.

I elbow him in the gut as I turn a reassuring smile on my boss.

"I twisted my ankle but I'm fine."

"What's this about getting shot at?"

"I was getting to that..."

I turn to shoot Dan a warning look before launching into my description of events. When I get to the part where the shooting starts, Wolff hands Ewing the rounds they collected.

"There may be more, but our focus was on finding Sloane," he offers.

"Can you show Deputy Schmidt where?"

"Sure. But there was something else," Wolff points out, piquing my attention. "We heard an ATV start up and take off farther up the mountain. I was going to go have a look."

"When was that?" I want to know.

"Right around the time we found you."

"You think it was the shooter?" Ewing asks.

"I'd think it would have to be," I volunteer. "This is a hiking trail, and not a particularly popular one. Why else would someone be heading up the trail on an ATV?"

"Where does this trail lead?"

"The trail meanders to a small lake about four miles from the trailhead. It loops around the lake and returns the same way," Bo answers the sheriff, showing him on the map.

"So whoever went up there has to come down the same route, basically," Ewing concludes.

"Is there anything else up there? Hunting cabin?" I probe further.

"Nothing visible on the satellite," Bo indicates. "But it wouldn't be unless it was built in a clearing. Lots of hunting shacks up in these mountains no one but the builder knows about."

"Is this BLM or US Forest Service land?" I follow up.

If it falls under Bureau of Land Management, you're not allowed to build anything, but with the USFS, you can apply for a permit to build a recreational cabin. A permit would mean a paper trail we could follow.

"Most of the land here is US Forestry," Wolff informs me. "There are a few pockets of BLM land, and some privately owned sections, but the bulk on this side of the Fisher River is national forest."

"Frank, you take one of the ATVs, and go with Wolff. Do the whole trail, see what you can find. Look for tracks, trails, shelters," the sheriff orders the deputy.

"I've got a forensic team coming in," he continues. "I'm going back to the trailhead to wait for them. Jillian, are you able to hang around to show the team the dumpsite?"

"I can show them," I pipe up, sensing which direction this is going in.

Junior pins me with a look. "No, because you're getting that ankle checked out."

Behind me I hear Dan mutter, "Thank you."

"I can stay," Jillian answers the initial question. "I'll head back to the trailhead with you for a bit though. I need to feed Emo."

I'm annoyed at being sidelined—this is my case, dammit —but I recognize when I'm outvoted. Maybe once that ankle has been looked at, I can come back out here.

Ewing nods at her, "Excellent. And Sloane? Call me for an update once that ankle is taken care of."

I outright reject the sheriff's suggestion to call an ambulance to pick me up from the trailhead, and concede instead to the least complicated option; to let Dan get me back to the ranch, and from there drive me to Libby.

Five minutes later, I'm back in Will's saddle, Dan behind me. I'm upset. I'm in pain, and I'm not in the mood for conversation. Luckily, he seems fine with the silence. Despite being annoyed with him, I lean back against his chest and close my eyes, lulled by the horse's steady gait.

When we get to the ranch, Dan directs his horse to where he has parked his truck right beside his cabin. As he lifts me down, I notice my mother is watching from the porch of my cabin, two doors down. She immediately gets up and walks over, while Dan helps me into the passenger seat of his pickup.

"What happened to you?"

I grab Dan's arm and dig in my fingers, silently warning him not to respond the way he did to Junior Ewing. My mom doesn't need to know I was shot at.

"I slipped and twisted my ankle. My boss insists I get it checked out. Where is Aspen?" I change the subject.

"Sleeping. I just put her down twenty minutes ago."

"Hey," Dan interrupts, "I'm quickly going to hand Will off at the barn."

"You looked cozy," Mom suggests as both of us watch Dan's fine ass lead the horse away.

"Hmmm."

"Nice of him to look after you."

I roll my eyes at her. "Nice? He's overbearing. Controlling. Oh, and stubborn."

Mom seems to find that funny.

"Are we talking about Dan? Because it sure sounded like you were describing yourself there for a minute," she scoffs. "What you describe as overbearing and controlling, looks to me to be protective. And you only call him stubborn because I'm guessing *you* didn't get your way. The pain is making you cranky."

I open my mouth, but my mother's pointedly challenging raised eyebrow stops me from speaking.

Dammit. I hate when I'm wrong.

The truth is, I *am* cranky from the pain, and from dehydration, and my stomach is trying to eat itself at this point. It's probably close to dinnertime by now.

"I need some water, and a snack."

It isn't exactly a concession, but I know Mom will understand it as one.

"It may not be a good idea to eat before you go to the hospital."

"I'm not going in for surgery, Mom," I counter.

"Let's hope you're right."

When Dan returns and gets behind the wheel, there are two bottles of water in the cupholders and a couple of freshly baked banana muffins in a Ziploc bag on my lap, courtesy of my mother.

Feeling a little ungrateful—thanks to Mom for that as well—and perhaps a tad remorseful, I put my hand on his arm.

"Thank you, by the way, for riding to my rescue. I don't think I could've made it up that ledge on my own."

"No problem."

I catch him glancing over with a grin on his face I choose to ignore. Instead, I give one of the muffins my full attention.

"Is the other one for me?" he asks.

I hold the Ziploc bag open for him. He's probably hungry by now too.

"Why don't you just drop me off and get yourself some dinner?"

He shoots me a look as he shoves half a muffin in his face.

I guess that's a no.

~

Dan

. . .

It didn't take her long to fall asleep.

The clock on my dashboard says nine fifteen when I turn onto the driveway to High Meadow.

She was poked and prodded, X-rays were taken, and the ultimate diagnosis is a second-grade torn ligament. Sloane's going to be in a walking boot, at least until she sees the doctor for a follow-up in two weeks. She was also given some pain meds and a prescription for more, for which we stopped at the drugstore on the way out of town.

She wasn't happy to be told she'd need to take it easy and wouldn't be driving for the immediate future. Understandable, since it'll likely make doing her job difficult, but I can't say I'm too unhappy about it. At least she'll be safe sticking around the ranch.

We both made some phone calls while waiting around the hospital. I was able to connect with JD, who said the window contractor is coming back in the morning to finish three upstairs windows, but the downstairs is done. It was a reminder for me to turn on the GoPro cameras with my app.

Sloane updated her mom, and called Sheriff Ewing who let her know the forensic team had arrived. Apparently, they'd come with floodlights so they could get started right away. I know Sloane is itching to get back out there, but I don't think she'll make it tonight. She doesn't even wake up when I pull up in front of her cabin and turn off the engine.

"Hey." I tap her on the knee. "We're home."

She grunts and rolls her head the other way, so I get out and round the truck to open her door. Next, I stick my head in the door and brush her lips with mine.

Now she cracks an eyelid.

"Come on. Let's get you inside and in bed."

The corner of her mouth pulls up in a crooked smile. "Yeah?"

I chuckle, she almost sounds drunk.

"Don't get any ideas, Sleeping Beauty. No sleepovers tonight. You have your mom waiting inside."

Her nose scrunches up, suggesting that reminder doesn't make her happy.

"Don't worry, we'll make up for it another time," I promise.

Instead of helping her out of the truck so she can walk under her own steam, I decide to capitalize on the fact she seems in a pliable mood. I slip an arm around her and one underneath her knees, lifting her out, with the romantic notion of carrying her inside.

Even though I'm in decent shape and have a good half a foot on her, Sloane isn't a petite woman, and this may be a bit more of a challenge to pull off than I anticipated. But Isobel is already waiting in the doorway, watching, and I'm not about to fall down on the job in front of her.

I do my best to make my trek to the front door look effortless, and Sloane seems to buy in, as she snuggles her head against my shoulder.

"Why don't you bring her straight through to her bedroom. I already put the baby's crib in mine," her mom suggests with a smirk.

I do believe the woman has an evil streak.

And it may well be genetic.

When I—as carefully as I can muster—lay Sloane down on her bed, she grins up in my face.

"An A for effort, but you may need a few ibuprofen after that."

~

"Why don't you hire someone?"

This from my sister, who called as I walked in my door. She wanted to know about the progress at the house and I mentioned we'd had a bit of a setback.

"I have the week off. I'll get back on track."

Although, her comment does give me an idea.

"I can't wait to see what it looks like," Lindsey continues. "But I don't think I'll be able to get out there before Thanksgiving."

My father wanted to host Thanksgiving this year, and Lindsey and her family were planning to come up for that. No way in hell my house will be done in two months or we could have it there, but she clearly wants to come see it.

"I'll take some pictures tomorrow. The sunsets are amazing from the porch."

In the background I hear one of my nieces start wailing.

Lindsey sighs. "That's my cue. Nightmares. It's a new thing," Lindsey explains. "Be glad you don't have kids. Talk to you later."

I immediately think of Aspen, and I'm tempted to tell my sister about her and her mother, but I don't get a chance because she's already hung up. It's probably a good thing, because I'd have been on the phone for another hour, and I really want to follow through on that idea she gave me.

Bo answers the phone immediately with, "How is she?"

"Grade two ligament tear. She'll be in a boot for a couple of weeks."

"Ouch. Bet she's not happy."

I think of the smiling woman I left in her bed half an hour ago, but I have no doubt that smile will be gone in the morning.

"Not really. Anyway, that's not the reason I was calling,"

234

I confess. "Do you know if Jackson is going to be around tomorrow morning? I'd like to drop by."

"Yeah, as far as I know. I can't guarantee he'll be up for a social visit, but you'll find out."

"It'll be more of a business proposal. I could use some help with the house. It's gonna be a challenge to do my job, work on the house, and manage trades all at the same time."

"Not to mention the new and incapacitated girlfriend," Bo contributes.

I hadn't even thought about that, but he makes a good point. No way to start a relationship if you don't have time to invest in it.

"Yeah, there's that," I admit.

"So what?" Bo pushes. "You wanna ask Jackson to work for you?"

"If I'm gonna hire someone, it might as well be him."

Bo laughs at me. "Is that what you plan on telling him?"

"I was thinking about it, now I'm not so sure."

That makes him laugh even louder.

"Ah, who knows. He may surprise you." Then he adds, "I'll make an extra big pot of coffee."

He doesn't wait for me to thank him before he ends the call.

I toss back the dregs of my beer and contemplate grabbing another, but then I get a whiff of myself. I guess I need a shower more than I need another beer. It's been a long-ass day and I'm about ready for bed anyway.

Grabbing my empty bottle and my phone, I head to the kitchen. I'm about to plug my phone in the charger, when a soft ping announces an incoming text.

How's your back?

Twenty-Two

DAN

I have a hard time keeping a straight face when he walks into the kitchen.

"Where's Lucy?" are the first words from his mouth.

"She said something about feeding the goats."

Aside from missing a leg, which still startles me, he's also lost a disturbing amount of weight. His face is gaunt, his eyes sunken in, and his expression is pure anger. He's not happy about me showing up here.

"And you're here because?"

Yeah, not happy at all.

I could try and beat around the bush for a bit, feed him some bullshit, but I have a feeling that's not going to do much to improve his mood. I may as well jump in, both feet, and see where it lands.

"Because I need your help."

"*My* help," he scoffs.

He hobbles on his crutches to the coffeepot, turning his back on me as he pours himself a mug.

"My mother put you up to this?" he asks over his shoulder.

"I haven't seen your mother since you guys got back from Fort Harrison," I answer truthfully. "No, I'm finally building my house."

He turns to face me, leaning his butt against the counter as he drinks his coffee. At least I have his attention.

"The shell is up, and I started on the interior framing, but I think I may have bit off more than I can chew. The guys give me a hand when they can, and I have trades coming in for some of the stuff, but I can't be there all the time. I already had to take this week off."

He hasn't said a word but he also hasn't moved and appears to be listening, which is encouraging.

"Anyway, I was talking to my sister last night and she's the one who suggested I hire someone. Like a construction manager or something. Someone who knows what needs to be done, can keep an eye on the trades, keep an eye on deliveries, maybe provide some security for the place."

"Security? Here?"

I drain the coffee Lucy poured me and approach Jackson, reaching around him for the coffeepot for a refill.

"A couple of nights ago, someone decided to spray-paint the shit out of the house. Inside and out."

"Seriously?"

"Yeah. JD, James, and I wasted a whole fucking day scrubbing it off all the logs."

"Know who did it?"

"I have my suspicions, but I haven't had a chance to look into it too closely. Wolff helped me put up some cameras in case they're stupid enough to try again, but we've got most of the windows and doors in there now, so at least the inside is protected."

"All it takes is a rock through the glass," Jackson points out.

"True, but that's where I'm hoping you'd come in."

He raises a skeptical eyebrow, but I'm hoping the proposal I came up with in the shower last night, and solidified with a phone call this morning, will pique his interest.

"You know that old motorhome Pippa used to travel around in? It's sitting idle behind their house and she's okay with us moving it up the road to set up next to my place. It has solar, a large water tank, a kitchen, bathroom, propane. Fuck, I think it even has a TV. It'd be your own private bachelor pad, away from prying eyes. You'd provide security at night, and manage the build during the day."

He hasn't told me to fuck off yet, which I'll take as a good sign.

"Why don't you move into the motorhome yourself?"

It's a fair question, which deserves an honest answer.

"I don't know if you heard, but Sloane is back in town. She moved into the cabin two doors down. She has a five-month-old baby, and I want to be close by. I'm into her."

Jackson snorts. "That's nothing new, although I would've thought you got over that."

"Turns out I didn't," I respond a little testily.

He sets down his coffee mug and raises his hands.

"Hey, man, if you wanna risk getting burned twice, be my guest."

He's pissing me off, but I have a feeling he's well aware, and I'm not about to let him suck me in. Determined, I get us back on track.

"So, are you interested?"

"I'm not some kind of charity case."

"I'm not fucking offering charity. I'm trying to hire someone to do the job, it can be you, or someone else." I shrug my shoulders and dump the rest of my coffee in the sink. "No skin off my nose as long as the work gets done."

Then I head for the door.

"I meant I'm not a charity. Not busting my ass for you for free."

I'm glad I have my back turned, otherwise he'd see the smug smile on my face. I have my hand on the door when I quote him what I figured would be a fair wage.

"Anyone ever tell you you're a cheap bastard?" he fires back.

This time I laugh out loud as I pull open the door, leaving him with my parting shot.

"Take it or leave it. I need to know by tonight."

I hear him yell, "*Asshole,*" as I head down the porch steps. But I'm grinning when I get in my truck. He's gonna call, I know he is.

Next, I'm making a quick stop to the cabin to pack a cooler, and then I'm heading back to the house to get to work.

Wolff is just coming out of Sloane's door when I pull up to my cabin. I never caught up with him last night after we got back from the hospital.

"Not at the house today?" he asks when I get out of the truck.

"I'm on my way, I'm just grabbing a few things here. What were you doing over at Sloane's?" I can't stop myself from asking.

The bastard grins, happy to try and get a rise out of me.

"She asked me to come."

"Because?"

"You missed it last night, but Deputy Schmidt and I

240

found a narrow access path to a cabin about half a mile from the lake up that trail. Sloane wanted me to show her exactly where on the map. She's gonna check for permits."

"Any sign of the ATV we heard?"

He shakes his head. "No. There were fresh tracks but I think he must've looped back down the trail while we were at the big clearing."

"So Sloane's already back to work," I observe.

"Were you expecting anything else?" Wolff points out. "Although, it's probably a challenge with her mom and the baby in the same space. Maybe I should've offered her the use of my cabin."

"If she needs quiet, she can use my place," I snap.

As he walks off, fucking Wolff laughs again, taunting me.

"You're too fucking easy, man."

Asshole.

～

Sloane

That was a frustrating forty-five minutes on the phone.

There's a US Forestry Services office here in Libby, but the lady I spoke to was a stickler for following proper procedure, which apparently is a written request signed by the proper authorities, which has to include an official fax number for the information to be sent to. That resulted in a phone call to Betty back at the office, who suggested contacting the sheriff, who apparently was up at the dumpsite waiting for the feds to arrive.

Long story short, I finally got hold of Junior, and with a

lot of back and forth, I just got word from Betty the official written request has been sent. Now all we have to do is wait. Hopefully, it won't be too long. I'd love to be able to get some leads going on this case before the FBI takes over.

At least I'm without interruptions here. As much as I adore my baby girl, she's a bit of a distraction, as is my mother. Yeah, that was pretty thoughtful of Dan. He popped in earlier for a quick visit and suggested I use his cabin to work, which I happily accepted. I have a sneaking suspicion Mom may have been a little relieved not to have me underfoot.

I pull up the Exxon video file I downloaded from the folder the sheriff sent me a link to. Wi-Fi can be sketchy here, and I'd rather have it on my hard drive so I can access it when I want. I know Ewing was going to get one of the guys to look at it, but I doubt anyone has had time in the last twenty-four hours.

It's going to take a while since we have about three hours' worth of video. Chelsea hadn't been too clear on exactly what time she passed through the Exxon gas station, but we were able to get an approximate timeframe.

Who knew there were so many white delivery trucks on the road? I've seen about five and I'm only half an hour into this video. Only one of them pulled into the gas station though, but it had the logo of a produce supplier on the side. The one I'm looking for had no markings or decals visible.

Leaning back, I stretch my arms over my head. I'm getting stiff from sitting. I'm almost tempted to make another pot of coffee, but I'm afraid I'll be up all night. I already need another pee break. Bracing myself on the table, I push myself up. Walking hurts, even with the boot, but the doctor said it's important to keep moving without over-doing it.

Dan's bathroom is pretty clean, I noticed as much the first time I was in here. I resisted nosing around, but this time the temptation is getting to me. After I do my business and wash my hands, I poke around the narrow glass shelf that serves as a medicine cabinet.

A container of Tylenol, some cold medication, a tube of cortisone cream, a bottle of aloe vera, and his Old Spice deodorant. No hair products, not even aftershave, just his Irish Spring soap and Old Spice deodorant, like my dad used to wear.

Jeff, Aspen's father, was all about the fancy fragrances—Tom Ford, Yves Saint Laurent, Armani—and he always wore a tad too much. I'd rather smell Old Spice with a hint of good, healthy man sweat any day.

There is nothing artificial about Dan. He is who he is, *what* he is, and I love that about him. He has this quiet confidence that seems to come naturally. Maybe it's the mountain air that breeds men like that up here.

The bottle of shampoo I've been sniffing slips from my hand, and clatters in the tub, when I hear my phone ringing from the living room. Wincing when I put weight on my bad ankle a little too enthusiastically, as I try to rush inside.

"Hello," I answer it, a little out of breath.

"Did I catch you in the middle of something?"

Of course, it would be Dan calling.

I try to ignore the embarrassed blush burning on my face.

"I was in the bathroom," I return casually. "What's up?"

"Where's your Jeep?"

"My Jeep? It's still parked at the sheriff's office. Why?"

"Uh, well, I was just thinking if we wanted to go somewhere, Aspen would need her car seat."

He may sound a little sheepish, but wow, there's a lot to unpack from what he says.

Not the least of which is the use of the word, *we*, casually identifying us as a unit, but more than that, a unit that includes my daughter. There doesn't even seem to be a question for him that she comes as part of me.

Also, what guy worries about a car seat?

My insides turn warm and gooey.

"Yeah. I can see if—" I was going to suggest maybe Sully would take Mom into town and she could drive my Jeep back, but I don't get a chance.

"I've got it," Dan interrupts. "I'll take care of it."

I must be getting soft, because my stubborn independent streak stays silent. Let him handle it if he wants to.

"Oh, and something else I was thinking about," he continues. "The ranch has a couple of ATVs but we rarely have more than one being used at a time. I could have one of the guys park one in front of your cabin. You don't need your foot to drive one of those, and you could take the trail that runs back to the river to get to your uncle's place. Or mine," he adds, making me smile.

"That would be awesome, if you think I could borrow one."

My mind is spinning with possibilities. If I wanted to, I could probably cross the river at the shallow part by the sandbar, or ride the shoulder of the highway to the other side of the bridge, and get up the mountain to check the progress at the site. Maybe even check out that cabin Wolff found.

"Yeah, for sure. By the way, use my place as long as you want. The guys brought over an extra generator and some floodlights, so I'll probably be working late anyway. I want to get as much done as I can."

"Thanks, I appreciate it. I think I'll join Mom for dinner and spend a little time with Aspen before her bedtime, but I may want to do some more work after she goes down."

"The place is yours. I may catch you later."

Then he ends the call.

He may not have meant that last comment to come across as a veiled promise, but the goosebumps on my skin certainly suggest I understood it as one.

Before the man completely scrambles my brain, I tap my trackpad to wake up my laptop, and try to redirect my focus on the video.

Twenty-Three

DAN

The lights are on inside my cabin when I pull up a little after nine thirty.

I like the thought of her in my space, even when I'm not there.

When I walk in, I don't see her at first, but when I close the door, she shoots up on the couch.

"Oh God, what time is it?"

"Twenty to ten."

She blows out a big breath. "Thank goodness."

"Did you get any work done?" I ask.

I kick off my boots and remove my socks, heading straight for the closet with the stackable washer and dryer.

"I did, but it's mind-numbingly boring to scan hours of security video. Especially when you have the same hours from three different camera angles. I'm only halfway through the second... What are you doing?"

I look over as I'm shoving my jeans and boxers down my legs.

"Taking off my dirty clothes," I point out the obvious. "You've seen me naked."

I stuff all my things in the washer and toss in some laundry soap before closing the door. Then I walk over and brace my hands on the back of the couch, leaning over to kiss the top of her head. I notice her attention is fixed on a certain part of my anatomy which always seems to be on alert when Sloane is around.

"Hold that thought," I whisper next to her ear. "I'm grabbing a quick shower."

Tossing my sweatpants and shirt on the vanity, I almost slip on my shampoo bottle when I step into the tub. I'm not sure how it ended up there, but I'm more concerned about getting myself clean in the least amount of time than worry about that. My very short shower is mostly cold, since I don't want to wait around for it to heat up. I'm in a hurry to get back to Sloane before she disappears on me.

She's still on my couch, and her enthusiastic, "Guess what?" greets me.

"I give up. What?" I return, heading for the fridge where I grab a couple of beers.

"I found her. Chelsea," she clarifies when I hand her a bottle and sit down next to her.

She turns the screen toward me and points. The video is frozen on a still shot of a gas station.

"There," she prompts.

I have to lean in to make out the shape of a girl with long hair just coming into frame, behind one of the pumps, only half in view.

"How can you tell that's her?"

"Watch."

She hits play and I watch the girl move away from the pump toward the actual building and slip around the side where you can see her pass an ice cooler.

"Watch," she repeats.

On the screen, the girl seems to move toward the street when you can see a white delivery truck come into the frame and pull up in front of her. She's forced to go around the truck where she disappears from sight. A few moments later the truck pulls into the street and drives off. There's no sign of the girl.

"Did you see?"

"He grabbed her."

She rewinds to where the back of the truck is in frame.

"Yes, and I have the time, and his license plate," she says triumphantly, reaching for her phone.

I sip my beer, and enjoy the view as Sloane animatedly talks to her boss, relaying the information she found.

"What time is that?" I hear her ask. "Yes, I can be there. I'll find a way."

"I'll drive you," I offer as soon as she gets off the phone.

"Because we're covering a big area, the FBI is putting together a task force and we're meeting at our office at ten tomorrow for a briefing."

I grin at her. "I thought you weren't happy the feds were swooping in on your investigation?"

She shrugs. "I wasn't, but this guy needs to be caught, and I realize our department is too small, and not really equipped to deal with a case of this magnitude. Especially with these other jurisdictions involved."

"Makes sense. So, are you done working for tonight?"

I reach for her laptop and let my hand hover while I wait for her answer.

"I think so," she answers, a knowing little smirk on her lips.

I close her laptop and slide it on the coffee table next to our beers. Then I reach for Sloane and stretch out on the couch, pulling her on top of me. She pushes up and rests her forearms on my chest, playing her fingers through my scruffy beard.

"Are you hurting?" I want to know, sliding my hands down to her lush ass.

She grins. "I'm feeling all kinds of things right now, but pain isn't one of them."

That's all the encouragement I need.

Sloane is ready for me, her fingers sliding in my hair as I slip my tongue past her lips. When her taste hits me, I groan down her throat. I've missed her.

It's been only three days since I first fell asleep with her in my arms, but I already can't remember a time when she didn't command all my senses.

I don't clue in immediately when she interrupts the kiss and presses her lips against the hollow of my neck, but I have a pretty clear idea where this is going when she moves her hands under the hem of my shirt, pushing it up.

I had plans to take my time with her this round, undress her slowly, giving each new exposed part of her my undivided attention before moving on to the next. I fully intended to taste every inch of her gorgeous body and have her beg for me to make her come.

Apparently, Sloane has similar plans, as she shimmies down my body and explores me with her mouth and hands. I'm not about to stop her—only an idiot would—and instead lace my fingers behind my head and watch as she slowly pulls down my waistband and exposes my cock.

She hasn't even touched it yet and I'm already leaking

precum. Every stomach muscle clenches in anticipation as she bends her head and her warm breath brushes the sensitive tip. Then she wraps a firm hand around my length, locks her blue eyes with mine, and with her little pink tongue licks up the drop, before she slides me down her throat.

I have to grab on to the armrest as she goes down on me with the same determination and enthusiasm she does everything else. I use every trick in the book to slow down my body's response, but there isn't anything that'll distract me from that blond head bobbing up and down on my cock. Christ, this exact image fed my fantasies for fucking years.

"Hey," she protests, when I lift her off my cock.

"I want inside you. Take off your pants," I urge her, even as I retrieve the condom I slipped in my pocket in the bedroom.

While I roll it on, I watch Sloane struggle, getting tangled up with her walking boot as she tries to get her yoga pants down. She gets them twisted up around her legs.

"Babe, leave it. On your knees on the edge and grab hold of the backrest."

She doesn't even question me, simply gets on her knees and bends forward, her ass in the air, and I almost swallow my goddamn tongue when I see she's already slick. I only trust myself to lean down for a quick taste, using the flat of my tongue.

I can't resist putting my teeth into the soft flesh of her butt cheek, hearing her hissed, "*Yesss.*"

Then I firmly grab her hips, line up my cock, and drive home.

Sheer fucking perfection.

∼

Sloane

"Oh God," I huff breathlessly.

My face is pressed into the back of the couch, and my body is still vibrating with aftershocks, as Dan's heart hammers against my back.

"Are you on the pill?" he mumbles against my skin.

"Mmm. Yes."

"Good."

My back is instantly cold when he straightens up and slowly pulls out. I'm empty and a bit exposed, but I feel him kiss the butt cheek he bit earlier. Then he sweetly pulls up my underwear and yoga pants, making sure I'm covered before he heads, with his business still hanging out of his sweatpants, to the bathroom.

"I've always used a condom," he announces as he walks back out, his pants in place. "But I'm paying my doctor a visit this week, getting a clean bill of health."

My mind is still a bit sluggish as I flop around on my back, but when I see the way he looks at me, the penny drops.

"I, uh...there has been no one since Aspen was born. Until you, of course," I add.

He bends down and brackets me with his arms on either side of me as he drops his forehead to mine.

"Gonna be good, sliding into you bare. Nothing between us."

A shiver rolls down my back at his low rumble. I slide my arms around his neck and offer my mouth for a kiss. He doesn't hesitate. The man knows how to use his mouth.

Sadly, the kiss is interrupted when a phone starts ringing.

252

"Yours?" Dan asks, grabbing my phone off the coffee table and handing it to me.

He grins when I flip it around to show him it's my mother calling.

"Hi, Mom."

"Should I lock the door? I'm gonna head to bed soon."

"No, leave it open. I'm on my way."

Tempting as it is to stay here, I want to wake up to my daughter's sweet face.

"I'll walk you home," Dan announces as he helps me up off the couch.

"You don't have to do that," I automatically say, like some kind of verbal muscle memory.

He shoots me a look. "Humor me."

I shove my laptop and my phone in the tote I brought over and hobble to the front door. Dan follows close behind, his hand on the small of my back. I sit down on the bench by the door and slip my good foot in the Birkenstock slide I wore here, when I notice Dan shoving his bare feet into a pair of Crocs.

"Now, there's something I never thought I'd see," I tease him.

He smirks and shakes his head. "My sister got them for me Christmas of last year. They're comfortable."

I raise my hands. "I'm not knocking them. I own a pair myself."

He plucks the tote off my shoulder, looping it over his. Then he wraps his left arm around my waist to support me, and walks me two doors down.

"What time tomorrow morning?" he asks when we stop outside my door.

"Nine thirty? I need to make a quick stop in at Rosauers, Aspen is running out of diapers."

Rosauers is Libby's major grocery and drug store, and not that far from the office.

"How about nine forty and I'll pick up diapers on my way home. Just shoot me a text with what you need."

I loop my arms around his neck and smile up at him.

"Be careful. Before you know it, I'm used to this kind of treatment."

He brushes my mouth with his.

"Mission accomplished."

Twenty-Four

SLOANE

"Come here, sleepy girl."

I pick Aspen up out of her bouncy seat and hobble toward the bedroom.

"I can put her down," Mom offers.

"It's okay, I've got it."

I have to grab what I can, when I can. Time is something you can't get back, and I'm more aware of it now than I was a few weeks ago. I bet you if I asked Nita's mother, she regrets every second of her daughter's too-short life she missed. It's the kind of regret that could destroy a person.

Aspen's eyes are getting heavy already when I put her on the big bed to quickly change her diaper. The moment I put her down in her crib, she rolls on her side, jams her little fist in her mouth, and closes her eyes. I watch her for a beat before I close the bedroom door and join my mother in the kitchen.

"Want another coffee?"

I grab my mug off the counter and hold it out for her to top up.

"When is Dan picking you up?"

"He said nine forty."

I sit down at the kitchen table and Mom sits down across from me.

"You're a natural," she says, smiling over the rim of her coffee cup at me. "Which, if I can be brutally honest, I wouldn't have guessed. Probably because I was expecting you to be as flustered and overwhelmed and clueless as I can remember being when I had you."

"I'm probably just a better actor than you are, believe me, I'm plenty clueless and overwhelmed," I confess, even though it makes me feel really good she thinks that. "It's funny how priorities change though. Ambitions change."

"What do you mean; ambitions change?"

"Well, before, I was dead set on having a career in law enforcement, and now all I think about is being home with Aspen because I'm afraid of all I'm missing. You stayed home after I was born, right?"

Mom smiles as her eyes drift off over my shoulder.

"Yeah. As out of my depth as I was, and as overwhelmed as I remember feeling at the time, I love the memories I have." Her eyes come to me. "But I wasn't a single parent."

"There's that," I concede. "Too bad I don't live in a state offering paid parental leave. I had to use up my sick leave and vacation days to get any time off. I could've at least had some more time at home with her."

"Would've helped if her father hadn't been a waste of space," Mom points out. "What happens if he shows up some day and demands to see his daughter?"

It's actually something I have thought about on occasion. I'm not going to stop him from seeing his daughter if he wants to, but if he ever shows up looking for any kind of custody—shared or otherwise—I will fight like hell for that not to happen.

"If he wants to see her, as long as it's on my terms, he can. But I won't let him lay any claim on her, and to be honest, I don't think he will."

"Well, if ever he shows his face, you better get that last part in writing."

"I will."

"By the way, I talked to Steve last night," she announces. "Told him about your ankle and this case you're working on, and he suggested I could stay longer than the two weeks, if you need me."

"Thanks, Mom, but I can't keep you here. You have a life in Panama, and at some point I'm gonna need to figure my life out on my own."

"Maybe you won't have to figure it out on your own," she offers with a smirk as she gets to her feet. "Here's Dan now."

"Detective Eckhart, I understand you have an update for us? A license plate, I believe?"

Special Agent in Charge Bellinger, as he was introduced at the start of the meeting, is a big, burly guy, probably in his fifties. He has the kind of presence that leaves no doubt as to who the top dog is. It's not that he's loud, or pompous, he just oozes a quiet authority you can feel in the room. He reminds me of Tom Selleck's character in *Blue Bloods*. Looks a little like him too.

We've already heard an update from the forensic team, who have apparently finished up in the gorge. Not including

Nita's body, they report up to a possible six additional bodies. One is believed to be male, and missing the right leg. We're told the others look to be female.

"Yes, a license plate, a name, and an address."

I hadn't been able to get to sleep last night and ended up working until three in the morning, running the plate number and pulling information on the owner.

"We received the security feed off three separate cameras from the Exxon gas station in Columbia Falls. The location from where Chelsea Littleton was abducted," I clarify.

Looking around the room, I go into a description of what I viewed on the video.

"It confirms Chelsea's own account of events, insofar as she can remember. As the truck drives off, you can catch a quick glimpse of the license plate."

I catch sight of Betty standing by the door, waving a stack of papers. "We'll pass around a still of the camera feed with the plate number visible, and the information we pulled on it. As you can see, the truck is licensed to Cedric Transport out of Eureka. A small one-truck delivery service owned and operated by Michael Cedric."

"Good work, Eckhart," SAC Bellinger states, assuming I'm done, which I'm not.

"Sir," I interrupt him. "I have additional information I literally received on my way in this morning."

He gives me a nod. "Go right ahead."

"I heard back from the US Forestry Service. They emailed me the copy of a permit they issued back in 1997 for the construction of the cabin our officers found near the trail on Kenelty Mountain."

"And?"

"A single permit holder, and only one name attached to

it; Cornelius J. Cedric. The address on the application looks to be in Eureka."

"That can't be a coincidence," one of the other law enforcement officers pipes up.

"My guess is the two are related," I agree.

"All right, Detective Eckhart, since you are already deep into this investigation, why don't you find out what background you can on both Cornelius Cedric and Michael Cedric. Find the connection. Also, forward me the video feed and the information from the USFS."

"Will do, sir."

When I get home, I can get on social media and see if I can find accounts in either of those names. That's usually the quickest and easiest way to get information on someone. People don't realize how much can be gleaned from the things they post on Facebook or Instagram. This kind of stuff is right up my alley. I'm a bit of a computer nerd and I love poking around, at times skirting the lines of what could be considered legal, but always for the greater good.

Bellinger continues to dole out responsibilities with a focus on identifying the victims and connecting them to missing person's reports, which is going to take some time. He instructs the various law enforcement departments he wants a BOLO issued for the truck and when spotted, to keep eyes on it until further instruction. His office will be looking into Cedric Transport.

"Any and all new information is to come directly to me. I'm central station, it's the only way to make sure we don't miss a thing. Let's stop this guy."

As we file out of the boardroom, Jillian falls into step beside me. I'd been surprised to see her still around.

"How's the ankle?" she inquires.

"Not too bad. The boot keeps it stable." I glance over at

her as we make our way down the hallway. "I figured you'd be gone already."

"I was asked to hang around. I took Emo down there one last time yesterday afternoon—once the forensic team removed all the remains—to make sure we hadn't missed anything in the surrounding area." She shrugs. "We didn't find anything else."

She holds open the door to the parking lot for me.

"So...when are you heading back?"

"Now. Emo is waiting for me in the car." She glances down at my boot. "Did you drive yourself?"

"Dan dropped me off. I have to call him for a pickup."

"Nonsense, I'm driving by the ranch anyway. I'll drop you off."

She pulls up in front of my cabin fifteen minutes later. Mom is on the porch with Aspen who is doing push-ups on her play mat.

"Is that your little one?"

"That's Aspen. Come on, you can meet her and my mom."

"Okay, five minutes. It'll give Emo a chance to stretch her legs before we hit the road."

Five minutes turn into twenty, which includes a cup of coffee and a muffin.

"Your daughter is precious," she says, getting to her feet as she hands her back to me. "And she has a lifetime fan in Emo."

The dog had her nose two inches from some part of Aspen at all times, and my daughter loved it.

"I may consult you about a puppy at some point. Once I find my own place to live," I tell her as I settle my daughter on my arm.

"Call me any time."

I hug her and say goodbye to Emo. I'm a bit sad to see them go, I liked the idea of having someone closer to my own age around.

I wave as Jillian drives off, heading down the driveway. When I turn to go inside, I notice my neighbor standing in the doorway of his cabin.

Wolff doesn't see me; his eyes are fixed on the back of her disappearing SUV.

~

Dan

I straighten up and stretch my back.

It's done. It took a bit longer than anticipated, but all the framing is complete.

A quick glance at my phone tells me it's three fifteen, not too bad. I'm going to quickly clean up my tools and straighten up what's left of the pile of two-by-fours outside. Then maybe I can pick up a pizza at the Red Dog Saloon and have a lazy night at home.

I've got both the HVAC and plumbing contractors coming in tomorrow morning. They'll have to work around each other, but we're on a pretty tight schedule. Electrical will be last, before insulation and drywall go up. That part —drywalling, taping, mudding, and sanding—will be the most time-consuming.

I carry the tools downstairs and organize them in the large storage bin near the side door. Next, I head outside to haul the table saw and generator in from the side porch. Then I head to the leftover lumber which is haphazardly tossed around the yard and try to wrangle it back into a neat pile. Finally, I gather up the trimmed pieces in a bin. Whatever I don't need, I can cut into kindling.

Spotting a few pieces that slipped under the porch, I lean down and fish them out, when my hand touches something metal.

It's a can of red spray paint.

For marking livestock.

Son of a bitch.

The vandalism to the house had kind of slipped down my list of priorities these past few days with so much else going on. I guess this is as good a time as any to confirm my suspicions.

Holding the can between my thumb and index finger, I carry it to my truck and find the Ziploc bag Isobel's muffins had been in, and drop the paint can inside. I toss it on the passenger seat before returning to the house to make sure everything is closed and locked up. Then I get behind the wheel and head into town.

She's behind the register cashing out a customer when I enter the store.

The moment she sees me walking up, she goes rigid. The customer says something to her as he grabs the bag of feed off the counter and flips it on his shoulder. Then he walks out the door and it's just her and me.

"What can I do for you?" she asks through clenched teeth.

Yep. She's still angry.

Her eyes drop down to the plastic bag in my hand and stay fixed there, a flush almost instantly appearing on her face. It speaks volumes, and is enough of a confession for me.

"Do you carry this brand, Shelby?"

"I don't think so."

"Would you mind checking for me?"

Right then Bill Vandermeer comes walking out of the warehouse in the back. He looks at his daughter and then at me.

"Is there a problem?"

"Shelby didn't recognize this brand, so I asked her to check," I explain, noticing Shelby squirm a little.

"Raidex Red?" he asks, noting the brand of the can in my hand. Then he turns to his daughter. "You just stocked the shelves in the warehouse with that stuff last week. Remember we got that shipment in right before the weekend?"

Shelby's face is now beet red, as she presses her lips together. Her father shakes his head at her before turning back to me.

"I'll grab 'em for you, how many cans do you need?"

I hadn't really planned on what I would do once I confirmed my suspicions—maybe go to the police—but now I'm thinking perhaps her father can keep his daughter in check.

"Actually, I just wanted to see if the can came from here," I tell him.

"I haven't sold any yet. You, Shel?" he asks his daughter, before catching himself. "Never mind, of course you haven't or you would've remembered we carry it."

"Could you check to make sure?" I press.

"Sure. I ordered twenty-four of the red, so it'll be easy to see. One sec."

He pokes his head back into the warehouse, and I glance at Shelby, who stays silent but is shooting daggers at me.

"I'll be damned. I've got two missing." Bill points at the can in my hand. "Where'd you get that?"

"I found it under my porch this afternoon. I'm building a log home just east of High Meadow along the Fisher River. Sometime during the night from Sunday to Monday, someone spray painted the inside and outside of my house with red paint." I hold up the plastic bag. "This red paint."

"What the hell?"

Bill seems genuinely baffled as he turns to his daughter and catches her glaring at me.

"I'm not sure what's going on here."

I'm pretty sure Vandermeer has no idea his daughter and I were briefly involved.

"Sir, your daughter and I saw each other very casually for a short while." Shelby audibly snorts, but I forge on. "I ended it, mainly because it became clear things weren't casual to your daughter anymore."

"I had nothing to do with it, asshole," she snarls, but it's like her father doesn't hear her.

He keeps his attention on me. "You think she did this?"

"Sir, I don't think it's a coincidence two cans of red paint went missing from your stock, one of which showed up under my porch."

The old man presses the palm of his hand against his forehead.

"Lord have mercy, Shelby. When are you gonna smarten up?" he laments. "You're thirty-two years old, and your mother and I have had it with you."

I listen to Shelby going off on her father. I feel for the man, but hell, I don't need to be a part of this discussion. I got what I came for, and her father can take it from here. I can still hear them yelling when I get to my truck. Tossing the empty can on the passenger seat, I get behind the wheel and head for the Red Dog Saloon.

My phone rings in my pocket as I'm sitting in the parking lot, waiting for my pizza. I grin when I see who's calling.

"You're an ass," I tell Jackson when I answer.

I had a feeling he was gonna make me wait an extra day, just to be a dick.

"Calling me fucking names already? Where the hell are you?" he grumbles.

"Picking up a pizza in town. Where are you?"

"Sitting on your goddamn porch with a six-pack and my fucking duffel bag, where do you think I am?"

Grinning, I shake my head. Guess my day isn't over yet.

"What do you want on your pie?"

Twenty-Five

"You have *got* to be shitting me."

Several months and not a word, a cell phone no longer in service, and no forwarding address. How ironic Mom and I were just talking about this possibility earlier.

"Come on, darlin', don't be that way."

That's how he used to talk to any woman who would sit down at his bar, except I was the fool who fell for it.

Well, I'm no longer falling for it, I'm spitting nails.

"You bailed months ago, no heads-up, no way to contact you. You just packed your bag and walked away, from your fucking daughter! And you sure canceled that phone number in a hurry, you useless piece of shit!"

I'm glad he caught me working at Dan's place, at least my yelling won't wake my daughter.

"I was in a bad place—"

I bark out an ugly laugh. "You? Give me a break, Jeff.

269

You got to stay home with our daughter while I had to go out and earn an income. Not what you'd call a hardship."

"It was stunting me, killing my muse."

Oh, my God. He is not to be believed. I don't know why I even bother talking to him.

"You're killing *me*. Why are you calling?"

When he hesitates, I already know what's coming.

"Well, I'm not sure where to find you. Things didn't work out west so...I came back to Billings, but I couldn't get into our place and I was told you left."

"It was never your place, Jeff. It was mine. My name on the lease, my money that paid for it. Mine."

"I lived there."

"For four months. That's it."

"Right, but here's the thing, I don't have anywhere else to go."

"And that's my problem, how?" I snap.

"You'd have your child's father living on the street?"

This time I laughed because that was hysterically funny. "I honestly can't believe you. Find yourself a place to live."

"Listen, I can probably get my job back at the pub, but I spent my last money on the flight home. There's a furnished studio apartment two blocks down from our old place I could move into today, but I don't have first and last month's rent."

I'm aggravated, get to my feet, and start pacing around the room.

"You're looking at me for money?"

"Unless you let me crash at your place until I'm back on my feet."

"You're delusional."

"Come on, Sloane, where are you living now?"

His whiny voice grates on me like nails on a chalkboard. How could I ever have thought we'd be able to turn what essentially was a one-night stand into a lasting relationship? I don't think I even like the guy.

I stop in the kitchen and look out the window over the sink. It got dark outside, but I can see there's a full moon out. Maybe that explains it.

"Certainly not in Billings," I let slip.

"You moved? I'm pretty sure you can't just move away. Aspen is my daughter too."

"Oh, *now* you remember?" I scoff. "And before you get any ideas, let's remember who disappeared for months. We've come full circle here and this conversation is done."

I still hear him railing as I take the phone away from my ear and end the call. Then I turn around and almost have a heart attack when I see Dan standing just inside the door. I grab for my chest.

"God, you scared the shit out of me."

He motions to the phone. "That the guy? The asshole who abandoned his baby daughter?"

Dan's voice is soft, but holds a threat I can feel across the room. I know for a fact if Jeff were to show his face here, he might well come to regret that.

"It was. How much did you hear?"

"Just the last bit," he shares, walking this way.

He stops right in front of me and leans down for a kiss. Then he takes a step back.

"I smell, I need a shower. Keep me company, and fill me in on why that asswipe called you?"

I follow him into the bathroom and sit on the toilet seat, enjoying the view as I tell him about the call. Despite a few growls, he doesn't interrupt me.

"He wants money."

"That's what it sounds like," I confirm. "But he's not getting a cent from me."

"Hold on a sec," Dan interjects as he steps out of the shower and grabs a towel, rubbing his hair vigorously. "I think you should give him the money."

My mouth falls open as I stare at him in disbelief.

"You're not serious, are you?"

"Yup. But on the condition he gives up his parental rights. It's not like he wants them, and he's using his rights as leverage over you. I don't think you've heard the last of him. I can call my sister, Lindsey, for advice. She's a legal assistant for her mother, who is a family lawyer in Durango. The law may differ from state to state, but they'll at least be able to tell us how to go about getting this done."

It takes me a moment to process. This is what Mom was suggesting this morning, making Jeff sign off on his rights. At the time it was something to consider for the future, but I guess Jeff's unexpected phone call makes it a reality to deal with now.

This would cost me legal fees and filing or whatever else is needed on top of his first and last month's rent, but it's probably cheaper in the long run than potentially having to deal with him long term. The only problem is, I'm not sure I'd be able to afford it. Even just first and last month's rent—which I'm guessing would be around fifteen hundred, so three grand total—would be a stretch for my meager savings. Of course, that also means I don't have first and last when I get around to looking for a place of my own.

"I can hear you thinking."

"I am." I grin up at him as he pulls me to my feet. "Your idea is kinda brilliant, but I'm not sure if it's going to be an option for me at this time."

He places his hands on my shoulders.

"Us," he corrects me. "You know where I see us going. I'm pretty sure you're at least on board with the concept of that. And that means we tackle shit as a team."

"But this isn't your problem," I point out.

"Sure it is. Anything that affects you, has an impact on me too. Isn't that the nature of relationships?"

"Honestly? I wouldn't know."

He shakes me gently and I'm suddenly aware that I'm standing in a small space with a very handsome, very naked man.

"Eyes up here, Sloane," he mumbles. "My point is, I benefit too. Once he's out of your and Aspen's life, there's more room for me."

Then he gives me the full force of his smile, and I feel the effect down to my toes.

"Okay," I give in with a nod. "If you could contact your sister to see if she knows what all of this would entail, that would be very helpful. Thank you."

"That wasn't too hard, was it?" he teases, still very naked.

The man is too tempting, and I'm having a hard time thinking of anything other than jumping him.

"Shouldn't you put some clothes on?" I suggest.

He slides his hands up my neck to cradle my face and drops a hard kiss on my lips, before letting go.

"I will, but only because I want to hear about the rest of your day and tell you about mine."

I'll be damned if that doesn't make me want to jump him harder.

Dan

. . .

"Seven victims."

I shake my head. It makes me a little sick to think what may have been happening in my backyard.

Sloane has been filling me in on the meeting at the sheriff's office this morning.

"Eight. Chelsea was a victim too," Sloane reminds me, snuggled up against my side.

"Of course, you're right."

"Anyway," she continues. "Remember the license plate on the video? I found the company it was registered under, and the name of the owner/operator. And guess what? It's the same last name as on the permit application for that cabin Wolff found up on the trail."

"Same guy?"

"No. There was a Cornelius on the permit application, but Michael is the listed name for the owner of Cedric Transport."

"Family, then," I guess, wondering why that name seems familiar.

"Yes, it turns out Cornelius was Michael's paternal grandfather. I just found an obituary for him earlier. From what I've been able to gather, Michael was the old man's only remaining relative."

"So Michael would've inherited the cabin?" I suggest.

"That seems the logical conclusion."

"So now what happens?"

"Well, before Jeff's call, I'd just fired off an email to the FBI special agent in charge with the information I dug up. It's up to him what'll happen with the information, but I assume they'll be paying Michael Cedric a visit."

There's that name again, followed by the same little niggle in the back of my mind, but I can't place it.

"Anyway," Sloane continues, tilting her head back to look at me. "I'm no longer in charge of this case, so I'll be waiting for instructions."

"That's gotta suck," I sympathize.

She shrugs. "Meh, before Aspen I would've been royally pissed, but to be honest, the scope of this case is more responsibility than I'd want to have rest on my shoulders." She rubs my chest with her hand. "But enough about me. How was your day?"

I tighten my arm around her shoulders.

"Good. Productive," I share. "I finished the framing just in time for the HVAC guys and the plumber to start tomorrow."

"Good for you. I bet that's a relief, getting it done before you have to go back to your regular day job."

"Sure is," I agree. "And remember I told you last night I'd asked Jackson to come on board?"

I'd brought it up when we were cuddled on this same couch, except with notably fewer clothes on at the time. I was thinking about Jackson because I hadn't heard anything yet.

"Yeah, did he call?"

"He did, actually. He showed up at the house and we had pizza and beers on the porch before we went to get your aunt's motorhome. It's now parked on the far side of the house, next to the river, and Jackson's already moved in."

"Wow," she whispers, and subsequently falls silent.

I wait her out for a bit before asking, "You don't think it's a good idea?"

She shakes her head. "It's not that, it's that I'm worried

about him, out there by himself. He was living alone when he tried to end it."

I press a kiss to the top of her head. "I hear you, but he's a grown man. Living under someone else's roof, under twenty-four seven monitoring, without a reason to get your ass out of bed in the morning doesn't seem like the better option."

She twists her body so she's looking straight at me.

"And living in a trailer at a building site does?"

"Yes, I think so," I tell her bluntly. "Being responsible for himself, responsible for the trades and security at the house gives him purpose. Being someone else's responsibility only erodes his self-worth further. He's a man, he needs to be reminded he still is, and missing a limb makes no damn difference."

She launches herself at me and lands on my lap, her mouth on mine and her hands tangled in my hair. She's smiling when she pulls back.

"You're a smart man, Daniel Blakely."

I scrunch my nose at the use of my full name, but grin back at her. I don't particularly want to address the next topic, but in the spirit of transparency...

"I went to see Shelby at the feedstore this afternoon."

"You did?"

Her body language tells me the casual curiosity in her question took effort.

"I was cleaning up the lumber at the house and found an empty spray-paint can under the porch. It was red live-stock marker paint."

"Son of a bitch," she mutters, which is pretty much what my own reaction was.

"Right. I was able to confirm two cans were missing from stock at the feedstore, but it's not exactly evidence."

"She had her hand in it," Sloane concludes firmly.

"Seems likely."

"Maybe she didn't do it herself," she offers. "But she was involved, if not the instigator."

I don't disagree with her.

"Didn't you say she was divorced? Could she have manipulated her ex into doing it?"

I feel like I've been zapped with a cattle prod, every synapses firing at the same time.

Of course, her ex.

That's what's been niggling at the back of my mind.

"Cedric."

Sloane looks at me, puzzled.

"Sorry?"

"She mentioned her ex once, told me he was a truck driver and they lived in Eureka before she moved back home. I'm pretty sure she mentioned the name Cedric. Mike Cedric."

Sloane is off my lap and on her feet in a flash.

"You're shitting me. Cedric is Shelby's ex?"

She massages her scalp with her fingertips, as if to help her think.

"I'm pretty sure that was his name," I state.

In fact, the longer I think about it, the more positive I am. Feeling the need to move, I get up off the couch and grab the empty beer bottles off the table to take to the kitchen.

"That would be wild," Sloane mutters.

"I've gotta admit, it's making me a tad uneasy," I confess, leaning over the sink as I stare outside. "That shit that went on right across the river on that mountain was already too close for comfort. This literally puts it in my backyard."

I feel her hand slide up my back.

"I'm sorry. And I'm sorrier yet to be all business but..."

I turn around to face her.

"What?"

She grimaces.

"Tell me you kept the spray can?"

Twenty-Six

SLOANE

"I think it's better if I talk to her alone."

I smile at Jason as I get out of the sheriff's cruiser.

SAC Bellinger was on the phone at the stroke of seven this morning. He'd seen my emails, both the one I sent before Jeff's call, and the one I followed it up with after I talked to Dan. He wanted me to go interview Shelby, see what I could find out about her ex without giving her too much information on why we're looking into him. He suggested I could always use the vandalism on Dan's home as my excuse for questioning her.

Ewing called shortly after. He'd also spoken with the special agent in charge, and insisted on sending over a deputy to pick me up and drive me to the feedstore. I was a little worried I might've been saddled with Frank Schmidt's miserable mug, but it was Jason who showed up. He'd been at the end of his shift, and kindly volunteered, which was a relief. I had him quickly stop at the office so I could drop off the spray-paint can for the sheriff to dust for prints.

"Sure thing."

I know she recognizes me when I walk in the door. Her mouth narrows into an angry slit as she watches my approach.

"Shelby Vandermeer? My name is Detective Sloane Eckhart with the Lincoln Sheriff's Office. I wonder if I could ask you a few questions?"

"What is this about?"

If she's intimidated or even surprised I'm here in an official capacity, she doesn't show it. She's oozing defiance.

"Actually, it's about Michael Cedric."

I watch her closely when I mention his name, and she seems surprised.

"Mike? What about him?"

"Michael is your husband, isn't that right?"

"Ex," she corrects me. "I divorced his sorry ass last year."

"Very well, ex-husband. Your ex owns a company I believe?" I flip through an almost empty notebook. "Yes, Cedric Transport."

She snorts. "Some company, it's just a stupid delivery truck he drives himself."

"Did you ever work for him? Take phone calls, schedule deliveries, things like that?"

"No. He did that himself. I had a job, at Watson's Market in Eureka." She tilts her head and narrows her eyes on me. "What the hell did he do?"

Hmm. I'm starting to wonder if her ex had anything to do with spraying Dan's place. She was surprised I brought him up, and so I can't detect any deception.

I ignore her question and change direction.

"When was the last time you were in contact with your ex?"

She scoffs at that. "That would've been the last time he split my lip in the parking lot outside the courthouse in Eureka after the divorce was final."

I feel a pang of sympathy for the woman. Now I understand a little better why she'd been so eager to hook herself to a good man like Dan.

"Did you report it?"

"Hell no," she responds instantly. "It would've meant another thing to tie me to that man. Nah, I figured it was a small price to pay for being rid of him once and for all."

"So he never called, never bothered you here?"

Her eyes drift over my shoulder and I see her lips press together. Then she lowers her gaze and straightens a stack of brochures. "No."

Hmm. Defiantly verbose before, she suddenly seems awfully subdued with that one-syllable response.

She could be lying, and *has* seen him since, in which case I'd love to know why, but if I push her she might shut down altogether, and I still have some questions I'd like her to answer.

"I only have a few more questions and then I'll get out of your hair," I mention, drawing a look of relief from her.

"Sure."

"Did you often go up to the cabin with him?"

I'm purposely making it sound like I already know she's familiar with the existence of the cabin.

"That hunting shack he has up on Kenelty Mountain? Hell no. He'd disappear there for days with...uh, with friends."

She appears to catch herself, which is interesting. Does she know something?

"Anyone in particular?" I prompt.

"No." She shakes her head firmly for good measure. "Hunting friends, I don't know them."

"Does he still go up there? To hunt?"

"How the hell am I supposed to know?" she snaps, annoyed. "Didn't I tell you I haven't seen him?"

An older man comes walking through a door that looks to connect with a storage space in the back. His eyes are sharp on me.

"Can I help you with anything?"

Shelby looks uncomfortable. "I've got it covered, Dad."

I get the vibe she doesn't want her father to clue in on what, or probably who, we were talking about. Not sure why but I understand a little something about family dynamics and decide to give her a break.

"Thank you," I address Shelby, scribbling my number on an empty page in my notebook and handing it to her. "Give me a call if you think of anything that might be helpful. I appreciate your time."

With a nod for the older man, I turn and head for the door. I can feel two pairs of eyes burning my back as I hobble outside. So much for a graceful exit.

"Get everything you need?" Jason asks when I get into the cruiser.

"I'm not sure," I admit. "Sounds like the subject was a dick, who didn't think twice about hitting her in the middle of the day outside the courthouse. She was forthcoming about that, but I get the sense there's something more, maybe she was aware of what Cedric was up to. She did suggest he wasn't up at the cabin by himself, but I never managed to get names because her father walked in. I'll try her again later, and in the meantime, I left her my number."

He takes me back to the office, at my request, and I

assure him he doesn't have to wait around for me; I'll find my way home. If worse comes to worst, I'm sure I can convince my aunt or Ira, who is a mechanic for Pippa at her Pit Stop Auto Shop, to run me home. I know I could call Dan and he'd probably drop everything, but I know he has his hands full today with trades showing up.

Junior is in his office and raises his head when I knock on his doorpost. Folding his hands behind his neck, he leans back in his chair as I walk in.

"How'd it go?"

"Found out our man didn't think twice to beat on her in public."

"Not a surprise," he grumbles.

"She knew of the cabin's existence; claims she never went up with him but he spent time there with *friends*." I use my fingers to make air quotes. "I think she knows something, but I didn't want to lean too hard and then we got interrupted. Left my number with her, and I can try again."

"Good. I'd like to have a name for those friends. Bellinger called again, turns out Cedric is in the wind and has been for some time."

"What do you mean?" I take a seat across from his desk.

"Agents went to check at his address, a rental place, but found new tenants in there. According to the landlord, Cedric forfeited his rent two months in a row, and when he went to collect he noticed mail had piled up with stamps dating back to early November and his pickup was parked outside, but the delivery truck was gone. The landlord ended up putting his belongings in storage and getting the truck towed. The feds discovered he hadn't been paying his bills and his cell phone account had been suspended since January. Looks like he's been off the grid for almost a year."

"Yet we have him and his truck on video," I point out.

"His truck, yes, but do we know it's him?"

"Who else?"

Ewing shrugs, "I don't know, but there were finger-prints found on one of the shells from the bullets that were fired at you that did not match fingerprints on file for Michael Cedric."

"That doesn't make sense."

"How about this then?" he follows it up with. "I scanned and emailed a thumbprint I was able to pull off that paint can you dropped off, and it was a match."

"A match to Cedric?"

Junior shakes his head. "A match to one of the prints on the shell."

This is getting weirder and weirder.

The more we discover, the less we seem to know.

～

Dan

"That's seriously fucked up, man."

I just finished telling Jackson about Shelby, who she was to me, and how she seems to be connected to the spray-painting of my house, and to the guy who was suspected of dumping the bodies found in the gorge.

"You're telling me."

We're just having a bite to eat, sitting under the awning outside the motorhome. It's a hot day for September, and the shade is a welcome break from the sun.

While the trades are working inside, Jackson and I have

been working on removing some stumps from what is to become my yard. Backbreaking work I wasn't sure Jackson would be up to, but he seems to be getting around okay on his prosthesis and offered to swing an ax to try and sever the roots.

I didn't stop him. He's a grown-ass man, and if he's feeling the need to prove himself still a man, for his own sake or mine, I'm not gonna stop him. Besides, I figure a bit more upper body muscle might come in handy for him.

"Want another one?" I ask with my hand in the cooler Ama ran out of the house this morning to give to me.

Stocked with water, apples, and probably a loaf's worth of bread in wrapped sandwiches. She must've heard Jackson's here too, although she didn't mention it.

"Is there another egg salad?"

I dig one up and toss it to him, grabbing a cheese and ham one for myself.

"You haven't asked."

It's a rhetorical question I don't even need clarification for. I know exactly what he means. What I take from his comment is he feels as uneasy as I do with the proverbial elephant in the room, and has decided to confront it.

"So you can tell me to fuck off? I figure you'll talk if you want me to know."

He seems to think on that, and I take the opportunity to take a bite of my sandwich.

"Honestly, aren't you pissed? Everyone else seems to be," he adds under his breath.

I fix my eyes on the river and the mountains beyond, trying to remain calm when I feel anything but.

Still, he wants honest, he's going to get it.

"Fuck, yeah, I'm angry as hell at you. Been tempted to take a swing at you, but the fact of the matter is, I can't pretend to know what would fucking drive you to do something like that. I'm not in your shoes."

I can feel him glancing this way but I need a minute to get a handle on my emotions before I turn to look at him.

"Shoe," he corrects me, with a wink.

I'll be damned if that doesn't set me off laughing. "You're an idiot."

"I think we've established that much," he responds somberly, before shoving the rest of his egg salad sandwich in his mouth.

The kicker is, when we get back to work a few minutes later, I no longer feel like I'm working side by side with a stranger. If anything, it almost feels like having my old friend back, the short interlude seems to have cleared the air.

The HVAC guys have already left—they'll be here tomorrow—but the plumber won't be back until Monday. I'm just watching him get into his truck, when I notice Sully and his daughter walking up the driveway.

"You guys done for the day?" he asks when they reach me.

"I think so. Jackson's already in the shower."

I jerk a thumb over my shoulder at the motorhome. He was pretty much done half an hour ago, driving himself too hard, but I figure that's okay. Sometimes physical pain can drown out psychological pain.

I turn my attention to Carmi. "How's school?"

She sticks a finger in her mouth and gags. "I hate school. It's boring."

I glance at Sully, whose eyes roll skyward. Maybe that wasn't the right question to ask.

"Where's Sloane?" Carmi looks around, trying to peek inside.

"Sloane? I don't know."

"Dad, I thought you said she was here," she directs at her father.

"That's what I assumed when she came by the ranch to borrow the ATV. You haven't seen her?"

The last is aimed at me.

"Not since last night."

Another night that ended with both of us at least partly naked, and Sloane sneaking back home so she could wake up with Aspen. But I'm not about to share that.

"Odd. She was supposed to be over for an early dinner with Isobel and the baby. They got there twenty minutes ago, and my sister says she can't get a hold of Sloane. So, I thought maybe Sloane got hung up here and her phone ran out of juice or something."

I'm officially tweaked, but I keep a straight face, mostly for Carmi's sake.

"She's not been here. Are you sure she came this way?"

"Yeah, I saw her head down the trail here."

Except there's a fork in the trail and if you hang right, you end up here, but if you turn left, it takes you straight to the shallow part where we crossed the river on horseback. It should still be shallow enough to do so by ATV.

"You figure she's gone back up the trail?" Sully asks.

"It's the only thing I can think of," I reply. "What time did she leave?"

Sully consults his watch. "Just after lunch, I think it was about two?"

It's four twenty now.

"Could be work-related," I suggest, despite the burning in my gut that tells me differently.

Sully nods and is already grabbing for his phone.

"I'll check with Ewing."

"In the meantime, I'm gonna go grab Will and have a look up there."

"Pick up a two-way. I'm gonna walk Carmi home and be right behind you."

Yeah, I'm not the only one worried.

Twenty-Seven

SLOANE

I glance at my cell phone.

Shit.

Maybe I should've thought this through more, but I was so eager to do something productive. I feel like a kid caught with their hand in the cookie jar.

After talking to Sheriff Ewing earlier, I was leaving the office to grab a coffee across the street and figure out who to hit up for a ride, when I bumped into JD in the parking lot. He'd been at the motor vehicle department next door renewing his license and offered to drive me back to the ranch.

JD doesn't talk a whole lot, so I had a chance to mull over this case. I was worried we weren't peeling away the layers of this case quickly enough. Sometimes the wheels of justice turn too slowly, and although this task force has a broader reach, it also needs to run through proper channels, losing some of the urgency. It could give our subject a chance to cover his tracks or—God forbid—reoffend.

Finding out Michael Cedric has basically been off the grid for ten months or more was unexpected, but discovering those prints don't belong to him really threw a wrench into the investigation.

Two perps? Or had we been barking up the wrong tree with Cedric? Did this mean we needed to start over?

No. Cedric had to be involved somehow. He owned the truck and inherited the cabin near the dumping ground. That could not have been a coincidence.

So when we got back to the ranch, I popped in to see my little girl, had a quick bite for lunch, and then went to see if I could borrow one of the ATVs.

My plan had been to head back up the trail and get a firsthand look at that cabin to see if there is any sign someone had been staying there recently. Just a little peek in the windows, see if there are any unlocked doors. I wasn't going to enter but maybe I could poke my head inside, and if I'd seen something of interest, I could've perhaps sped up a search warrant for the place, since that's in the FBI's hands now.

The river crossing was a piece of cake, I only got a little wet, and the trail has been easy so far. I stopped near where Dan and Wolff pulled me from the gorge and—using a big stick I found for better balance—walked to the rock edge above where Emo found the remains.

There wasn't anything left to see down below, except for trampled ferns. All the pale bones gone, and for a moment I just stood there in respect to the poor souls whose lives ended up at the bottom of the gorge.

I was about to turn around when my phone started vibrating in my pocket, almost making me jump.

Special Agent in Charge Bellinger's number is displayed on my screen.

"Special Agent Bellinger, word of warning," I start off. "Reception may be spotty where I am."

"Detective Eckhart, I'm not sure what happened, ... an issue with the files you sent me."

"An issue?" I parrot.

"As in, ... are glitches in the security feeds around the time markers you .... A section of six minutes in total is missing ... three videos provided."

"What? How is that even possible?"

"I was hoping ... able to tell me." He sounds none too pleased.

"Sir, I have no idea. I even made sure to send you the Google Drive link to the original files instead of the ones I downloaded to my computer to review."

"Did ... download them ... last Wednesday?"

The wind is starting to pick up which seems to make reception even worse.

"On Tuesday, actually."

"And those downloaded ... the only ones you reviewed?"

"Yes, sir. Why?"

"Because it ... Drive ... accessed last ... morning ..."

Abruptly, the line goes dead.

I try to reconnect, but notice where I had a single bar before, I now have none.

It's a short walk back to the ATV, where I check my phone again. *Nothing.* I can turn back, but I'm probably more than halfway to the cabin already. I really don't want this to be a wasted trip.

I just wish I could give the sheriff a heads-up, but I've heard sometimes text messages make it out when you have spotty reception, so I quickly type one out to my boss.

. . .

Call Bellinger: Exxon security video tampered with?
Who all had access?
I'm checking the cabin, spotty reception here, will call when
I can.

Then I sit down on the ATV with my walking stick between my legs, fire up the engine, and continue on up the mountain. I may need that walking stick because these machines make a lot of noise, and I'd prefer not to advertise my approach should someone be there. Wolff showed me where it is on the map, and I know there's a narrow path off the trail that takes you to the cabin. I figure I can find some place to hide the ATV from sight, and move in on foot.

The whole way up there I replay the conversation with the SAC. Was he saying someone accessed the files Wednesday morning? He must have, because there was obviously nothing missing from the files I downloaded.

Who *did* have access to that folder? Ewing, obviously, and whoever sent it to him in the first place. I remember him mentioning he'd ask one of the guys to have a look at the tapes, but I don't even know if he got around to it. Things have been rather hectic this past week.

I almost end up driving past the cutoff to the cabin on my left. The path is narrower than the trail, but would still fit the ATV if I wanted to drive it all the way up. Instead, I roll the vehicle off the trail and into some underbrush a few hundred feet farther down. Then I grab the walking stick and start to backtrack.

It's not until I'm only a few feet from the pathway, I

notice tire tracks in the looser sand on this side of the trail. They appear to turn onto the path. Someone seems to have come up the trail from the other side of the loop. They may actually be there right now.

I stop and pull my phone out to check how many bars. I have none, but I must've hit a pocket with some reception at some point, because my text to Junior seems to have gone through. I quickly type out an update.

Instead of walking up the smaller trail, I duck into the trees. At least they give me some coverage. I check my belt for my sidearm on my hip and the small of my back for handcuffs. At this point, all I want to do is confirm someone is there and wait for others to arrive, but I won't hesitate to stop them if they try to leave.

I don't see an ATV, but from what I can see from my vantage point in the trees, the cabin itself is pretty basic, a front door with a small window on either side. It's nestled in the trees, which is good for me, because it gives me cover while I check out the sides and the back to see if anything is parked back there. It'll also give me a chance to check for possible additional access or exit points. My goal is to gather information so when backup arrives—I hope—we can draw up a plan of attack.

The going is tough with that damn walking boot hampering me, and I'm tempted to take it off, but I don't think that's gonna get me far. Instead, I do my best to keep cover as I circle the cabin.

No vehicles, and only two small windows at the back. No door, which means only one way in or out, since those windows wouldn't be big enough for someone to get through.

Encouraged by the fact whatever ATV made those

tracks coming up here appears to be long gone, I approach the rear of the cabin, hoping to get a glimpse inside.

The window is caked with dirt and I use a tissue I had wadded in my pocket and some spit to clean a tiny corner, enough for me to see through.

The inside looks like one open space, no doors, no plumbing, just what appears to be a chemical toilet in one corner and several jugs of what I assume is water, lined up against the far wall. There's a kitchen chair with its back underneath one of the front windows, and there appears to be an animal hide of some sort on the floor.

I move to the next window, giving a small patch a quick clean before I bring my eye close to it. I have a slightly different perspective from this angle and just catch the corner of a mattress which must be butting up against this wall.

As fast as I can manage, I round the cabin to the front to see if I can get a peek into one of the front windows. These ones seem to have been cleaned a bit more recently than the ones in the back. I peek over the windowsill and almost have a heart attack when I hear a scream from inside.

The hair on the back of my neck stands on end, as I process what I'm looking at.

A woman, huddled on the mattress in a corner of the room, shackled to the wall, mouth wide open as she screams. It's not until she finally quiets and stares straight at me, I recognize her face.

Shelby Vandermeer.

My brain is trying to grapple with the fact a woman I saw just a few hours ago, at her parents' store, is now held captive inside a cabin on the mountain. She's even wearing the same clothes she had on earlier.

While I'm still trying to process, my body is already in motion, moving toward the door, only to find it locked.

It's a very basic mechanism; a hinged metal plate that slips over a ring through which a padlock is hooked. A good kick might do the trick, but I don't think my ankle would survive. I put my shoulder into it but that doesn't do much good, and the last thing I need is a bum shoulder to go with my ankle.

I scan my surroundings for anything I could use, pick up a brick-sized rock, and slam it on the lock. It likely won't do much for the padlock, but I might be able to loosen the metal bracket from the wood it's screwed into.

A series of well-aimed whacks, and I notice the door having a bit more give. I put my shoulder in again, and then once more, when I hear the wood splinter as the ends of the screws break away from the post. Picking up the walking stick I dropped, I push open the door and walk inside.

"Are you okay?" is my first question as I crouch down beside Shelby.

Her blouse is ripped open, exposing a lacy shelf bra supporting ample breasts. She's shaking and clearly terrified, eyeing the open door behind me. Any edge she had this morning at the feedstore is long gone.

"He'll be back," she sobs.

If someone is coming back, I realize they'd be able to tell something was wrong from a distance with the door open. If it's the same person who shot at me, they have a rifle and could shoot up this place and us in it without coming close enough for me to stand a chance with my gun.

I get up and close the door. He'll have to come close enough to see the broken hinge. It'll give me a fighting chance.

Unless I can get us out of here first, but looking at those

heavy metal chains bolted into the wooden beams, I'm not so sure. Those are bolts, not like the wood screws holding the door lock together. The cuffs on her wrist are not standard handcuffs but look like something from the Middle Ages; rusted, with a wider metal band and an actual keyhole.

"Who is coming back?" I ask her as I crouch back down.

I notice dried blood on the side of her neck and follow it up past her ear and into her hairline. A knock on her head? She does seem out of it, could be with fear, could also be a head injury of some kind.

"Shelby?" I prompt her. "Who is coming back?"

"He thought I told you, but I never told," she suddenly rattles, grabbing my hand so tight I'm afraid she'll snap my fingers. "*Don't tell on family*, and I never did, but he didn't believe me. He's going to kill me…" Her eyes, wide and terrified, turn on me. "You too."

"No one is going to kill us," I assure her. "I'm going to get us out of here."

Family? Is she talking about Cedric or someone else?

Her father?

As soon as the thought enters my mind, I shake it off. I can't imagine her father doing something like this. Then again, I would never have thought my own father would almost kill my mother and then himself.

At this point it doesn't matter, all that matters is getting us safely out of here.

I check the cuffs again. If I had a piece of metal wire, I might be able to jiggle the old lock, but I don't carry paperclips on me, and my hair's too short for pins.

I look around the cabin, checking to see if there's anything I might be able to use, but there's nothing that would serve the purpose.

For once I wish I was partial to underwire bras, but I

hate the way those cut into my chest. I turn to look back at Shelby, huddled on the mattress, her blouse gaping open.

"Hey, Shelby?" I sit on my knees in front of her. "I need to get you out of these cuffs, but I'm going to need the underwire in your bra to do it."

My initial thought is my request caused the panic in her face, but then I hear it...

The sound of an engine approaching.

"It's him," she whispers.

Her eyes are wild as she turns to me.

"My cousin."

Twenty-Eight

DAN

"What are you doing?"

I look over my shoulder at Wolff, who catches up with me just as I'm starting up the trail.

"Coming with you."

His tone is matter-of-fact, as if following me on what could be a wild-goose chase is not even a question.

I bumped into him in the barn when I was saddling Will, and I mentioned I was heading up the mountain to see if I could find Sloane. I guess he finished what he was doing, grabbed his horse, Judge, and decided to come after me.

"She may not even be up here," I point out.

"Oh, she's up here," Wolff counters, pointing at the fresh ATV tracks on the trail. "Although why she'd come up by herself, I don't know."

"Doing her job, would be my guess." I dart him a sharp glance, feeling suddenly protective, even though I had those same thoughts myself earlier. "She doesn't have the luxury of a team, like we do. Or even a partner," I point out.

Wolff throws me an amused glance as he calls my bluff. "Is that your party line, or is it how you really feel?"

I don't bother answering, we both know I'm not happy she's up here on her own, or I wouldn't be going after her, knowing it'll piss her off.

It's not until we pass near the spot where we found the rifle shells, Wolff breaks the silence.

"Looks like she may have pulled off here."

He's just pointing out some flattened vegetation on the side of the path when my radio crackles to life.

"Sully here. Dan, come in."

"Dan here, what's up?"

"Sheriff Ewing showed up at the ranch, looking for Sloane. Do you have eyes on her?"

"Negative. Not yet."

"Dan..." Junior Ewing's voice replaces Sully's. *"I need you to get to her...we're on our way, but you're closer. New information has come to light she is not aware of that could put her in a lot of danger."*

Then he proceeds to explain the kind of danger he thinks she is in, and my blood runs cold in my veins.

"On it," I bark as I give Will my heels.

Wolff—having heard every word—is right on my tail as we urge our horses to hotfoot it up the trail.

I'm fucking terrified out of my mind for her.

There's no way she would've seen this coming.

~

Sloane
Forty-five minutes earlier

304

. . .

"Cousin?"

I'm already getting to my feet and my hand is reaching for my weapon.

"He's going to kill us," she whispers, her eyes fixed on the door.

Her body is shaking so hard, the chains she's shackled with rattle. She's petrified and I don't think she can even hear me.

Outside the sound of and engine abruptly dies, and I try to listen for other sounds. Anything to indicate someone might be approaching, but I can't pick up anything.

Well, I'm not about to twiddle my thumbs here, waiting for whoever is out there to dictate what happens next. Determined to take charge of the situation right off the bat, I crouch down and ease to the front of the cabin. There, I squeeze myself in the corner by the window to the right of the door, so I have some cover when he opens the door coming in. I hold my gun in front of me as I try to peer outside without being seen.

An ATV is parked outside, but I don't see anyone. No one seems to be out front. I shift to the other side of the window, trying to get a better look toward the side of the house, when I catch a flash of a familiar uniform rounding the corner of the cabin.

I blow out a big breath of relief. *Backup*.

Swinging around, I focus on Shelby.

"It's okay, the cavalry arrived. Sit tight, we'll get you out of here," I assure her before tucking my gun in its holster and reaching for the door.

Pulling it open I step outside and swing toward the deputy I'd seen coming around the corner.

"Glad to see you here. Do you have a toolbox on your quad? I've got Shelby Vandermeer held captive inside, and I need something to get her out of those shackles."

"Shackles? Show me," Jason says, following closely as I start leading the way inside.

I aim a reassuring smile at Shelby when I walk in the door, but she's not looking at me.

She's looking straight over my shoulder, her face a picture of sheer terror.

There's an instant flashback to this morning, when Shelby and I were in the feedstore talking, and I caught her glancing over my shoulder with a weird expression on her face.

Jason had been behind me then too, sitting in his cruiser outside.

Jason?

He'd been at the end of his shift, offered to drive me to the feedstore. He even mentioned heading straight home when he dropped me off at the sheriff's office.

So what is he doing here?

Not understanding, I turn my head to look over my shoulder, when I catch sight of something swinging toward me.

Then my world goes dark.

Dan

"Do you smell smoke?"

I slow Will down and sniff a few times.

Fuck.

306

He's right. I can smell it, but I can't see anything.

August and September are the worst months for wild-fires here, especially the past couple of years. But something tells me this is no wildfire.

"How much farther?"

"The cutoff to the cabin is up there past that next bend," Wolff provides. "We can't come storming up though. We have to approach with caution. Stay behind me."

I reluctantly hold Will back to fall in line behind Judge. It's costing me, not forging ahead, but Wolff has training for this kind of stuff. He leads the way off the trail, cutting a diagonal path through the trees in the approximate direction of the cabin.

The smell of smoke is definitely thicker here, but as I'm about to mention that, I hear the sound of an engine firing up. For a moment Wolff appears to hesitate. Then he urges his horse forward, no longer worried about approaching with caution.

I have to duck out of the way of low-hanging branches whipping at me, and one too-close pass by a tree trunk almost takes out my left knee. But, I'm still in the saddle when our horses burst out of the trees just as an ATV whips past, speeding away from the cabin.

One look to my left and my heart lodges in my throat. A small structure in a clearing at the top of the trail appears to be fully engulfed in flames, and I swear I can hear a woman screaming.

Fuck the guy on the ATV. My gut tells me Sloane is in trouble up there.

By the time I bring Will to a sliding halt, I've already noticed the roof of the cabin isn't quite engulfed, but tall flames are shooting up along the entire front of the structure. Including the front door. My guess is an accelerant was used.

Fire tends to be loud, but it still doesn't drown out the frantic screams coming from inside. I dive into my saddle-bags and dig up my folding axe before leaping off Will's back. The axe is the only tool I could think of that might be useful. Unfortunately, I can't even get close enough to the front door to reach it.

Growing frantic, I start running around the side, hoping for a window or another door I can get in.

"Dan! Give me a hand!"

I whip my head around and see Wolff trying to drag a dead tree across the clearing. I immediately rush to help him. I have a good idea what he has in mind. Between the two of us, we're able to lift the tree and run with it toward the cabin.

It only takes two hits before the door swings in. I don't hesitate and drop the tree, rushing through the opening, even as I pull my shirt over my mouth as makeshift protection for the smoke. The heat of the flames singes the hair on my body.

My eyes are watering from the smoke as I try to take in the scene before me.

The flames seem to be contained to the front and halfway down the sides of the cabin and leaking across the ceiling. The fire hasn't gotten to the back wall yet, where I see two figures huddled together on a mattress on the floor.

I have no trouble recognizing Sloane, her walking boot gives her away, and I immediately reach for her. The only thing on my mind is getting her out of here before the ceiling comes down on us. But as I grab for her arm, she shakes me off.

"Help me," she forces out in a raw voice.

It's only then I pay attention to the second figure. It takes me a moment to recognize the screaming, half-naked woman is Shelby. She's cuffed to a length of rusty chain hooked into the wall. Sloane is desperately trying to work the lock on the iron cuffs around Shelby's wrists with a length of wire, while the other woman appears to be fighting her all the way.

I grab the fold-up axe I hooked on my belt and push Shelby closer to Sloane.

"Hold her still," I bark, lifting the axe.

I aim where the chain hooks onto the bracket on the wall, hoping there's a weakness in one of the links. But before I can swing, the axe is plucked from my hand

"Take Sloane out, I've got her," Wolff orders me.

I don't hesitate and pull Sloane up off the floor. Then I wrap one arm around her waist, and with my other hand force her head in my neck as I half-drag her with me.

The flames have almost blocked the entire doorway and all I can do is hold my breath as I leap through. I don't stop moving until I no longer feel the heat and sink down on my knees on the ground, still clinging on to Sloane. When I look over my shoulder, I just see Wolff jumping clear of the fire, carrying Shelby.

"You're okay," I rasp against Sloane's singed hair. "You're both okay."

Then I release the back of her head and notice my hand is covered in blood.

Twenty-Nine

SLOANE

"It's a scratch."

Wolff grins and shakes his head at my challenge, but I'm clearly pissing off Dan.

"It's a gash," he returns sharply.

I roll my eyes.

"Not anymore," I remind him. "The stitches fixed it. Now, if you don't mind, I have a visit to make."

I've been lucky, I know that. Things could've been a hell of a lot worse than fourteen stitches on my scalp, a concussion, and some smoke inhalation. The baton he apparently hit me with could've easily cracked my skull, but it turns out, I have a hard head.

What is more painful than anything else is the feeling of betrayal. Of all my new colleagues, he was the one I felt most closely connected to. That I could've misjudged him so put a serious dent in my confidence.

Jason Heany had been apprehended right there on the trail.

Sheriff Ewing had the foresight to put together two teams, each comprised of sheriff's deputies and several High Mountain Trackers, and sending them up the trail in both directions of the loop. Ironically, the person who ultimately placed him in handcuffs, was none other than Deputy Frank Schmidt. Which only goes to show my judgment of character is off.

Schmidt was the deputy Sheriff Ewing had tasked with reviewing the Exxon security tapes, but when confronted, he admitted he'd passed on the job to Jason Heany when he offered to do it. When Junior heard that, he accessed the deputy's personnel file and pulled Jason's mandatory employee fingerprints. Those turned out to match the ones taken from the bullet shell and paint can.

While we were all packed off to the hospital with varying injuries, the FBI, led by SAC Bellinger, arrived in town to take over. We weren't here long before Wolff, Dan, and I were separately interviewed by the feds but, apparently, they haven't been able to get Shelby to talk. She is somewhere else in the hospital being treated and, as Bellinger was just here to explain, is in a state and unwilling to talk to anyone other than me.

The agent came in to request I talk to her. He hopes it will give us a better idea how the individual pieces fit together into a bigger picture. My, "Hell yes," to the request did not go over well with Dan. His protective instincts have gone into overdrive, and even though part of me loves him for it, even understands it, I'm not about to sit the conclusion of what started as *my* investigation out on the sidelines.

"Fine," he grumbles. "But I'm sticking close."

He lifts his hand to stop me when I start to object. "Out of sight, but close," he insists.

I nod, letting him have that one. I'm sure this afternoon's events were traumatizing for him as well. Also, if not for Dan's protective tendencies, I recognize I likely would not have survived that fire.

I'm not sure how long I'd been out for when Shelby's frantic screams penetrated. I was disoriented at first, the cabin had already been filling with smoke and I could feel the heat of the flames on my skin, but reality set in fast enough. I had to fight my instincts to get the hell out of there, because there was no way I could even contemplate leaving Shelby behind.

She'd been incoherent with fear and given our very precarious situation, I didn't waste time coaxing her out of her bra gently. I needed my hands on those wires if I had any chance of getting her, and therefore myself, out of there alive.

Truth be told, I'd already been losing hope by the time I heard a loud bang behind me. When we were getting sprayed with embers, I was convinced the roof had started caving in. Next thing I knew, I was being dragged through a wall of flames by Dan, who'd come sweeping in like some fictional action hero.

So, I let him push me, in the wheelchair he insisted on, to Shelby's hospital room. A curtain is partly pulled around her bed, which is not visible from the door. I can see why when I spot SAC Bellinger already in the room, but out of sight of the bed. He presses his index finger to his lips. I nod at him as I roll myself around to the other side of the bed.

Shelby has her eyes closed, and only now do I notice the bruising around her eyes and the dark marks around her neck. When I touch her hand, she startles awake. As soon as she sees me her eyes fill with tears.

"Thank you," are the first words from her mouth. "You stayed."

"Technically, I think those thanks belong to Lucas Wolff and Dan, because I wasn't having a whole hell of a lot of luck getting you out."

At the mention of Dan's name, I notice her wince.

"When we were young, he always protected me," she starts, and for a moment I'm not sure if she's talking about Dan or Jason. "I'd get teased in school, and he would take care of the bullies, like an older brother might. His mom and mine are close, they're sisters, so he was a constant presence growing up."

Yeah, that has to be Jason.

She sniffles and I hand her a box of tissues from the nightstand. I choose not to say anything and risk disrupting her flow. As it turns out, she doesn't need my prompting, since she continues after she blows her nose.

"He's the one who actually introduced Michael and me. It was at a baseball game I went to see. Both of them played in the same league, just on opposing teams."

I let her talk through the years of her marriage, understanding that for her it's probably all part of the same story. However, my interest is piqued when she explains how he started spending stretches of time away from home—indicating she had no idea where he was—and when he'd return, he'd become increasingly violent with her.

"My parents never knew, but when I showed up at home that last time he put his hands on me, after our divorce was finalized, Jason was there. He told me he'd make sure no one would ever hurt me again." She shakes her head as she stares past me out the window. "I swear I didn't ask him to, but I think he may have done something to Michael."

I finally break my silence, wanting more information from her.

"Do you know if Jason was one of those hunting buddies of Michael you told me about before?"

I get a quick flash of her eyes. "As far as I know, Jason was the only one."

The way she avoids looking at me directly for long, I have to wonder whether she may have had some inkling her cousin and her ex-husband were engaged in some questionable things. I have a good sense she wouldn't admit it if she did.

"How did you end up at the cabin?" I ask instead.

"Jason came back to the store after he saw me talking to you. He told me if I didn't come with him, he could make it look like my father spray-painted Dan's house and would make sure he'd end up in prison."

"But that wouldn't have been true, would it?" I prompt her.

She shakes her head. "No, Jason did that..." She leaves a big pause before adding, "At my request."

A nurse walks in, wheeling a medical cart.

"I'm sorry, I just need to take your vitals," she addresses Shelby. "And then I really need you to get some rest," she adds.

She doesn't look at me but I know the last comment was meant for me.

"I will leave you to it," I announce, wheeling my chair back to make room for the nurse. "We'll be in touch."

"Sloane?" she calls as I'm heading for the door.

"Yes?"

"Can you tell Dan I'm really sorry?"

~

Dan

It's past four in the morning when I park the truck next to my cabin.

Wolff and I had been good to go hours ago, but Sloane was still waiting on the outcome of a few tests before they were comfortable letting her go. She was none too happy about the delay and when it was suggested she simply spend the night, she threatened to leave against medical advice.

Sully and Jonas had shown up at the hospital to check on us and brought my truck so we'd have wheels home. They ended up giving Wolff a ride home while I stayed behind with Sloane.

I'm not sure if she is in pain, tired, or what is going on, but she's grown very quiet these past few hours since she had a hissy fit over spending the night at the hospital. She almost seems flat, with little reaction to what is happening around her.

Even now, she's sitting in the passenger seat of my truck, engine off, just staring out the windshield.

"Can I make a suggestion?"

She turns her head to me, and looks like she only now realizes where she is. But at least I have her attention.

"Sorry?"

"Rather than waking up Aspen and your mom now, why don't you come with me? I can help you shower off some of that grime without getting those stitches wet. We can sleep for a few hours and then you can head home a bit more refreshed."

I know they said no shower for twenty-four hours but,

surely, they don't expect her to walk around covered in dirt and soot, reeking like the inside of a chimney until tonight. I can use the handheld shower to keep the water away from the cut, which is at the hairline behind her right ear.

"Okay."

Another flatly delivered response, which is so out of character for Sloane, who generally is highly animated and fully engaged. I get the sense something more than pain or fatigue is brewing.

"Sit tight, I'll come get you."

Once inside the cabin, I lead her straight to the bathroom. I turn on the water as she strips down. Then I help her in the tub, getting her to sit on the edge to keep the weight off her ankle. I manage to avoid getting the stitches wet by having her lean forward as I do my best to wash the smoke out of most of her hair.

There's little to no conversation from either of us during her brief shower or after, when I wrap a big towel around her and help her out of the tub. I guess this very long day is getting to me too.

In the bedroom, I hand her one of my T-shirts and flip back the cover on the bed.

"I'm just gonna throw our clothes in the washer and grab a quick shower myself."

Ten minutes later, feeling much better, I'm surprised to find Sloane still up, watching me as I walk into the bedroom.

The moment I crawl under the covers she turns to me, putting her head on my shoulder and her hand in the middle of my chest.

"I've been thinking..."

I cover her hand with mine. "I was wondering what was

going on in your head." Then I press a kiss to her hair. "Talk to me."

"I'm no better than Jeff."

"What?" I shift on my side so I can look at her. "What are you talking about?"

"I've been so focused on my job, so eager to get this case resolved, I didn't even think twice about Aspen, I just went up that mountain."

"I call bullshit," I counter. "You didn't abandon your daughter for a bunch of lofty dreams. You left your child in the capable hands of your mother while you went out to do the very important job of trying to make sure no more young girls end up like Nita or even Chelsea."

"But I risked my life. I wasn't thinking about my daughter when I chose to stay in a burning building with a virtual stranger to try and get her free. If something had happened to me—"

"But it didn't," I interrupt, squeezing her hand in mine. "You're right here."

That's when she turns those big blue eyes on me, swimming with tears.

"I wouldn't have made it out if you hadn't shown up, and we both know it."

I bring her hand to my lips. I haven't allowed myself to think about what might've happened, but I'm thinking about it now. Overwhelmed with it, actually.

My voice is hoarse, and not from the smoke, when I tell her, "We make a good team," and gather her in my arms.

"I want to be a good mother."

"You already are," I mumble into her hair.

"I'm thinking maybe I should quit my job," she throws out there.

I scoot back so I can look her in the eye.

318

"Wanna know what I think? I think you...make that *we*...have had an extremely fucked-up day, and we definitely should not be making any decisions or binding declarations until we've had at least a couple of normal days, and definitely a few solid nights."

Bending down, I press a soft kiss to her lips.

"With perhaps one exception," I add.

Then I take a deep breath before finally voicing what I should've told her eight years ago.

"I love you, Sloane Eckhart."

Thirty

SLOANE

"Aren't you clever. Look at you."

Aspen proudly rolls over and reaches for her favorite toy. Of course, that toy is immediately shoved into her mouth, where everything goes these days. She seems mighty pleased with herself as she smiles wide.

"She's as determined as her mother."

I glance over at Thomas, who is beaming a smile at my daughter. He is totally enamored with her, and given he never experienced the joys of grandchildren, I'm more than happy to have him claim standing as her great-grandfather. Aspen is going to grow up with a big family.

We're sitting out on the porch of the big house, enjoying a beautiful fall afternoon, and watching Alex working with a fearful horse in the corral. Her ability to communicate with these animals is something to behold.

Mom is inside with Ama, hanging out in the kitchen, and probably talking about me. It's been a little over a week since she got here and—even though she hasn't brought it up with me—I'm guessing she's struggling to figure out what to do. She has a flight back home to Panama and Steve on Sunday, which is only four days away.

I know she's worried about me in a variety of ways. Two weeks ago that would've annoyed, even upset me. As I sit here today, I understand, because I have some concerns myself.

What happened up on that mountain has given me cause for a lot of thought. My first response had been reactive and I'm grateful to Dan for talking me down off that ledge, but even five days later, I still believe perhaps this job is not the right one for me. At least not while Aspen is this young.

"I can hear the wheels turning from here," Thomas observes. "I'll be sittin' in this chair until Ama tells me dinner is ready anyway, so you might as well talk to me."

I hide my grin. I've always liked Jonas's father, who is a straight shooter.

"Not even sure where to start. I came here about a month ago now, aiming to get my life together, and I'm not sure I've accomplished much of anything."

"You mean, other than catch a serial killer?" the old man interrupts.

I open my mouth to point out that was at the very least a joint effort, but decide against it. His point is still valid.

"I guess there's that," I give him. "But the question is; should I even be trying to catch dangerous criminals if I don't even have something as basic as a house or childcare organized for my daughter?"

I turn to look at Aspen, who still seems happy enough on her play blanket with her toys.

"If I hadn't been told to stay home until I'm completely

cleared by the doctor, and would've missed her reaching for and grabbing that toy just now. I recently missed her rolling over for the first time and don't want to miss these milestones in her life. I don't want to have to make choices that don't have her as a priority, and these past few weeks have shown that's exactly what this job would require. But I can't just quit my job."

As much as I've mulled this over in the past few days, I feel I've not really gained any clarity. Dan has patiently listened, encouraging me to take my time to figure things out, but he hasn't really given me much feedback, claiming it's a decision I have to come to myself.

"Hmmm." Thomas rocks his chair and rubs his chin. "Why can't you?"

"Quit my job? Because it's a great job, and I need an income."

He nods. "Fair enough, but as I understand it, the sheriff's department now has a position for a deputy they need to fill. Predictable shift hours so you can schedule care for the little one in advance. Maybe not the job you want, but a job you can handle right now. Doesn't seem that complicated."

Back to being a deputy?

I give a mental shrug. Why not?

It might've felt like giving up my dream not that long ago, but it's amazing how quickly perceptions can change. The idea actually lifts a huge burden off my chest.

I turn my head at the sound of voices and catch Dan chatting with Alex outside the barn, but his eyes are fixed on me.

"That boy loves you," Thomas states behind me.

"I know. The feeling is mutual."

"Right, then you know neither you nor that little one of

yours ever has to worry about a roof over your heads or food on the table."

We make a good team. It's what he said to me the morning we got home from the hospital, right before he told me he loved me.

Apparently, it's that simple for these men; you take care of what and who you love.

The old man is right, it's not that complicated, I just need to tackle things one at a time.

When I see Dan start coming this way, I get to my feet and turn to Thomas, bending over to kiss his cheek.

"Thank you."

Thomas clears his throat as he waves me off.

Grinning, I crouch down to pick Aspen up off the floor and prop her on my hip, just as Dan comes up the porch steps.

He doesn't even hesitate, hooks me behind the neck and lays a heavy one on me. After he lets me up for air, he reaches for Aspen, who greets him with a gummy smile. He props her on his arm and blows a raspberry in her neck.

"What's the smile for?" he asks.

"I'm having a good day."

He grins back at me. "Yeah?"

"Yeah. Can you keep an eye on her while I make a few phone calls?"

A few minutes later, I sit down on the couch in my cabin, and dial the number I ended up saving in my phone.

"Did you change your mind?"

The smug tone of Jeff's voice annoys me, and it's tempting to tell him to go fuck himself, but that won't do anyone any good. He can be an asshole all by himself.

Two days ago, Dan handed me a piece of paper with the name and number of a lawyer in Billings. Courtesy of his sister Lindsey and her mother, who provided the contact. According to Dan, the lawyer was waiting for my call, which I will follow up with as soon as I get Jeff's agreement.

"As a matter of fact, I did," I tell him. "I will pay you five thousand dollars..." I can hear him whoop it up, but keep talking right over him. "...on one condition; you give up your parental rights to Aspen."

"Sorry, what?"

"You will be contacted by a lawyer in Billings in the next few days, who will have five thousand dollars and a document for you to sign. Once you place your signature, you will receive the money. And once that's done, Jeff, I want you to lose my number."

Ending that call feels pretty damn satisfying.

Next, I call the law office and set up a Zoom appointment for tomorrow morning to get the paperwork in order and transfer the money. My savings account is going to take a serious hit, leaving me little cushion, but I'll build again. Or *we* will.

My final call is to Junior Ewing.

"I was about to call you," he starts. "How are you doing?"

"I'm good."

"You home?"

"Yes, why?"

"Because I'm pulling up to the ranch now."

Not much later I'm sitting on the porch of the ranch house again, this time joined by Jonas and a few of the guys, listening to the sheriff giving us an update on the case. Aspen is on my lap with a bite ring in her mouth, still working on those bottom two teeth to come through.

"What are the fucking odds two sick bastards with the same violently perverse fantasies randomly meet doing something innocuous like playing baseball?" JD, who is leaning against one of the posts, questions.

"You'd be surprised. Maybe not playing baseball, but you have online interest groups for everything and anything under the sun. Many individuals don't get further than fantasies, but put them in a group of like-minded perverts, and suddenly they feel powerful enough to act out on those fantasies," Wolff supplies.

Ewing nods in agreement. "With Heany and Cedric, they each had a certain role to play. Even though it appears Heany was the brains of the operation, Cedric was the muscle responsible for kidnapping the girls. From what I understand, Cedric got off on the physical abuse of those girls, but for Heany the psychological torture was what motivated him. The control game. By his own admission, he never quite felt the same satisfaction after he'd killed Michael."

"Did he ever explain why he killed him?" I probe, as Aspen starts to chew on my knuckle.

"His cousin. Shelby Vandermeer," the sheriff states. "She was his obsession. He couldn't have her, so he introduced her to Michael."

"That way he could still control her," I conclude. "So when he discovered Michael had been abusing her without his knowledge, it would've been the worst kind of betrayal."

"Right. He could not handle the loss of control."

A shiver runs down my spine when I think about how this all could've ended much differently.

When Ewing gets to his feet a few minutes later, I stand as well.

"Before you go, do you have a minute for me?"

"Sure."

"I've got her," Dan offers, plucking Aspen from my arms as he gives me an encouraging nod.

I haven't had a chance to tell him what I've decided yet, but he makes it clear he'll support whatever that might be.

I send him a grateful smile before following the sheriff down the steps.

~

Dan

"People are fucked up, man."

Once again, I'm sitting on my new porch with Jackson, sipping a beer and downloading as we watch the sun go down.

Sloane is spending some time with her mother tonight, which she hasn't done a whole lot of since Isobel got here. Her mother has decided to stick to her original plan to head back to Panama in four days. She indicated as much over dinner, citing she'd rather come back again in two months with her husband to celebrate Thanksgiving here.

It'll be a big family gathering, too big for my dad's place in Kalispell, but I'm thinking if I push hard we could do it right here.

I've just finished relaying what the sheriff's visit revealed this afternoon, and Jackson reacts as expected.

"It never ceases to amaze me, the messed-up shit people do to each other," he adds. "The dark crap we carry around inside, hidden from those around us. It's ugly."

I'm not sure at this point if we're still talking about what happened here or whether he is referring to something I'm not privy to. But when I shoot him an inquiring look, he shakes his head. It's my warning not to pursue, which I honor.

Instead, I steer the conversation to construction progress.

"How much longer do you figure before we can start putting up some drywall and insulation?"

"Plumbing is done for now, HVAC will be by the end of this week, and the electrician said he'll need another five or six days to finalize the rough-ins. We should be able to follow behind room by room. In a hurry?" he asks.

I tell him about the plans for Thanksgiving.

"Lucky bastard. You go from a bachelor's existence with no family to a fucking instant houseful, including a woman and a baby."

I bend my head, grinning, as I pluck at the label on my beer bottle.

"Yeah, well...trust me, I never thought I'd be that guy."

"You did once," he reminds me.

"I know, and then I gave up on that dream."

Jackson shakes his head. "Like I said, lucky bastard."

We sit in silence as the sinking sun turns the sky a deep orange. A light rustle to the left draws my attention and I see the beautiful bull elk make an appearance. I can't really be sure it's the same one I've seen before or not, but I'd like to think it is.

"*Look*," I alert Jackson on a whisper.

"I've seen him before, this time of night," Jackson shares. "He likes to snack on that patch of grass along the riverbank."

Sure enough, he bends his neck, lowering his large rack of antlers as he starts munching away. We watch for a while, until all of a sudden his head comes up, ears alert. He must've heard something, because the next moment he is gone again.

"I'd forgotten how beautiful it is here."

I turn to Jackson, who is leaning forward, looking out at the darkening mountain range.

"Even living here, I forget sometimes," I admit, before cautiously adding, "Have you thought about staying here permanently?"

"Mom wants me to, and Jonas offered me a spot on the team." He snorts derisively. "Not sure what he thinks I can contribute."

It's on my lips to remind him there is plenty, but I hold back, because I realize it's not so much about what others value in him, but in how he values himself.

Instead, I challenge him.

"Only one way to find out."

"You're an asshole," he mumbles, throwing me a dirty look.

"Water off my back, my friend," I tell him as I get to my feet.

I gather up the empties and drop them in the case we left just inside the house. Jackson follows me down the porch steps to my truck.

"Maybe on the weekend we can sneak off for a short ride," he suggests when I get behind the wheel.

As far as I know, he hasn't yet been back in the saddle, so this feels like a huge step. I hold back on the fist pump though, I'm sure he doesn't want to turn this into a big deal.

"Sure. You can take Will. I'll grab Blitz, he's due for some exercise."

He nods and lifts his hand as he walks over to the motorhome.

I'm grinning when I drive off, feeling pretty damn pleased with myself.

Tonight my friend is showing signs of coming back to life, and Saturday we're hitting the trails, something I wasn't sure we'd ever get to do again.

In addition, I only have four more days to wait before I can either move into Sloane's bed, or have her move into mine. Then two more months to finish up the new place and get us permanently situated and ready to start our life together.

Fuck, I can't wait.

Thirty-One

"Not yet."

My nails dig into his glutes as I try and speed up his movements, but he holds firm to his excruciatingly measured pace. His jaw is clenched, and sweat is dripping down his face with the effort to maintain control.

"You're not human," I accuse him, as he keeps me teetering on the edge of a climax I just know is going to blow my head off.

It feels like it was hours ago he woke me up with his mouth between my legs. The man has fast become an expert at playing my body like a finely tuned instrument. He's at his most playful in the early morning hours, when there is less chance of Aspen waking up, so he can torture me mercilessly.

"Dan, *please*..." I plead.

It's almost painful, every nerve in my body vibrating with a need only he seems able to elicit. But when he slides his hands behind my knees to spread them wider, I know he's reached the edge of his restraint.

Release comes fast and violently, with Dan's face shoved in my neck and his cock planted deep. It feels like I'm having some sort of out-of-body experience, and if not for his weight keeping me anchored to the mattress, I might have levitated off the bed.

"Christ, baby," he pants against my skin. "I don't think I can move."

"Hmm," is all I manage. I'm content lying here, surrounded by Dan, suspended in time.

Lounging in bed is a luxury I haven't had much opportunity for since I returned to work as a sheriff's deputy. Both Dan and I start at seven in the morning, and I drop Aspen off at the wonderful daycare I found for her on the way into town. On the weekends we've been working on the house. So I'm enjoying these few extra mindless moments.

But eventually thoughts of the busy days ahead creep in. They'll be different from the hectic few months behind us to get the house done, or the crazy weekend to get us all moved in. Today is my first of three vacation days leading into the holiday weekend, but I won't have time to relax.

First to arrive today are Mom and Steve. They're renting their own car in Kalispell so won't need a pick up, but I should probably get this house in order. My parents are staying with Sully and Pippa, but I still have to get our house ready for guests. Last night we rolled into bed but there are still plenty of boxes to be unpacked, and I haven't even started on putting together the guest rooms where Dan's family will be staying on Thanksgiving.

I actually suggested that. Since Lindsey and her family are already at Dan's father's place in Kalispell, initially the plan had been for them to head back there after Thanksgiving dinner before they return to Durango again the next day. That way we have a chance to spend some quality time with everyone. We'll have a few days to spend with Mom and Steve before the holiday, and we've already visited with David, Dan's father, a couple of times since he's only an hour or so away. However, I haven't met Lindsey or her family yet, although I've spoken to her on the phone, and I thought it might be nice to get to know them.

"I'm guessing the fun is done?"

Dan nuzzles my neck and presses what feels like a brand-new morning erection against my thigh.

"You're inhuman," I accuse him.

He pushes off me and grins down. His hair is standing every which way and he still has the imprint of his pillow on the side of his face, but his eyes sparkle, his smile is contagious, and he is by far the most beautiful man I've ever known. Inside and out.

I'm about to tell him so when the baby monitor jumps to life with a loud squeal. Our little alarm clock is up and ready for the day.

"I'll get her," Dan volunteers, hopping out of bed.

Another thing that makes him beautiful is the way he adores Aspen as much as he adores me, and is not afraid to show us every day. I want my daughter to grow up knowing she deserves nothing less.

"Hey," I call out when he disappears into the hallway.

He pokes his head back around the corner. "Yeah?"

"You know I love you, right?"

In two steps he bridges the distance to the bed, and I find myself half hauled up in his arms and kissed breathless. When he lifts his head, he has a tiny smirk on his face.

"Yeah, I know. You show me every day, still good to hear the words though."

I immediately make a mental note to get in the habit of telling him more often.

"Somebody's out of patience," he points out.

You definitely don't need the monitor to hear the loud wailing coming from down the hall. As easy and compliant a baby as she was not that long ago, she appears to have run low on patience at seven months old. She lets us know when she wants something, and right now she wants some attention.

Dan kisses the tip of my nose before darting back out of the room.

For the next few minutes, I sit on the edge of the bed, the baby monitor pressed against my ear, a smile on my face, listening to the two of them chat it up.

This is my life now, and I love it.

Dan

"Good to see you."

I try not to show my surprise when I open the door to find Jillian Lederman standing on our porch with a large shopping bag in her hand.

I know Sloane stays in touch with her, but she never mentioned she'd invited her for Thanksgiving.

"Come in," I quickly add, stepping aside and inviting her into the chaos the house has turned into.

My family already arrived a couple of hours ago, which apparently is enough time for four-year-old Cherry and almost two-year-old Chloe to lose any and all inhibitions. Chloe is currently running around the room, buck naked, with her diaper stuck around one ankle, while big sister

Cherry is giggling her little ass off as she tries to catch up with her.

The football game is on TV in the living room with Sully and Wolff watching, while Pippa, and my brother-in-law, Wapi, are talking engines. Carmi is on her belly on the floor, playing with Aspen, and Steve—who turns out to be a huge NASCAR fan—is at the dining table with my father in deep conversation, not really bothered by the mayhem around them. Isobel, Lindsey, and Sloane are in the kitchen, hanging around the island drinking wine.

"Jillian! You made it," Sloane calls out when she catches sight of her.

As Jillian makes her way to the kitchen I notice Wolff, halfway out of his seat, a shocked expression on his face as he follows her with his eyes. He seems to catch himself and sits back down, but not before Sully takes note as well. Interesting.

"Can I get anyone another drink?" I ask the group in the living room. "Wolff? Another beer? Something stronger?"

Sully chuckles as Wolff shoots me a dirty look.

"I'm good," he grumbles.

Sully hands me his empty, and Wapi does the same.

When I walk into the kitchen to get them fresh beers, I notice the conversation between the women huddled around the kitchen island stops abruptly.

"Am I interrupting?"

Sloane shakes her head, her eyes innocently wide. A sure sign she's lying through her teeth.

"No, no. Jillian was just telling me she brought dessert, would you mind getting it from the back of her SUV?"

Dessert? We have five pies sitting on the kitchen counter.

A strangled sound comes from my sister and when I

turn to her, she slaps a hand over her mouth. Something's definitely going on.

Still, I focus on Jillian, whose expression is completely blank. "Sure, gimme your keys."

I drop the beers off for the guys and head outside. Using her key fob, I open the gate on the SUV, and am greeted with an excited yip.

No pies, but a dog crate takes up almost all the space in the back. Inside is a giant puppy, wild fur, tongue lolling, and tail wagging. The remnants of a red bow, I'm sure was originally tied to the crate, is now laying at the pup's massive feet.

When I look back at the house, I catch sight of Sloane coming toward me, a smile on her face, as Jillian, my sister, and my mother-in-law have come out on the porch.

"We agreed no presents," I remind Sloane.

We had this conversation last month when she asked what I wanted for my birthday, which was last week. I told her I already had everything I could want, and to keep her money in her pocket. She agreed on the condition I didn't buy her anything when hers comes around either.

"We agreed no *birthday* presents," she corrects me, a smile on her face. "And before you bring up the money thing, River is a rescue."

"River?"

"He already had the name," she clarifies with a shrug." I thought it was kismet."

The dog is getting impatient and starts gnawing at the metal bars. The moment I slide back the lock, he shoves the crate door open and launches himself at me, leading with his tongue.

"He's house-trained and Jillian says he's good with kids and with other animals," Sloane adds.

I lift the dog out of the vehicle, holding him up in front of me. He's going to be a big boy, he's heavy already. When I put him down, he immediately moves to greet Sloane, his whole body wiggling with excitement.

This morning I would've told you there's nothing more I could wish for, but Sloane managed to find the one thing our house was missing.

I slide my arm around her, and with my other hand, turn her face to me.

"You realize my promise to you is null and void now, right?"

She rolls her eyes and I press a hard kiss on her mouth.

Little does she know I already have my eye on a pretty paint filly at High Meadow.

With the pup already stumbling up the porch steps ahead of us to meet the rest of the family, I lead Sloane back to our very full, now even more chaotic house.

Damn, how'd I get so lucky?

∼

"You guys be good, okay?"

I get whines and whimpers from Hunter and Murphy, who are crowding around my legs as I try to get out. Emo is being his aloof self, curled up on the carpet in front of the fireplace, pretending not to care whether I come or go, but I know the moment I walk out the door, she'll be up on the chair by the window to watch me go.

I already put Peanut and Nugget in the back of the SUV. They have their noses pressed against the glass, tongues lolling, excited to be the ones to come with me this time. More often than not it's one of the others, needed for their specialized noses. Today, however, it's Peanut's sweet disposition, and Nugget's cuddly nature that are important. Where we're going no one will care Peanut is partially blind or Nugget has deformed hind legs.

This will be our first visit to Wellspring Senior Living, an assisted living facility in Kalispell. I got this gig through my friend Sloane, who is also the one who suggested I move up here from Missoula in the first place.

It was less than five months ago, I was called out to Libby with Emo to search for human remains in the mountains. I still have occasional nightmares about the boneyard my dog sniffed out; a dumping ground for what turned out to be a pair of serial killers.

That's when I met Sloane, who was a detective for the Lincoln Sheriff's Department, and my local contact. She and I connected right away and stayed in touch after I returned home, forging the kind of friendship I've been lacking in recent years. All my old friends have slowly disappeared over time, and I haven't exactly done much to hang on to them. They'd all been part of a life I no longer fit into.

Connecting with the dogs had been the first tentative step on a new path. The friendship with Sloane had been the next one. If not for her, I wouldn't have been able to gather up the courage to pull up stakes in Missoula, and seek out a fresh start here.

When I was up here to celebrate Thanksgiving with Sloane, her fiancée Dan and their families, the subject of relocation came up. It was over a cup of tea on her front porch early the morning after. She asked why I'd seemed preoccupied during dinner, and I mentioned toying with the idea of a fresh start, even though I didn't give her the background. She didn't ask why—which is one of the reasons I like her so much—and simply suggested moving closer to her. She pointed out there would be likely be plenty of work for me and the dogs here in the mountains, since I already had connections with law enforcement in the region and left a good impression.

The idea had been churning through my head the entire drive back home that afternoon, and by the time I got to Missoula, I'd mostly had my mind made up. The next day I called the realtor who helped my buy my property on the outskirts of Missoula five years prior, and set the wheels in motion.

Two months later, and here I am; just settled into the dog's and my new digs, off Terrace View Road, halfway between Libby and Sloane and Dan's place. The single-story, rustic ranch house came with a couple of acres of property backing onto the banks of Big Cherry Creek. The place even had an outdoor run and kennels since the previous owner had hunting dogs.

As I drive away I glance back at the house and catch sight of Emo's shadow in the large front window. Then I notice the cutter hanging down from the corner and the missing downspout, and realize the term 'rustic' may be giving the place more credit than it deserves.

The bones of the house are good, and the previous owner had made a good start on renovations, but ran out of money and steam, which is why I was able to pick it up for a relative steel and on very short notice. And the property itself is amazing, with beautiful views from the back deck, which had been put in new in the past two years.

Most of the windows have been replaced, but the roof definitely needs work, as does some of the stonework on the big river-rock chimney. The siding is actual wooden boards that were stained a gray-blue color. I don't hate it, but it's looking a little weathered.

Inside isn't too bad; the only thing left to do are the extra bedrooms and main bathroom. The kitchen cabinets and concrete counter look fairly new, and so do the floors; nice light, extra wide, hardwood boards. The focus in the living space is the large stone fireplace, which—along with the view—is what sold me on the house.

The day before yesterday, when the movers arrived, I had them place the big pieces of furniture, but leave the boxes in one of the extra bedrooms for me to tackle bit by bit.

Which is what I'll get back to later today when I get home.

There is snow on the ground, but the roads are clear and it's a beautiful day for a drive. Despite the cold outside air, I have the window behind me open a crack so Peanut can stick her large nose outside. She easily gets car sick otherwise. Mostly Great Dane, she is large enough to stick her head over the backseat and I can hear her sniffing at the fresh air.

Nugget is probably already asleep in the large dog bed I have in the back of the SUV. These two are my therapy dogs. They love affection and they love people, which is a bit of a miracle, given where they came from. As unmatched a pair as they are, these two are best friends.

I pull my knit beanie farther down over my ears against the cold chill. Then I turn up the radio and sing along full-blast to Duran Duran's *Hungry Like the Wolf* as I make my way to Kalispell. I can't hold a tune to save my life, but luckily my dogs don't care.

"You must be Ms. Lederman," the sweater-vest-wearing administrator waiting for me at reception greets me. "David Gentry, we spoke on the phone."

I shake his offered hand. "Please, it's Jillian. Nice to meet you."

"Of course. Jillian, would you follow me? We already have quite a gathering in the community hall. Sadly, our facility isn't equipped to handle live-in animals, so a lot of our residents had to give up a pet. They miss them."

"I can only imagine," I reply. "I don't know what I would do without my guys."

Ten minutes later, Nugget charms his way from lap to lap, doing the rounds as he's bound to do. Peanut is a tad more discerning with her affections and has picked out her favorite person in the room; a frail-looking elderly woman in a wheelchair. Peanut is sitting down beside the chair, her head resting on the lap of the woman, who absent-mindedly scratches Peanut behind the ears.

Both woman and dog have their eyes closed, a look of satisfaction on their faces.

I catch David's eye, who seems pretty pleased as well. It's amazing how simple and effortless it really is to bring a little joy to people's lives.

It brings me joy as well, and provides me with some balance for the rewarding, but often heart-breaking search and recovery work I do.

*****

Wolff

"Did you find everything okay?"

I pile the items I picked up on the counter.

"I think so." I quickly check the list on my phone. "Yeah, that's it."

And thank God for that.

Even just being in the proximity of a shopping mall gives me fucking hives, so after wandering the aisles of the women's clothing department in Target for the past half hour, I'm sweating like a pig. Good thing I only need to do this once, maybe twice a year.

I wait for the woman to ring me up and pull out my credit card. Then I watch her pack up my purchases, and with a curt nod for her, grab the bags, and walk as fast as I can out to the parking lot.

My phone vibrates in my pocket as I'm getting into my truck.

"Yep."

"Ama says you're in Kalispell?" Dan asks.

Ama is both housekeeper and office manager at High

Meadow. She's also the most well-informed person at the ranch; she seems to know everything about everyone. So, I'm not surprised she was able to tell Dan my whereabouts, even though she didn't get that information from me.

"Yep."

"Good. I have a favor to ask."

"What do you need?"

"Any chance you could swing by Home Depot on your way back? I just started a new project and need a few things."

I chuckle. "A new project? Aren't you still doing work on your house?"

Dan and Sloane moved into the new log home Dan built just before Thanksgiving a little over two months ago. I thought he was still finishing up the inside.

"I am, but something else came up that has priority."

"Oh?"

"Yeah..." I hear him chuckle. "Don't tell Sloane, but I'm building a stable out back. I'm buying Aspen a pony for her birthday in April."

Aspen is Sloane's baby daughter. Dan is not the biological father, but you'd never know from the way he dotes on the kid. The fact he's buying her a pony shouldn't surprise me. Still, I stifle a bark of laughter.

"You realize she's just turning one, right?"

"So? She's already starting to pull herself up, and have you seen her crawl? She can cross the room in three seconds flat. Mark my words; she'll be able to walk by her birthday, and getting her in the saddle is the next step."

"If you say so. Happy to lend a hand on the new project, but in the meantime, shoot me a text with your wishlist and I'll swing by Home Depot on my way back."

"Will do. I appreciate it."

I'm still grinning when I take off my hat and walk into the lobby at Wellspring fifteen minutes later. I wave at Marcela, the receptionist, in passing. I'm halfway down the hall to my mother's unit, when her voice calls me back.

"Lucas! Your mother isn't there."

Anyone calling me by that name is associated with my mother in one way or another. The rest of the world knows me by my last name.

I backtrack my steps and stop in front of her desk.

"She's not? We were supposed to have lunch."

The pretty woman smiles at me as she shakes her head.

"Guess she got a better offer, she's in the community hall. But..." she adds with an over-the-top flirty hair-flip. "I'm free for lunch."

"I'll be sure to keep that in mind," I tell her with a wink.

Marcela is happily married woman with a couple of cute kids, and the flirting is all in good fun. She'd never step out, and I'd never step in.

I head down a different hallway, leading to the communal areas. When I walk into the main hall, I spot my mother's wheelchair right away. Hard to miss, since she's half obscured by a dog the size of a small horse, cuddled up to her.

"She made a new friend."

I turn around to find David Gentry, the home's administrator, standing behind me.

"I see that. Since when do you allow pets in here?"

"Certified therapy animals are allowed," he clarifies. "Board approved and all. Your mother was instrumental in getting that approval."

I vaguely recollect her telling me about a resident petition she was having everyone sign last month. Feeling a little bad I was only listening with half an ear at the time. Despite her small stature, and her failing health, my mother still is a force to be reckoned with.

I turn my head to look at her and catch her eye.

"Lucas! Come meet Peanut."

Who the hell would call an oversized animal like that, Peanut?

The dog lifts its head off my mother's lap when I walk over. That's when I notice it's missing an eye. The animal looks scary enough and I'm sure could snap my mother in half with those jaws, but it seems friendly enough, its tail thumping the linoleum floor as I approach. Bending down, I kiss my mother's papery cheek.

"Peanut?"

Mom beams up at me. "Isn't she precious?"

Precious is not exactly the term I would've come up with for the less than attractive dog, but she's definitely sweet, leaning her weight against my leg and staring up at me with one adoring eye, as I rub her head.

"Good girl," I mumble at her.

The next moment the hair on my neck stands on end when I hear someone walk up behind me, and say, "It's almost time to go, Peanut."

I don't need to turn around to know who the owner of that voice is, but I don't have a choice when my mom speaks up.

"Oh, Jillian, I'd like you to meet my son Lucas."

I meet those pretty green eyes, now sparkling with amusement. Of course a dog named, Peanut, would belong to this woman. She named her cadaver dog, Emo, after all.

Hell, I knew she recently moved to the area—Sloane mentioned it more than once—but I wasn't expecting to run into her at my mother's assisted living home. That's a little too close for comfort.

"So you *do* have a first name; Lucas, huh?"

"You already know each other?" Mom looks back and forth between us.

"I do. How are you doing, Jillian?"

She adjusts the small fur ball she's holding in her arms. "Good, thanks."

I turn to my mother to explain. "Jillian and I met working on a search last summer."

Despite my immediate attempt to identify our connection as a professional one only, I see Mom's mind already at work behind the gleam in her eyes.

Great.

"Is that so? Well, what a happy coincidence this is then," she says in a chipper voice and with a satisfied smirk on her face.

My mother has never passed up on an opportunity to try and hook me up with any seemingly available female we've come across. She has never given up hope to get me tied down and settled, despite the fact I've told her often enough I'm not looking for anything permanent. Certainly not with someone my mother hooked me up with.

"It certainly is a coincidence," Jillian agrees with a kind smile for my mother. "Unfortunately, I have to run. My time is up here and I have to take these guys home and fed, but I'll be back in two weeks."

Mom leans forward to give that ugly mutt a hug, before Jillian heads out with both dogs. Then she nudges my hip with her elbow.

"She seems like a nice girl. Maybe you should walk her out."

"*Mom,*" I warn her.

348

The tiny redhead with the big smile is already enough of a temptation without my mother's interference.

UP NEXT ARE JILLIAN AND WOLFF IN HIGH INTENSITY.
GET YOUR COPY HERE.

Also by Freya Barker

High Mountain Trackers:

HIGH MEADOW

HIGH STAKES

HIGH GROUND

HIGH IMPACT

Arrow's Edge MC Series:

EDGE OF REASON

EDGE OF DARKNESS

EDGE OF TOMORROW

EDGE OF FEAR

EDGE OF REALITY

EDGE OF TRUST

EDGE OF NOWHERE

GEM Series:

OPAL

PEARL

ONYX

PASS Series:

HIT & RUN

LIFE & LIMB

LOCK & LOAD

LOST & FOUND

On Call Series:

BURNING FOR AUTUMN

COVERING OLLIE

TRACKING TAHLULA

ABSOLVING BLUE

REVEALING ANNIE

DISSECTING MEREDITH

WATCHING TRIN

IGNITING VIC

CAPTIVATING ANIKA

Rock Point Series:

KEEPING 6

CABIN 12

HWY 550

10-CODE

Northern Lights Collection:

A CHANGE OF TIDE

A CHANGE OF VIEW

A CHANGE OF PACE

SnapShot Series:

SHUTTER SPEED

FREEZE FRAME

IDEAL IMAGE

Portland, ME, Series:

FROM DUST

CRUEL WATER

THROUGH FIRE

STILL AIR

LuLLaY (a Christmas novella)

Cedar Tree Series:

SLIM TO NONE

HUNDRED TO ONE

AGAINST ME

CLEAN LINES

UPPER HAND

LIKE ARROWS

HEAD START

Standalones:

WHEN HOPE ENDS

VICTIM OF CIRCUMSTANCE

BONUS KISSES

SECONDS

SNOWBOUND

About the Author

USA Today bestselling author Freya Barker loves writing about ordinary people with extraordinary stories.

Driven to make her books about 'real' people; she creates characters who are perhaps less than perfect, each struggling to find their own slice of happy, but just as deserving of romance, thrills and chills in their lives.

Recipient of the ReadFREE.ly 2019 Best Book We've Read All Year Award for "Covering Ollie, the 2015 RomCon "Reader's Choice" Award for Best First Book, "Slim To None", Finalist for the 2017 Kindle Book Award with "From Dust", and Finalist for the 2020 Kindle Book Award with "When Hope Ends", Freya spins story after story with an endless supply of bruised and dented characters, vying for attention!

www.freyabarker.com

9 781988 733944